GENA SHOWALTER

HEART OF THE DRAGON

HQN™

Recycling programs
for this product may
not exist in your area.

ISBN 13: 978-0-373-77525-5

HEART OF THE DRAGON

www.HQNBooks.com

Printed in U.S.A.

Dear Reader,

Since the first title in my Atlantis series, *Heart of the Dragon,* was published in 2005, I've been asked how I thought to combine the lost city of Atlantis with the creatures of lore. The answer is simple: what if. What if the gods hid their greatest mistakes inside Atlantis and that's why it's buried under the sea?

That single question branched into a thousand others, each more intriguing than the last. What if a dragon shape-shifter is forced to guard the portal that leads to his home, tasked with killing anyone who enters—even the woman of his dreams (*Heart of the Dragon*)? What if a modern man is sent inside the forbidden city to steal its greatest treasure... who just happens to be a beautiful female he can't resist *(Jewel of Atlantis)*? What if the king of the nymphs can seduce everyone he encounters—except the woman he loves (*The Nymph King*)? I hope you'll join me on these journeys through Atlantis, where the creatures of myth and legend walk, peril lurks around every corner and forbidden passions ignite. Even readers familiar with the books might find a few new surprises in these slightly revised versions!

And be sure to check out *The Vampire's Bride,* my newest tale of Atlantis, where I answer the question readers have been asking for years: what if the villain in all those earlier stories, the vampire king who has tortured and hated and warred, got a story of his own?

Wishing you all the best,

Gena Showalter

Other sexy, steamy reads from

GENA SHOWALTER

and HQN Books

The Lords of the Underworld series
The Darkest Night
The Darkest Kiss
The Darkest Pleasure
The Darkest Whisper

The Atlantis series
Jewel of Atlantis
The Nymph King
The Vampire's Bride

Tales of an *Extra*ordinary Girl series
Playing with Fire
Twice as Hot

Other must-reads
The Stone Prince
The Pleasure Slave
Animal Instincts
Catch a Mate

From Harlequin Teen
Intertwined

More stunning tales from Gena Showalter are coming your way!

In May 2010, look for the next installment of the
Lords of the Underworld series
Into the Dark

In September 2010, watch for the
sequel to *Intertwined*,
Unraveled

You survived a childhood of mind-numbing pain and abject humiliation. You survived a childhood of utter terror and unimaginable horror. Somehow, some way, you survived a childhood with me as your babysitter. Thankfully I've found a better outlet for my...creative spirit.

To Auston and Casey Dowling. I love you both.

To Debbie Splawn-Bunch, who wouldn't let me title this book *Extra Crispy Love*.

HEART OF THE
DRAGON

PROLOGUE

Atlantis

"DO YOU FEEL IT, BOY? Do you feel the mist preparing?"

Darius en Kragin squeezed his eyes tightly closed, his tutor's words echoing in his mind. Did he feel it? Gods, yes. Even though he was only eight seasons, he felt it. Felt his skin prickle with cold, felt the sickening wave of acid in his throat as the mist enveloped him. He even felt his veins quicken with a deceptively sweet, swirling essence that was not his own.

Fighting the urge to bolt up the cavern steps and into the palace above, he tensed his muscles and fisted his hands at his sides.

I must stay. I must do this.

Slowly Darius forced his eyelids to open. He released a pent-up breath as his gaze locked with Javar's. His tutor stood shrouded by the thickening, ghostlike haze, the bleak walls of the cave at his back.

"This is what you will feel each time the mist summons you, for this means a traveler is nearby,"

Javar said. "Never stray far from this place. You may live above with the others, but you must always return here when called."

"I do not like it here." His voice shook. "The cold weakens me."

"Other dragons are weakened by cold, but not you. Not any longer. The mist will become a part of you, the coldness your most beloved companion. Now listen," he commanded softly. "Listen closely."

At first Darius heard nothing. Then he began to register the sound of a low, tapering whistle—a sound that reverberated in his ears like the moans of the dying. *Wind,* he assured himself. *Merely wind.* The turbulent breeze rounded every corner of the doomed enclosure, drawing closer. Closer still. His nostrils filled with the scent of desperation, destruction and loneliness as he braced himself for impact.

When it finally came upon him, it was not the battering force he expected, but a mockingly gentle caress against his body. The jeweled medallion at his neck hummed to life, burning the dragon tattoo etched into his flesh only that morning.

He crushed his lips together to silence a deep groan of uncertainty.

His tutor sucked in a reverent breath and splayed his arms wide. "This is what you will live for, boy. This will be your purpose. You will kill for this."

"I do not want my purpose to stem from the deaths of others," Darius said, the words tumbling from his mouth unbidden.

Javar stilled, a fiery anger kindling in the depths

of his ice-blue eyes, eyes so unlike Darius's own—unlike every dragon's. All dragons but Javar possessed golden eyes. "You are to be a Guardian of the Mist, a king to the warriors here," Javar said. "You should be grateful I chose you among all the others for this task."

Darius swallowed. Grateful? Yes, he should have been grateful. Instead he felt oddly…lost. Alone. So alone and unsure. Was this what he truly wanted? Was this the life he craved for himself? His gaze skimmed his surroundings. A few broken chairs were scattered across the dirt and twig-laden ground. The walls were black and bare. There was no warmth, only cold, biting reality and the lingering shadow of hopelessness. To become Guardian meant pledging his existence, his very soul to this cave.

Gaze narrowed, Javar closed the distance between them, his boots harmonizing with the drip, drip of water. His lips pulled in a tight scowl, and he gripped Darius's shoulders painfully. "Your mother and father were slaughtered. Your sisters were raped and their throats slit. Had the last Guardian done his duty, your family would still be with you."

Pain cut through Darius so intensely he nearly clawed out his eyes to blacken the hated images hovering before them. His graceful mother twisted and bent, lying in a crimson river of her own blood. The bone-deep gashes in his father's back. His three sisters… His chin trembled, and he blinked away the stinging tears in his eyes. He would not cry. Not now. Not ever.

Mere days ago, he had returned from hunting and found his family dead. He had not cried then. Nor had he shed a tear when the invaders who plundered his family were slaughtered in retribution. To cry was to show weakness. He squared his shoulders and raised his chin.

"That's right," Javar said, watching him with a glint of pride. "Deny your tears and keep the hurt inside you. Use it against those who hope to enter our land. Kill them with it, for they only mean us harm."

"I want to do as you say. I do." He glanced away. "But—"

"Killing travelers is your obligation," Javar interrupted. "Killing them is your privilege."

"What of innocent women and children who mistakenly stumble through?" The thought of destroying such purity, like that of his sisters, made him loathe the monster Javar was asking him to become—though not enough to halt this course he had set for himself. To protect his friends, he would do whatever was asked of him. They were all he had left. "May I set them free on the surface?"

"You may not."

"What harm can children do our people?"

"They will carry the knowledge of the mist with them, ever able to lead an army through." Javar shook him once, twice. "Do you understand now? Do you understand what you must do and why you must do it?"

"Yes," he replied softly. He stared down at a thin, cerulean rivulet that trickled past his boots, his gaze following the gentleness and serenity of the water. Oh, that he possessed the same serenity inside himself. "I understand."

"You are too tender, boy." With a sigh, Javar released him. "If you do not erect stronger defenses inside yourself, your emotions will be the death of you and all those you still hold dear."

Darius gulped back the hard lump in his throat. "Then help me, Javar. Help me rid myself of my emotions so that I might do these deeds."

"As I told you before, you have only to bury your pain deep inside you, somewhere no one can ever hope to reach it—not even yourself."

That sounded so easy. Yet, how did one bury such tormenting grief? Such devastating memories? How did one battle the horrendous agony? He would do anything, anything at all, to find peace.

"How?" he asked his tutor.

"You will discover that answer on your own. Much sooner than you think."

Magic and power began swirling more intently around them, undulating, begging for some type of release. The air expanded, coagulated, leaving a heady fragrance of darkness and danger. A surge of energy ricocheted across the walls like a bolt of lightning, then erupted in a colorful array of liquid sparks.

Darius stilled as horror, dread and yes, anticipation sliced a path through him.

"A traveler will enter soon," Javar said, already tense and eager.

With shaky fingers, Darius gripped the hilt of his sword.

"They always experience disorientation at first emergence. You must use that to your advantage and destroy them the moment they exit."

Could he? "I'm not ready. I cannot—"

"You are and you will," Javar said, a steely edge to his tone. "There are two portals, the one you are to guard here and the one I guard on the other side of the city. I am not asking you to do anything I would not—and have not done—myself."

In the next instant, a tall man stepped from the mists. His eyes were squeezed shut, his face pale, and his clothing disheveled. His hair was thick and silvered, and his tanned skin was lined with deep wrinkles. He had the look of a scholar, not of war or evil.

Still trembling, Darius unsheathed his weapon. He almost doubled over from the sheer force of his conflicting emotions. A part of him continued to scream to run away, to refuse this task, but he forced himself to remain. He would do this because Javar was right. Travelers were the enemy, no matter who they were, no matter what their purpose.

No matter their appearance.

"Do it, Darius," Javar growled. "Do it now."

The traveler's eyelids jolted open. Their gazes suddenly clashed together, dragon gold against human green. Resolve against fear. Life against death.

Darius raised his blade, paused only a moment—

stop, run, do not—then struck. Blood splattered his bare chest and forearms like poisoned rain. A gargled gasp parted the man's lips, then slowly, so slowly, his lifeless body sank to the ground.

For several long, agonizing moments, Darius stood frozen by the fruit of his actions. *What have I done? What have I done!* He dropped the sword, distantly hearing a clang as the metal thudded into the dirt.

He hunched over and vomited.

Surprisingly, as he emptied his stomach, he lost the agony inside him. He lost his regret and sadness. Frigid ice enclosed his chest and what was left of his soul. He welcomed and embraced the numbness until he felt only a strange void. All of his heartache—gone. All of his suffering—gone.

I have done my duty.

"I am proud of you, boy." Javar slapped his shoulder in a rare show of affection. "You are ready to take your vows as Guardian."

As Darius's shaking ceased, he straightened and wiped his mouth with the back of his wrist. "Yes," he said starkly, determinedly, craving more of this detachment. "I am ready."

"Do it, then."

Without pausing for thought, he sank to his knees. "In this place I will dwell, destroying the surface dwellers who pass through the mist. This I vow upon my life. This I vow upon my death." As he spoke the words, they mystically appeared on his chest and back, black and red symbols that stretched from one shoulder to the other and glowed with inner fire. "I exist for no other purpose. I am Guardian of the Mist."

Javar held his stare for a long while, then nodded with satisfaction. "Your eyes have changed color to mirror the mist. The two of you are one. This is good, boy. This is good."

CHAPTER ONE

Three hundred years later

"He doesn't laugh."

"He never yells."

"When Grayley accidentally stabbed Darius's thigh with a six-pronged razor, our leader didn't even blink."

"I'd say all he needs is a few good hours of bed sport, but I'm not even sure he knows what his cock is for."

The latter was met with a round of rumbling male chuckles.

Darius en Kragin stepped inside the spacious dining hall, his gaze methodically cataloging his surroundings. The ebony floors gleamed clean and black, the perfect contrast for the dragon-carved ivory walls. Along the windows, gauzy drapes whisped delicately. Crystal ceilings towered above, reflecting the tranquillity of seawater that enclosed their great city.

He moved toward the long, rectangular dining table. The tantalizing aroma of sweetmeats and fruit should have wafted to his nostrils, but over the years his sense of smell, taste and color had deteriorated.

He smelled only ash, tasted nothing more than air, and saw only black-and-white. He'd willed those senses away. Better, easier to exist in a void. Only sometimes did he wish otherwise.

One warrior caught sight of him and quickly alerted the others. Silence clamped tight fingers around the chamber. Every male present whipped his focus to his food, as if roasted fowl had suddenly become the most fascinating thing the gods had ever created. The jovial air visibly darkened.

True to his men's words, Darius claimed his seat at the head of the table without a smile or a scowl. Only after he'd consumed his third goblet of wine did his men resume their conversation, though they wisely chose a different subject. This time they spoke of the women they had pleasured and the wars they had won. Exaggerated tales, all. One warrior even went so far as to claim he'd gratified four women at the same time while successfully storming his enemy's gate. For a nymph, that was possible. A dragon? No.

Darius had heard the same stories a thousand times before. He swallowed a mouthful of tasteless meat and asked the warrior beside him, "Any news?"

Brand, his first in command, leveled him a grim smile and shrugged. "Perhaps. Perhaps not." His light hair hung around his face in thick war braids, and he hooked several behind his ears. "The vampires are acting strangely. They're leaving the Outer City and assembling here in the Inner City."

"They rarely come here. Have they given no indication of why?"

"It cannot be good for us, whatever the reason," Madox said, jumping into the conversation. "I say we kill those that venture too close to our home." He was the tallest dragon in residence and always ready for combat. He perched at the end of the table, his elbows flat on the surface, both hands filled with meat. "We are ten times stronger and more skilled than they are."

"We need to obliterate the entire race," the warrior on his left supplied. Renard was the kind of man others wanted to guard their backs in battle. He fought with a determination matched by few, was fiercely loyal and had studied the anatomy of every species in Atlantis so he knew exactly where to strike each to create the most damage. And the most pain.

Years ago, Renard and his wife had been captured by a group of vampires. He'd been chained to a wall, forced to watch as his wife was raped and drained. When he escaped, he brutally destroyed every creature responsible, but that had not lessened his heartache. He was a different man than he'd been, no longer full of laughter and forgiveness. What Darius hated most was that a rogue group of dragons had mimicked the tale, doing the same thing to the vampire king, who had not been responsible for Renard's tragedy, but who now blamed Darius for it. Thus, a war erupted between their races.

"Perhaps we can petition Zeus for their extinction," Brand replied.

"The gods have long since forgotten us," Renard said with a shrug. "Besides, Zeus is like Cronus in so many ways. He might agree, but do we really want him to? We are all creations of the Titans, even those we loathe. If Zeus annihilates one race, what is to stop him from wiping out others?"

Brand gulped back the last of his wine, his eyes fierce. "Then we will not ask him. We will simply strike."

"The time has come for us to declare war," Madox growled in agreement.

The word "war" elicited smiles across the expanse of the room.

"I agree that the vampires need to be eliminated. They create chaos and for that alone they deserve to die." Darius met each warrior's stare, one at a time, holding it until the other man looked away. "But there is a time for war and a time for strategy. Now is the time for strategy. I will send a patrol into the Inner City and learn the vampires' purpose. Soon we will know the best course of action."

"But—" one warrior began.

He cut him off with a wave of his hand. "Our ancestors waged the last war with the vampires, and while we might have won, our losses were too great. Families were torn asunder and blood bathed the land. We will have patience in this situation. My men will not jump hastily into any skirmish."

A disappointed silence slithered from every man present, wrapping around the table, then climbing up the walls. He wasn't sure if they were considering his words, or revolt.

"What do you care, Darius, if families are destroyed? I'd think a heartless bastard like you would welcome the violence." The dry statement came from across the table, where Tagart reclined in his seat. "Aren't you eager to spill more blood? No matter that the blood is vampire rather than human?"

A sea of angry growls grew in volume, and several warriors whipped to face Darius, staring at him with expectation, as if they waited for him to coldly slay the warrior who had voiced what they had all been thinking. Tagart merely laughed, daring anyone to act against him.

Do they truly consider me heartless? Darius wondered. Heartless enough to execute his own kind for something so trivial as a verbal insult? He was a killer, yes, but not heartless.

A heartless man felt nothing, and he felt *some* emotions. Mild though they were. He simply knew how to control what he felt, knew how to bury it deep inside himself. That was the way he preferred his life. Intense emotions birthed turmoil, and turmoil birthed soul-wrenching pain. Soul-wrenching pain birthed memories… His fingers tightened around his fork, and he forced himself to relax.

He would rather feel nothing than relive the agony of his past—the same agony that could very well become his present if he allowed a single memory to take root and sprout its poisonous branches.

"My family is Atlantis," he finally said, his voice disturbingly calm. "I will do what I must to protect her. If that means waiting before declaring war and angering every one of my men, then so be it."

Realizing Darius could not be provoked, Tagart shrugged and returned his attention to his meal.

"You are right, my friend." Grinning broadly, Brand slapped his shoulder. "War is only fun if we emerge the victor. We heed your advice to wait most readily."

"Kiss his ass any harder," Tagart muttered, "and your lips will chap."

Brand quickly lost his grin, and the medallion hanging from his neck began to glow. "What did you say?" he demanded quietly.

"Are your ears as feeble as the rest of you?" Tagart pushed to his feet, leaving his palms planted firmly on the glossy tabletop. The two men glared at each other from across the distance, a charged stillness sparking between them. "I said, kiss his ass any harder, and your lips will chap."

With a growl, Brand launched himself over the table, knocking dishes and food to the ground in his haste to attack Tagart. In midspring, reptilian scales grew upon his skin and narrow, incandescent wings sprouted from his back, ripping his shirt and pants in half, transforming him from man to beast. Fire spewed from his mouth, charring the surface of everything in its path.

The same transformation overtook Tagart, and the two beasts grappled to the ebony floor in a dangerous tangle of claws, teeth and fury.

Dragon warriors were able to change into true dragons whenever they desired, though the transformation happened of its own volition whenever raging emotions gripped them. Darius himself had not experienced a change, impromptu or otherwise, since he discovered his family slaughtered over three hundred years ago. To be honest, Darius suspected his dragon form was somehow lost.

Tagart snarled when Brand threw him into the nearest wall, cracking the priceless ivory. He quickly recovered by whipping Brand's face with his serrated tail, leaving a jagged and bleeding wound. Their infuriated snarls echoed as deep and sharp as any blade. A torrent of flame erupted, followed quickly by an infuriated hiss. Over and over they bit and lashed out at each other, separated, circled, then clashed together again.

Every warrior save Darius leapt to his feet in a frenzy of excitement, hurriedly taking bets on who would win. "Eight gold drachmas on Brand," Grayley proclaimed.

"Ten on Tagart," Brittan shouted.

"Twenty if they both kill each other," Zaeven called excitedly.

"Enough," Darius said, his tone even, controlled.

The two combatants jumped apart as if he'd screamed the command, both panting and facing each other like penned animals, ready to attack again at any moment.

"Sit," Darius said in that same easy tone.

Rather than obey this time, they growled gutturally at each other. Not so the rest. They sat. While they might wish to continue cheering and taking bets, Darius was their leader, their king, and they knew better than to defy him.

"I did not exclude you from the command," he

said to Tagart and Brand, adding only slightly to his volume. "You will calm yourselves and sit."

Both men leveled narrowed gazes on him. He arched a harsh brow and motioned with his fingers a gesture that clearly said, "Come and get me. Just don't expect to live afterward."

Minutes passed in suspended silence until finally, the panting warriors assumed human form. Their wings recoiled, tucking tightly into the slits on their backs; their scales faded, leaving naked skin. Because Darius kept spare clothing in each room of the palace, they were able to grab a pair of pants from the wall hooks. Partially dressed now, they righted their chairs and eased down.

"I will not have discord in my palace," Darius told them.

Brand wiped the blood from his cheek and flicked Tagart a narrowed glare. In return, Tagart bared his sharp teeth and released a cutting growl.

They were already on the verge of morphing again, Darius realized.

He worked a finger over his stubbled chin. Never had he been more thankful that he was a man of great patience, yet never had he been more displeased with the system he had fashioned. His dragons were divided into four units. One unit patrolled the Outer City, while another patrolled the Inner. The third was allowed to roam free, pleasuring women, losing themselves in wine or whatever other vice they desired. The last had to stay here, training. Every four weeks, the units rotated.

These men had been here two days—a mere two days—and already they were restless. If he did not think of something to distract them, they might very well kill each other before their required time elapsed.

"What think you of a tournament of sword skill?" he asked determinedly.

Indifferent, some men shrugged. A few moaned, "Not again."

"No," Renard said with a shake of his dark head, "you always win. And besides that, there is no prize."

"What would you like to do, then?"

"Women," one of the men shouted. "Bring us some women."

Darius frowned. "You know I do not allow females inside the palace. They pose too much of a distraction, causing too many hostilities between you. And not the easy hostilities of a few moments ago."

Regretful groans greeted his words.

"I have an idea." Brand faced him, a slow smile curling his lips, eclipsing all other emotions. "Allow me to propose a new contest. Not of physical strength, but one of cunning and wits."

Instantly every head perked up. Even Tagart lost his wrathful glare as interest lit his eyes.

A contest of wits sounded innocent enough. Darius nodded and waved his hand for Brand to continue.

Brand's smile grew wider. "The contest is simple. The first man to make Darius lose his temper, wins."

"I do not—" Darius began, but Madox spoke over him, his rough voice laden with excitement.

"And just what does the winner gain?"

"The satisfaction of besting us all," Brand replied. "And a beating from Darius, I'm sure." He offered them a languid shrug and leaned back in the velvet cushions of his chair. He propped his ankles on the tabletop. "But I swear by the gods every bruise will be worth it."

Eight sets of eyes swung in Darius's direction and locked on him with unnerving interest. Weighing options. Speculating. "I do not—" he began again, but just like before he was silenced.

"I like the sound of this," Tagart interjected. "Count me in."

"Me, too."

"And me, as well."

Before another man could so easily ignore him, Darius uttered one word. Simple, but effective. "No." He swallowed a tasteless bite of fowl, then continued with the rest of his meal. "Now, tell me more of the vampires' doings."

"What about making him smile?" Facing Brand, Madox shoved eagerly to his feet and leaned over the table. "Does that count? It's a show of emotion and as rare as his temper."

"Absolutely." Brand nodded. "But there must be a witness to the deed, or no winner can be declared."

One by one, each man uttered, "Agreed."

"I will hear no more talk of this." When had he lost control of this conversation? Of his men? "I—"

Darius snapped his mouth closed. His blood was quickening with darkness and danger, and the hairs at the base of his neck were rising.

The mist prepared for a traveler.

Resignation rushed through him and on the heels of that was cold determination. He eased up, his chair skidding slightly behind him.

Every voice tapered to silence. Every expression became curious.

"I must go," he said, the words flat, hollow. "We will discuss a tournament of sword skill when I return."

He attempted to stride from the room, but Tagart leapt up and over the table and swiveled in front of him. "Does the mist call you?" the warrior asked, casually leaning one arm against the door frame and blocking the only exit.

Darius gave him no outward reaction. But then, when did he ever? "Step out of my way."

Tagart arched an insolent brow. "Make me."

Someone snickered behind him.

With or without his approval, it seemed the game had already begun. This wasn't like his men. They must be more bored than he'd thought.

Darius easily lifted Tagart by his shoulders and tossed the stunned man aside, slamming him into the far wall. He thudded to the floor in a gasping heap. Without facing the others, Darius asked, "Anyone else?"

"Me," came an unhesitant and unrepentant reply. A blur of black leather and silver knives, Madox rushed to stand at his side, watching him intently, gauging his reaction. "I want to stop you. Does that make you angry? Make you want to scream and rail at me?"

An unholy light entered Tagart's eyes as he scrambled to his feet. He curled his fingers around the hilt of a nearby sword and stalked to Darius, his motions slow and deliberate. Never once pausing to consider the stupidity of his actions, he pointed the razor-sharp tip of the blade at Darius's neck.

"Would you show fear if I vowed to kill you?" the infuriated man spat.

"That's taking things too far," Brand growled, joining the growing group around him.

A drop of blood slithered down Darius's throat. The nick should have stung, but he felt nothing, not a single sensation. Only that ever-present detachment.

No one realized his intentions. One moment Darius stood still, seemingly accepting of Tagart's assault, but the next he had his own sword unsheathed and directed at Tagart's neck. The man's eyes widened.

"Put your weapon away," Darius told him, "or I will kill you where you stand. I care not whether I live or die, but you, I think, care greatly for your own life."

One second dragged into two before a narrow-eyed Tagart lowered his sword.

Darius lowered his own weapon; his features remained stony. "Finish your meal, all of you, then retire to the practice arena. You will exercise until you have not the strength to stand. That's an order."

He strode from the chamber quite aware he had not given his men the reaction they craved.

DARIUS DESCENDED the cave steps four at a time. Ready to finish the deed and resume his meal in private, he removed his shirt and tossed the black fabric into a far corner. The medallion he wore, as well as the tattoos on his chest, glowed like tiny pin-pricks of flame, waiting for him to fulfill his vow.

Expression blank, mind clear, he tightened his clasp on his sword, positioned himself to the left of the mist…and he waited.

CHAPTER TWO

GRACE CARLYLE ALWAYS hoped she'd die from intense pleasure while having sex with her husband. Well, she wasn't married, and she'd never had sex, but she was still going to die.

And not from intense pleasure.

From heat exhaustion? Maybe.

From hunger? Possibly.

From her own stupidity? Absolutely.

She was lost and alone in the freaking Amazon jungle.

As she strode past tangled green vines and towering trees, beads of sweat trickled down her chest and back. Small shards of light seeped from the leafy canopy above, providing hazy visibility. Barely adequate, but appreciated. The smells of rotting vegetation, old rain and flowers mingled together, forming a conflicting fragrance of sweet and sour. She wrinkled her nose.

"All I wanted was a little excitement," she muttered. "Instead I end up broke, lost, and trapped in this bug-infested sauna."

To complete her descent into hell, she expected the

sky to open and pour out a deluge of rain at any moment.

The only good thing about her current circumstances was that all this hiking and sweating might actually help her lose a few pounds from her too-curvy figure. Not that losing weight did her any good here. Except, perhaps, in the newspapers.

New Yorker found dead in Amazon
A shame. She was hot!

Scowling, she swatted a mosquito trying to drink her arm dry—even though she'd applied several layers of ucuru oil to prevent such bites. Where the hell was Alex? She should have run into her brother by now. Or, at the very least, stumbled upon a tour group. Or even blundered upon an indigenous tribe.

If only she hadn't taken an extended leave of absence from AirTravel, she'd be soaring through the air, relaxed and listening to the hypnotic hum of a jet engine.

"I'd be in an air-conditioned G-IV," she said, slashing her hand like a machete through the thick, green foliage. "I'd be sipping vanilla Coke." Another slash. "I'd be listening to my coworkers discuss stiletto heels, expensive dates and mind-shattering orgasms."

And I'd still be miserable, she thought, *wishing I were anywhere else.*

She stopped abruptly and closed her eyes. *I just want to be happy. Is that too much to ask?*

Obviously.

So often lately she battled a sense of discontent, a desire to experience so much more. Her mother had tried to warn her what such discontent would bring her. "You're going to get yourself in trouble," she'd admonished. But had Grace listened? *Noooo.* Instead she'd followed her aunt Sophie's lovely bit of wisdom. Aunt Sophie, for God's sake! The woman who wore leopard print spandex and cavorted with mailmen and strippers. "I know you've done some exciting things, Gracie honey," Sophie had said, "but that's not really living. Something's missing from your life and if you don't find it, you'll end up a shriveled old prune like your mom."

Something *was* missing from Grace's life. She knew that, and in an effort to find that mysterious "something," she'd tried speed dating, Internet dating and singles bars. When those failed, she decided to give night school a try. Not to meet men, but to learn. Not that the cosmetology classes had done her any good. The best stylists in the world couldn't tame her wild red curls. After that, she'd tried race-car driving and step class. She'd even gotten her belly button pierced. Nothing helped.

What would it take to make her feel whole, complete?

"Not this jungle, that's for sure," she grumbled, jolting back into motion. "Someone please tell me," she said to the heavens, "why satisfaction always dances so quickly out of my reach. I'm dying to know."

Traveling the world had always been her dream, and becoming a flight attendant for a private charter had seemed like the perfect job for her. She hadn't realized she would become an airborne waitress, jaunting from hotel to hotel, never actually enjoying the state/country/hellhole she found herself in. Sure, she'd scaled mountains, surfed the ocean waves and jumped from a plane, but the joy of those adventures never remained and like everything else she'd tried, they always left her feeling more unsatisfied than before.

That's why she had come here, to try something new. Something with a bit more danger. Her brother was an employee of Argonauts, a mythoarchaeological company that had recently discovered the crude glider constructed by Daedalus of Athens—a discovery that rocked the scientific and mythological communities. Alex spent his days and nights delving deep into the world's myths, proving or disproving them.

With such a fulfilling job, he didn't have to worry about becoming a shriveled old prune. *Not like me,* she lamented.

Wiping the sweat from her brow, Grace increased her pace. About a week ago, Alex had shipped her a package containing his journal and a gorgeous necklace with two dangling, intertwined dragon heads. No note of explanation accompanied the gifts. Knowing he was in Brazil and looking for a portal that led into the lost city of Atlantis she'd decided to join him, leaving a message on his cell phone with details of her flight.

With a sigh, she fingered the dragon chain hanging at her neck. When Alex failed to pick her up at the airport, she should have returned home. "But nooo," she said with deep self-loathing, suddenly more aware of her dry, cotton mouth. "I hired a local guide and tried to find him. '*Sí, senhorina,*'" she mimicked the guide. "'Of course, *senhorina.* Anything at all, *senhorina.*'"

"Bastard," she muttered.

Today, two miserable days into her trek, her kind, considerate, I-only-want-to-help-you guide had stolen her backpack and abandoned her here. Now she had no food, no water, no tent. She did, however, have a weapon. A weapon she had used to shoot that bastard in the ass as he ran away. The memory caused her lips to curl in a slow smile, and she lovingly patted the revolver resting in the waist of her dirty canvas pants.

Her smile didn't last long, however, as the midday heat continued to pound against her. In all her wildest dreams, her need for fulfillment had never ended like this. She'd envisioned laughter and—

Something hard slammed into her head and jostled her forward. She yelped, her heart pounding in her chest as she rubbed her now throbbing temple and skimmed her gaze over the ground, searching for the source of her pain.

Oh, thank you, thank you, she mentally cried when she spied the rosy-colored fruit. Mouth watering, she studied the delicious-looking juice seeping from the smashed remains. Was it poisonous? And did she care if it was? She licked her lips. No, she didn't care. Death by poison was preferable to walking away from this unexpected treasure.

Just as she reached down to scoop up what she could, another missile crashed into her back.

She gasped and jerked upright.

Spinning, she sent her narrowed gaze through the trees. About ten yards away and fifteen feet up she discovered a small, hairy monkey holding a piece of fruit in each hand. Her jaw dropped open in disbelief. Was he…smiling?

He swung back both of his arms and launched each piece at her. She was too stunned to move and simply watched as they splattered against her pants, stinging her thighs with their impact. Laughing, proud of himself, the monkey jumped up and down and waved his limbs wildly through the air.

She knew what he was thinking: *ha, ha, there's nothing you can do about it.* This was too much. Robbed, abandoned, then assaulted by a primate who should pitch for the Yankees. Scowling, at her wit's end, she picked up the fruit, claimed two mouth-watering bites, paused, claimed two more bites, then launched what was left. She nailed her target in the ear. He lost his smile.

"Nothing I can do about it, huh? Well, take that, you rotten fuzz ball."

Her victory was short-lived. In the next instant, fruit sailed at her from every direction. Monkeys littered the trees! Realizing she was outnumbered and outgunned, Grace grabbed what fruit she could, ducked behind a tree, jumped over a swarm of fire ants and ran. Ran without knowing what direction she traveled. Ran until she was certain her lungs would collapse from exertion.

When she finally slowed her pace, she sucked in a breath, then bit into her bounty. Sucked in another breath, then bit into the fruit again, continually alternating between the two. As the sweet juices ran down her throat, she moaned in surrender.

Life is good, she thought.

Until another hour passed. By then her body forgot that she'd had any nourishment, and lethargy beat rough fists inside her, causing her feet to drag. Her bones were liquefying, and her mouth felt dryer than sand. But she kept walking, each step creating a mantra in her brain. Find. Alex. Find. Alex. Find. Alex. He was out here somewhere, looking for that silly portal, perhaps blithely unaware of her presence. Why couldn't he have been at the coordinates his journal had claimed he'd be? Where the hell was he?

Unfortunately the deeper she roamed through the jungle the more lost and alone she became. The trees and liana thickened, as did the darkness. At least the scent of rot evaporated, leaving only a luscious trace of wild heliconias and dewy orchids. If she didn't find shelter soon, she would collapse wherever she found herself, helpless against nature. Though her vaccinations were up-to-date, she hated snakes and insects more than hunger and fatigue.

Several yards, a tapir and two capybaras later, she

had made no progress that she could see. Her arms and legs were so heavy they felt like steel clubs. Not knowing what else to do, she sank to the ground. As she lay there, she heard the gentle song of the insects and the— Her eardrums perked. The peaceful trickle of water? She blinked, listening more intently. Yes, she realized with excitement. She was actually hearing the glorious swoosh of water.

Get up, she commanded herself. *Get up, get up, get up!*

Using every bit of strength she possessed, she pushed to her hands and knees and crawled into a thick tangle of vegetation. Forest life pulsed vibrantly around her, mocking her weakness. Brilliant, damp green leaves parted and the ground became wetter and wetter until becoming completely submerged by an underground spring. The clear, turquoise water smelled clean and refreshing.

Shaking with the force of her need, she cupped her hands together, scooped up the cool, heavenly liquid and drank deeply. Her parched lips welcomed every wet, delicious drop…until her chest began to burn, hotter and hotter, like she was swallowing molten lava. Except, the sensation came from the outside of her body, not the inside.

The heat became unbearable, and she shrieked. Jolting up, her gaze locked on to the twin dragon heads dangling from the silver chain around her neck. Both sets of ruby eyes were glowing a bright, eerie red.

She tried to jerk the thing over her head but was

suddenly propelled forward by an invisible force. Arms flailing, she broke past an amazingly thick wall of flora. Light gave way to muted dark as she was dragged, grunting and fighting, several yards. Finally, she stilled, and the medallion cooled against her chest.

Her eyes grew impossibly round as she studied her new surroundings. She had entered some sort of cave. *Drip. Drip.* Droplets of water beat against the rocky floor. A cool, welcoming breeze kissed her face as relief nearly buckled her knees. The tranquil ambiance flowed into her, helping to calm her racing heart and labored breathing.

"All I need now is the powdered eggs, canned beans and coffee that were in my pack and I'll die happy."

Too exhausted to care what might be inside, waiting for a tasty human to appear, she scrambled deeper inside the passage and down a steep incline. The ceiling constricted and lowered, until she had to crouch and kneel. How long she crawled, she didn't know. Minutes? Hours? She only knew she needed to find a smooth, dry surface so that she could sleep. Gradually a ribbon of light appeared. The welcome beam snaked around the corner like a summoning finger. She followed.

And found Paradise.

Light crowned a small, iridescent pool of…water? The dappled ice-blue liquid seemed thicker than water, almost like a clear, transparent gel. Instead of lying on the ground, however, the pool hung upright at a slight angle, much like a portrait on a wall. Yet there was no wall to support it.

Why wasn't it spilling over? she wondered dazedly. Her foggy brain couldn't quite sort through the bizarre information. Balmy tendrils of mist enveloped the entire haven. A few ethereal strands reached the cavern top, swirling, circling, then gently dipping back down.

She uttered a nervous laugh, and the sound echoed all around her.

Grace reached out carefully, meaning only to touch and examine the strange substance. At the moment of contact, a violent jolt exploded within her, and she felt as if her entire being was sucked into a vacuum, pulling her, tugging her in every direction.

The world crumbled, breaking around her piece by fragile, needed piece, until finally ceasing to exist. Terror unfurled and consumed her. She was falling slowly, falling down. Her arms reached out, desperate for a solid anchor, yet no tangible object greeted her palms.

That's when the screams began. High-pitched, disharmonized, like a thousand screeching children running all around her. She covered her ears to block the sound. She needed the noise to stop, had to make it stop. But the screams only grew louder. More intense.

"Help me!" she cried.

Stars burst like fireworks at her side, spinning her round and round. Spinning her up and down. Waves of nausea churned inside her stomach, and she tried valiantly to regain any sense of time or place.

Suddenly everything quieted.

Her feet touched a hard surface; she swayed but didn't fall. The nausea slowly receded. Cautiously she shifted her feet, ascertaining that she truly stood on a stable foundation.

In. Out. Relieved, she drew in a breath and slowly let it out. In. Out. When her head cleared, she cracked open her eyelids. A haze of dew still rose from the small pool like strands of pale, glistening ivy composed entirely of fairy dust. The beautiful sight was spoiled only by the stark contours of the gloomy cavern—a cavern that was different from the one she'd first entered.

Her brows furrowed. Here, the rocky walls were covered with strange, colorful markings, like liquid gold upon forgotten ash. And…was that splattered blood? Shuddering, she tore her gaze away. The floor was damp, burdened with odd-shaped twigs, rocks and straw. Several crudely carved chairs pushed against the far corner.

Instead of miserable humidity, she inhaled air as cold as winter ice. Air that possessed a sickeningly metallic bite. The walls were taller, wider. And when she'd first entered, the dappled pool had been on the right side, not on the left.

How had her surroundings changed so drastically and quickly without her moving a step? She shivered. What was going on? This couldn't be a dream or a hallucination. The sights and smells were too real, too frightening. Had she died? No, no. This certainly wasn't heaven, and it was too cold to be hell.

So what had happened?

Before her mind could form an answer, a twig snapped.

Grace's chin whipped to the side, and she found herself staring up into cold, ice-blue eyes that swirled in startling precision with the mist. She sucked in an awed breath. The owner of those extraordinary eyes was the most ferociously masculine man she'd ever seen. A scar slashed from his left eyebrow all the way to his chin. His cheekbones were sharp, his jaw square. The only softness to his face was his gloriously lush mouth that somehow gave him the hypnotic beauty of a fallen angel.

He stood in front of her, at least six foot five and pure, raw muscle. He was shirtless, his stomach cut into several perfect rows of strength. A six-pack, she mused, the first she'd ever seen in real life. Shards of mist fell around him like glittery drops of rain, leaving glistening beads of moisture on his bronzed, tattooed chest.

Those tattoos were glowing, but more than that, they appeared alive. A fierce dragon spread crimson wings and seemed to be flying straight out of his skin, like a 3-D image come to dazzling life. The dragon's tail dipped low, past the waist of the black leather pants. Around its body were black symbols that boasted curling slashes and jagged points. These stretched the length of his collarbone and around the biceps.

The man himself proved more barbarous than his tattoos. He held a long, menacing sword.

A wave of fear swept through her, but that didn't stop her from staring. He was utterly savage. Fascinatingly sensual. He reminded her of a caged, wild animal. Ready to strike. Ready to consume. Danger radiated from his every pore, from the dark rim of his crystalline, predator eyes, to the blades strapped to his boots.

With a flick of his wrist, he twirled the sword around his head.

She inched backward. Surely he didn't mean to use that thing. My God, he was lifting it higher as if he really did mean to… "Whoa, there." She managed a shaky laugh. "Put that away before you hurt someone." *Namely me.*

He gave the lethal weapon another twirl, brandishing the sharp silver with strong, sure hands. His washboard abs rippled as he moved closer to her. Not a trace of emotion touched his expression. Not anger, fear, or mischievousness, offering her no clue as to why he felt the need to practice sword-slicing techniques in front of her.

He stared at her. She stared back, and told herself it was because she was too afraid to look away.

"I mean you no harm," she managed to croak out. Time dragged when he didn't respond.

Before her horror-filled eyes, his sword began to slice downward, aimed straight for her throat. He was going to kill her! On instinct, she swiped her gun from the waist of her pants. Her breath snagged in her throat, burning like acid as she squeezed the trigger. *Click, click, click.*

Nothing happened.

Shit. *Shit!* The cylinder was empty. She must have used all of her bullets on her bastard of a guide. The gun shook in her hand, and terror wrapped around her with the chill of a wintry storm. Her gaze scanned the cave, searching for a way out. The mist was the only exit, but the savage warrior's big, strong body now blocked it.

"Please," she whispered, not knowing what else to do or say.

Either the man didn't hear her, or he didn't care what she said. His sharp, deadly sword continued to inch closer and closer to her neck.

She squeezed her eyelids tightly shut.

CHAPTER THREE

DARIUS UTTERED a fierce curse and allowed his sword to pass just in front of the woman, never actually touching her. The action danced a delicate breeze through the red tendrils of her hair. The fact that he could see the actual color, a tempest of carmine that tumbled around her shoulders, startled him enough that he hesitated to destroy the possessor of such brilliance.

He fought past his shock and gripped his weapon at his side, trying to prepare his limbs to wreak destruction. Trying to force icy determination through his veins and push away any thoughts of mercy or sorrow. He knew what he had to do. Strike. Destroy.

That was his oath.

But her hair… His eyes basked in their first intake of color in over three hundred years. His fingers itched to touch. His senses longed to explore. He should have hated it. He'd *wanted* his senses barren. Hadn't he? But he'd looked at her, thought of the family he'd once loved, and his determination had cracked. That crack had been all his senses needed to activate.

Kill, his mind demanded. *Act!*

His teeth gnashed together, and his shoulders tightened. His tutor's voice echoed through him. *"Killing travelers is your obligation. Killing them is your privilege."*

There were times, like now, he loathed the tasks he performed, but never once had he hesitated to do what was needed. He'd simply continued on, assassination after assassination, knowing there was no other alternative for him. His dragon life force had long since overpowered his mortal side. There was a conscience living inside him, yes, but it was shriveled and decayed from lack of use.

So why was he hesitating now, with *this* traveler?

He studied her. Freckles dotted every inch of her skin, and streaks of dirt marred her jaw. Her nose was small and elfin, her lashes thick, sooty, and so long they cast spiky shadows on her cheeks. Slowly she opened her eyes, and he sucked in a heated breath. Her eyes were green and flecked with ribbons of blue, each color dusted with determination and fear. These new colors mesmerized him, enchanted him. Made his every protective instinct surface. Worse…

It shouldn't have—gods, it shouldn't have—but desire coiled inside him, powerful coils that refused to loosen their grip.

When the woman realized his sword tip pointed to the ground, she crouched down ever so slightly, clutching an oddly shaped metal object. He could only assume she was in attack position. She was frightened, true, but to survive she would fight him with all of her strength.

Could he really destroy such bravery?

Yes. He must.

He would.

Mayhap he truly was the heartless beast Tagart had called him. No, surely not, he thought in the next instant. The very actions that made him evil made him a keeper of the peace and provided safety for all residing in Atlantis.

There could be no other way.

Yet looking at this newest intruder, really looking at her, he *felt* like a beast. Her features were so guileless, so angelic, sparks of some unfamiliar emotion crackled within him. Concern? Regret? Shame?

A combination of all three?

The sensation was so new, he had trouble identifying exactly what it was. What made this traveler so different from the others that he hesitated—and, gods forbid, felt desire? The fact that she resembled a delicate fairy queen? Or the fact that she was everything he'd always secretly wanted—beauty, gentleness and joy—but knew he could never have?

Unbidden, his gaze drank in the rest of her. She was not tall, but had a regal bearing that gave her an air of height. Her skin was smudged with grime and sweat that did nothing to detract. Her clothing fit her rounded curves to perfection and paid her beauty proper homage.

More unwelcome sensations pulsed through him, unnamable sensations. Hated sensations. He should feel nothing; he should remain detached. But he felt; and he wasn't. He yearned to trace his fingertips all over her, to immerse himself in her softness, to bask in her colorful brilliance. He yearned to taste, yes, actually taste her entire body and drive away the flavor of nothingness.

"No," he said, more for his benefit than her own. "No."

He *must* destroy her.

She had broken the law of the mist.

All those years ago a Guardian had failed to accomplish his duty, had failed to protect Atlantis, and in turn brought about the deaths of many people—people Darius had loved. He could not, *would* not allow even this fairy queen to survive.

Knowing this, Darius still remained in place, unmoving. His cold, hard logic warred against his primitive, male appetite. If only the woman would glance away…but seconds turned to minutes, and her gaze remained fixed on him, studying. Perhaps even appreciating.

Desperate to escape the mental hold she had on him, he demanded, "Turn your gaze, woman."

Slowly, so slowly, she shook her head, whisking red tendrils around her temples. "I'm sorry. I don't understand what you're saying."

Even her voice was innocent, soft and lyrical, a caress of his senses. Yet he had no idea what she had said.

"Damn this," he muttered. "And damn me."

The corners of his lips twitched in a scowl. He

commanded himself to remain indifferent to her even while he sheathed his sword and closed the distance between them. There was no reason to do what he was about to do, but he could not stop himself. His actions were no longer controlled by his mind, but by some force he didn't understand or want to acknowledge.

She gasped at his approach. "What are you doing?"

He pressed her back, crowding her until she met the rock-lined wall; she kept the metal object directed at him, the silly thing clicking over and over again. Did she truly expect to protect herself from a dragon warrior with such a useless object? He easily pried it from her fingers and tossed it behind his shoulder. Unbeaten, she lashed out, kicking and hitting and scratching like a wild demon.

He secured her by the wrists, pinning them above her head. "Cease," he said. When she continued to squirm, he sighed and waited for her to tire. Only a few minutes passed before her movements slowed, then halted altogether.

"You'll go to prison for this," she said, dragging in breath after breath.

Her warm exhalations caressed his chest, their intoxicating sweetness a tangible entity that prodded his memory, another gentle reminder of the family he couldn't quite banish from his mind. He almost jerked away from her, but the scent of fear and orchids enveloped him, a sensual declaration of her appeal. He'd smelled nothing but ash for so long; he couldn't help but luxuriate in this new fragrance. Inhaling deeply, he pressed against her, brushing her body with his, closing all hint of separation. The need to touch her, any part of her, refused to leave him.

She shivered. From the cold? he wondered. Or from a turbulent desire similar to his own? Her nipples were pebbled against his ribs, erotically abrading, and as he watched her nibble her soft bottom lip, the arousal he felt for her became a storm. A desperate, wild storm. A storm so intense it was like a supernatural entity. His dragon's blood flowed to his cock like a freshly sprung river, hot and consuming.

His lips curled into a self-disparaging smile. The moment he realized he was actually smiling, he frowned. How his men would have laughed to crown this dainty creature the winner of their wager. Yet he couldn't seem to make himself care. By the gods, he'd never felt anything so perfect, so right.

His captive blinked up, and their gazes collided. Had white-hot sparks of awareness visibly enveloped them at that moment he would not have been surprised.

This woman is your enemy, he reminded himself, gritting his teeth and shifting his hips so that his erection remained a safe distance away.

"The mind is open, the ears will hear," he bit out. "Understand we do, apart or near. My words are yours—your words are mine. This I speak. This I bind. From this moment, through all of time."

Still watching her, he said, "Do you understand my words now?"

"Yes. I—I do." Her eyes widened, darkening with renewed flecks of alarm. Her mouth opened and closed several times as she struggled to form a coherent rejoinder. "How?" was all she could manage. Her voice was strained. Then, she added more strongly, "How?"

"I cast a spell of comprehension over your mind."

"Spell? No, no. That's not possible." She shook her head. "I speak three languages, and I had to work hard to learn every one of them. What did you do to me? What did you do to my brain?"

"I have already explained that to you."

"Don't tell me the truth, then." She laughed, the sound emerging desperate rather than humorous. "None of this matters, anyway. Tomorrow morning I'll wake up and discover this was all a horrible nightmare."

No, she wouldn't, he thought, hating himself more at that moment than ever before. Tomorrow's dawning she would not wake at all. "You should not have come here, woman," he said. "Do you care nothing for your life?"

"Is that a threat?" She fought against his hold. "Let me go."

"Cease your struggles. Your actions merely press your body deeper into mine."

She immediately stilled.

"Who are you?" he demanded.

"I'm an American citizen, and I know my rights. You can't keep me here against my will."

"I can do anything I like."

All color drained from her face because there was no denying the truth of his words.

To prolong her demise like this is cruel, his mind shouted. *Close your eyes and strike.*

Once again his mind and body acted as separate entities. He found himself releasing her and stepping backward. She leapt away from him as if he were a bloodsucking vampire or a hideously misshapen Formorian.

He focused all of his might on her destruction, looking anywhere except her enigmatic, sea-colored eyes, thinking of anything except her fierce, admirable spirit. Her shirt was torn and gaped down the middle, revealing the hint of two perfect breasts encased in pale pink lace. Another spark of desire flared inside him. Until his gaze locked on the two sets of rubied eyes that hung in the valley of her breasts.

His breath snagged as he studied the ornament more intently. Surely that was not…could not be…

But it was.

A frown cemented his features, and his fingers fisted so tightly his bones almost snapped. How had this woman come to possess such a sacred talisman? The gods awarded every dragon warrior a Ra-Dracus, a Dragon's Fire, upon reaching manhood, and a warrior never removed his gift, not for any reason save death. The markings etched at the base of this one were familiar to him, but he could not recall exactly to whom it belonged.

Not this woman, that much he knew. She was not a dragon, nor was she a child of Atlantis.

His frown deepened. Ironically the very oath that commanded him to harm her also compelled him to keep her alive until she explained how and why she had the medallion. Reaching out, he attempted to remove it from her neck. She slapped his palm and scampered backward.

"Wh-what are you doing?" she demanded.

"Give me the medallion."

She didn't cower at his hard tone as most would have done. Nor did she jump to obey. No, she returned his gaze with unflinching courage. Or stupidity. She remained firmly in place now, hands at her side.

"Don't come any closer," she told him.

"You wear the mark of a dragon," he continued. "And you, woman, are no dragon. Give me the medallion."

"The only thing I'll give you is an ass-kicking, you rotten thief. Stay back."

He leveled her with a resolute gaze. She was defensive and fearful. Not a good combination when trying to obtain answers. He almost sighed. "I am called Darius," he said. "Does that ease your fears?"

"No, no it doesn't." Contrary to her words, her muscles relaxed slightly. "My brother gave me this necklace. It's my only link to him these days, and I'm not giving it up."

Darius worried a hand down his face. "What is your name?"

"Why do you want to know?"

"What is your name?" he repeated. "Do not forget who holds the sword."

"Grace Carlyle," she reluctantly supplied.

"Where is your brother now, Grace Carlyle?" Her name floated easily from his tongue. Too easily. "I wish to speak with him."

"I don't know where he is."

And she did not like that she did not know, he realized, studying the worry in her eyes. "No matter," he said. "The medallion does not belong to him, either. It belongs to a dragon, and I *will* have it back."

She studied him for a long, silent moment, then offered him a sunny if brittle smile. "You're right. You can have it. I just need a moment to take it off." She raised her arms as if she meant to do as she'd claimed—take it off. But in the next instant, she darted forward until she stood poised at the mist's entrance. His arm snaked out and jerked her back into the hard circle of his body. She gasped on impact.

Had his reflexes not been so quick, he would have lost her.

"You dare defy me?" he said, perplexed. As leader of this palace, he was used to having his every command obeyed. Well, before today and his army's game. That this woman opposed him was shocking, yet somehow added to her appeal. She was not a warrior and had no defense against him.

"Let me go!"

He held steady. "Struggling is pointless and merely delays what must be done."

"What must be done?" Instead of calming, she beat her pointy little elbows into his stomach. "What the hell must be done?"

He whirled her around and used one of his hands as a shackle, locking her against him, chest to chest, hardness to softness.

"Be still!" he shouted. Then blinked. Shouted? Yes, he'd actually raised his voice.

Amazingly enough, she stilled. Her breath came shallow and fast. Amid the growing quiet, he began to hear the beat of her heart, a staccato rhythm that reverberated in his ears. Their gazes narrowed on each other and looking away proved impossible. Minutes ticked by unnoticed.

"Please," she at last whispered, and he wasn't sure if she was asking him to release her or hold her more tightly.

He used his free hand to smooth up the velvety soft expanse of her neck, then gently flick her hair out of the way. The heat of her beckoned him to linger, and he fought the urge to glide his hands across her every feminine peak and hollow, from the plumpness of her breasts, to the slight roundness of her stomach. From the exotic slope of her legs, to the hot wetness of her center.

Was she the kind of woman who could accept and return his animal passion? Or would she find him more than she could handle?

The thought jarred him, and he gave a brutal

shake of his head to dislodge it. Whether she could handle him or not didn't matter. He wasn't going to bed this woman.

And yet…

He easily imagined Grace naked and in his bed, her body splayed for his view. Her arms open and waiting for him. She would smile slowly, seductively, and he would inch his way atop her, graze his tongue over every curve and hollow, enjoy her as he'd never enjoyed another—or let her enjoy him—until they both collapsed.

The fantasy caused his desire to intermingle with tenderness, each sensation sparking off the other as they raced through him.

Desire he could tolerate. Tenderness he could not.

For years he'd tried to suppress his physical needs, but he'd learned that was impossible. So he'd begun to allow himself the occasional woman, taking them hard and fast, then leaving them quickly afterward. He didn't kiss, didn't savor. Just took them with utter detachment, an easily forgettable coupling.

He needed that same detachment now, which meant he needed to ignore Grace's appeal. With that firmly rooted in his mind, he hurriedly unhooked the chain's clasp from around her neck, though he was careful not to bruise her.

"Give that back," she demanded, pulling against his hold. "It's mine."

"No. It is *mine*."

Her expression turned venomous.

Without removing his gaze from her, Darius secured the medallion around his own neck, causing it to clang against the other Ra-Dracus. "I have many questions for you, and I expect you to answer every one," he told her. "If you utter a single untruth, you will regret it. Is that clear?"

A strangled breath slipped past her lips.

"Do you understand?" he reiterated.

Wide-eyed, she nodded slowly.

"Then we will begin. You told me you want to give the medallion back to your brother. Why? What does he plan to do with it?"

"I—I don't know."

Did she lie? The angelic cast of her features suggested no untruth had ever passed from her lips. Thinking of her lips brought his gaze to them. They were plump lips. Lips made for a man's pleasure. He ran his hand down his face, unsure what to believe, but knowing he should not imagine those lips slipping up and down his shaft, her red hair spilling over his thighs.

"Where did he acquire it?" Darius ground out.

"I don't know," she said hollowly.

"From who did he acquire it?"

"His boss."

His boss…Darius's jaw ticked. That meant there were more surface dwellers involved. "How long has the chain been in your possession?"

She closed her eyes for a moment, silently counting the days. "A little over a week."

"Do you know what it is? Or what it does?"

"It does nothing," she said, her brow furrowed. "It's just a necklace. A piece of jewelry."

He regarded her intently, studying, gauging. "How, then, did you find the mist?"

She pushed out a breath. "I don't know, okay. I was walking around that damn jungle. I was hot and tired and hungry. I discovered an underground spring, stumbled upon the cave and crawled inside."

"Did anyone enter the cave with you?"

"No."

"Are you certain?"

She glared up at him, daring him to do what he would. "Yes, damn it. I'm certain. I was alone out there."

"If you have lied…" He allowed his threat to hang in the air unsaid.

"I told you the truth," she snapped.

Had she? He honestly didn't know. He only knew that he wanted to believe every word she uttered. He was too captivated by her beauty. Too entranced by her scent. He should kill her here and now, finally, but still he couldn't bring himself to hurt her. Not yet. Not until he'd had time and distance to put her in proper perspective.

I'm a fool, he thought. Darius grabbed her by the waist and hoisted her over his shoulder. She began kicking immediately, and her nails raked down his back.

"Put me down, you Neanderthalic bastard!" Her shrieks echoed in his ears. "I answered your questions. You have to let me go."

"Perhaps a little time in my chamber will make those answers of yours improve. Surely you can do better than 'I don't know.'"

"Improve? Improve! If I'd given you different answers, I would have been lying."

"We shall see."

He strode up the cave stairs and into the palace above. She continued to squirm and kick, and he continued to hold her firmly with his arms. He was careful to avoid his men as he carried her to his chamber. Once there, he tossed her atop the velvet covered mattress and tied her flailing arms and legs to the posts. Seeing her splayed on his bed made him sweat and ache. Made him rock-hard. Gods, he couldn't deal with her now, not when she looked so…eatable. Without another glance in her direction, he turned and strode into the hall. The door closed behind him of its own accord.

Sooner or later, the woman would have to die…by his own hand.

CHAPTER FOUR

ALONE IN THE ROOM, Grace tugged and squirmed until she freed her wrists. She untied the knots at her ankles and jerked upright. Alex had tied her up many times when they'd been children, so escaping seemed like child's play. Besides that, her captor had not tied the knots that tight. As if he'd been afraid to hurt her. She dragged in a shaky breath as her gaze darted throughout the spacious interior, taking in every detail. Other than the gloriously soft bed she sprawled upon, a tiered ivory chest was the only other furnishing. Colors…so many colors glistened from the jagged walls like rainbow shards trapped in onyx. There was a cream and marble hearth, unlit and pristine. The only exit was a door with no handle.

Where the hell am I? she wondered, panic rising.

Fear and adrenaline pounded furiously through her blood. A man who could afford this type of luxury could afford an impregnable security system. She fisted her hands on the sapphire velvet coverlet as another thought invaded her mind. A man who could afford this type of luxury could afford to kidnap and torture an innocent woman with no consequences.

Shooting to her feet, she tried to fight past her fear. *I'll be okay. I'll be okay.* She just needed to find a way out of here. Before *he* returned. She raced to the door, clawing at the tiny seam. When that didn't work, she pushed, trying to force the doors to split down the middle. The thick ivory remained firmly in place, refusing to budge even a little. She expelled a frustrated screech. She should have expected no different. Like he'd make escape that easy.

What was she going to do?

There were no windows to crawl through. And the ceiling…she glanced upward and gasped. The ceiling was comprised of layered crystal prisms, the source of the room's light. A thin crack stretched across the middle from one end to the other, giving way to a spectacular view of swirling, turquoise liquid. Yet the liquid didn't drip through. Fish and other sea creatures—those were *not* mermaids, she assured herself—swam playfully through the water.

I'm underwater. Underwater! She banged her fists against the door. "Let me out of here, damn you!"

No response was forthcoming.

"This is illegal. If you don't let me out, you'll be arrested. I swear you will. You'll go to prison and be forced to have intimate relations with a man named Butch. Let. Me. Out."

Again, no response. Her punches slowed, then stopped altogether. She rested her cheek against the coolness of the door. *Where the hell am I?* she wondered once more.

Something tugged at her memory…something

she had read. A book or a magazine, or…Alex's journal! she realized. The bottom dropped from her stomach, and she squeezed her eyes shut as the full implication hit her. Her brother had written about a doorway from earth to Atlantis, a portal surrounded by mist. Her mouth formed an O as a section of his text invaded her mind, clicking in place like the piece of a puzzle. Atlantis was not the home of an extraordinary race of people, but of horrible creatures found only in nightmares, a place the gods had hidden their greatest mistakes.

Her knees weakened and her stomach clenched. Turning, placing her back to the door, she sank to the cold, hard ground. It was true. She had traveled through the mist. She was in Atlantis. With horrible creatures even the gods feared.

Let this be a dream, a dream I'll awaken from any moment. I promise I won't complain about anything ever again. I'll be content.

If the gods heard her, they ignored her.

Wait, she thought, shaking her head. She didn't believe in ancient Greek gods.

I have to get out of here. She'd wanted danger and fulfillment, yes, but not this. Never this. En route to Brazil, she'd imagined how intrepid she would feel helping Alex, how accomplished she would feel proving or disproving such a well-loved myth.

Well, she'd just proved it—and she felt anything but accomplished.

"Atlantis," she whispered brokenly, staring over at the bed. The comforter appeared quilted from glass, yet she knew exactly how soft it was. She was in Atlantis, home of minotaurs, Formorians, were-wolves and vampires. And so many more creatures her brother hadn't been able to name them all. Her stomach gave another painful clench.

Just what type of creature was her captor?

She searched her memory. Minotaurs were half bull and half human. While *he* may have acted like a bull, he had not possessed the physical character-istics of one. Formorians were one-armed and one-legged creatures. Again, he didn't qualify. Could he be a werewolf or a vampire? Yet neither of those seemed right, either.

With his dragon tattoos, he seemed more like, well, a dragon. Could that be right? Didn't dragons have scales, a tail and wings? Perhaps he was the only human here. Or perhaps he was a male nymph, a creature so sexual, so potent and virile, he could not be released into human society. That certainly ex-plained her hopelessly powerful reaction to him.

"Darius," she said, rolling his name across her tongue.

She shivered twice, once in fear and once in something she didn't want to name, as his image filled her mind. He was a man of contradictions. With his swirling, ice-blue eyes, harsh, demanding tone and rock-solid muscles, he personified every-thing cold and callous, everything incapable of offering warmth. And yet, when he touched her, she'd felt molten lava run through her veins.

The man reeked of danger, resembling a warrior

who lived with no laws but his own. Like the deliciously tantalizing warriors she read about in romance novels. This was no novel, however. This man was real. Raw and primal. Purely masculine. When he spoke, his voice resonated a dark, barely leashed power reminiscent of midnight tempests and exotic, foreign lands. Despite everything, she had been drawn to him in the cave.

Despite everything, she was *still* drawn to him.

Never, in all of her twenty-four years, had a man stirred such sensuous awareness inside her. That this man did, a man who had threatened her—several times—blew her mind. He'd even tried to slice her in half with that monstrous sword of his. *But he didn't hurt you,* her mind whispered. *Not once.* His touch had been so gentle…almost reverent. At times, she'd thought his gaze was pleading with her to touch him in return.

"You need your head examined, young lady, if you actually find that man attractive." Her mother's stern voice reverberated in her mind. *"Tattoos, swords. Not to mention the beastly way he carried you over his shoulder. Why, I was horrified."*

Then her aunt Sophie piped in, *"Now, Gracie baby, don't listen to your mother. She hasn't had a man in years. You should offer him a little somesome. Does Darius have a single, older brother?"*

"I truly do need my head examined," she muttered. Her relatives were taking residence inside her mind, dispensing bits of advice whenever they wanted.

A wave of homesickness hit her in a way she hadn't experienced since her first week of summer camp all those years ago. Her mother might be reserved and exacting from years of caring for Grace's sickly father, but she loved and missed her. Her aunt loved her, too, and would have hugged her tight.

She drew her arms around her stomach, trying to mask the hollowness. Where had Darius gone? How long before he returned?

What did he plan to do with her?

Nothing good, that much she suspected.

The air here was warmer than in the cave, but the cold refused to leave her, and she trembled. Her gaze flicked up the jagged walls, to the ceiling. Climbing up might earn her scratched and bloody palms, injuries she'd willingly endure if the crystal ceiling opened wide enough for her to slip through and swim to safety.

She eased to her feet, her legs shaky. First she needed sustenance or she'd collapse—and then she'd never escape.

On top of the dresser was what looked to be a bowl of fruit and a flagon of wine. Drawing in a deep breath of sea-kissed air, she approached. Her mouth watered as she reached out and palmed an apple. Without giving herself time to contemplate the likelihood of poison, she quickly ate—more like inhaled, she thought—the delicious fruit. Then another. And another. Between bites, she sipped the sweet red wine straight from the flagon.

By the time she stepped to the edge of the wall, she felt stronger, more in control. She gripped two small ledges and hoisted herself up, balancing her feet on the sharp ebony. Up, up she scaled. She'd once climbed the Devil's Thumb in Alaska—not her favorite memory since she'd frozen her butt off—but at least she knew how to climb properly. She dared a peek down, gulped, and thought lovingly of the harness she had used on Devil's Thumb.

She reached the top, and her palms were indeed bruised and raw, throbbing. Using all of her might, she pushed and clawed at the crystal. "Come on," she said. "Open for me. Please open for me." Hope curdled in her stomach as the damn thing remained firmly closed. Near tears, she maneuvered her way down to the lowest outcropping and hopped to the floor.

She shoved her hair out of her face and took stock of her options. There weren't many since she was stuck in this room. She could passively accept whatever Darius had planned for her, or she could fight him.

No deliberation was required. "I'll fight," she said, resolved.

By whatever means necessary, she had to get home, had to find and warn her brother about the dangers of the mist—if it wasn't too late already. An image of Alex popped into her mind. His dark red hair artfully arranged around his pale face; his body lying motionless in a coffin.

She pressed her lips together, refusing to consider

the possibility a moment longer. Alex was alive and well. He was. How else would he have sent her his journal and the medallion? Stamps were not sold in the afterlife.

Her gaze scanned the room again, this time looking for a weapon. There were no knickknacks. No logs in the hearth. The only item that might work was the bowl holding the fruit, but Grace wasn't sure how much damage she could do to Darius's fat (okay, sexy) head with a surprisingly flexible bowl.

Disappointment swam through her. What the hell could she do to escape? Make a trip cord of the sheets? She blinked. Hey, that wasn't a bad idea. She raced over to the bed. When she lifted the silky linen, her palms ached sharply.

Despite the pain, she tied each end on either side of the sliding doors. Darius might look indomitable, but he was as vulnerable to mishap as everyone else. Even the myths of old spoke of every creature, be they human or god, as being fallible. Or in this case, fallable.

Though she lived in New York now, Grace had grown up in a little town in South Carolina, a place known for its friendliness and politeness to strangers. She'd been taught to never purposely hurt another human being. Yet she couldn't stop a slow smile of anticipation as she studied the sheet.

Darius was about to take a tumble.

Literally.

DARIUS STALKED into the dining hall. He paused only a moment when he realized he no longer saw colors, but once again saw merely black-and-white. He inhaled a disappointed breath. When he realized he smelled nothing, he stilled. Even his newly developed sense of smell had deserted him.

Until now, he hadn't realized just how much he missed those things.

This was Grace's doing, of course. In her presence, his defenses had crumbled and his senses had come alive. Now that there was distance between them, he had reverted to his old ways. What kind of power did she wield that she could so control his perceptions? A muscle ticked in his jaw.

Thankfully his men had not waited for his return. They had already adjourned to the training arena as he'd ordered. Though they were several rooms over the sounds of their grunts and groans filled the air.

Lips drawn tight, Darius moved to the immense wall of windows at the back of the room. He gripped the ledge above his head and leaned forward. As high upon the cliffs as this palace sat, he was granted a spectacular view of the city below. The Inner City. Where creatures were able to relax and intermingle. Even vampires, though he did not spy the masses his men had encountered.

Crowds of Sirens, centaurs, cyclops, griffins, and female dragons ventured from shops and strolled the streets as merchants peddled their wares. Several female nymphs frolicked in a nearby waterfall. How happy they appeared, how carefree.

He craved that same peace for himself.

With a growl, he pushed himself from the ledge and paced to the edge of the table, where he gripped the end with so much force the fire resistant wood-stone snapped. He had to get himself under control before he approached the woman—Grace—again. There were too many emotions churning inside him: desire, tenderness, fury.

He stabbed and pounded at the tenderness; he kicked and shoved at the desire. They proved most resilient, hanging on to him with a viselike grip. The lushness of her beauty could charm the strongest of warriors from his vows.

By the gods, if he experienced these sensations simply from holding her wrists, from gazing into her vibrant eyes, what would he feel if he actually palmed her full, lush breasts? What would he feel if he actually parted her luscious thighs and sank the thickness of his erection inside her? His tormented moan became a roar and echoed from the crystal above. Were he ever to have that woman naked and under him—he might perish from an overload of sensation.

He almost laughed. He, a bloodthirsty warrior who was thought to possess no heart and had felt nothing more than detached acceptance for three hundred years, was agonizing over one small woman. If only he hadn't smelled her sweetness, a subtle fragrance of flowers and sunshine. If only he hadn't caressed the silkiness of her skin.

If only he didn't want more.

What was it about her that defeated centuries of

safeguards? he wondered. If he figured out the answer to that, he could easily resist her.

Fight, man. Fight against her enchantment. Where is your legendary discipline?

With an almost brutal slash, he jerked a shirt from one of the wall hooks. He pulled the black material over his head, covering both of the medallions he wore. The etchings at the bottom of the one Grace had worn flashed before his mind, and in a sudden burst of clarity he placed the stolen medallion with its owner. Javar, his former tutor.

Darius frowned. How had Javar lost such a precious treasure? Did Grace's brother wield some strange power that allowed him to slip through the mist, fight Javar and win the sacred chain? Surely not, for Javar would have come to Darius for aid—if he still lived, his mind added.

Darius had spoken to his former tutor by messenger only a month ago. All had seemed well. But he knew better than anyone that a life could change in the space of a single heartbeat.

"You have to do something, Darius," Brand growled, flying into the room. The long length of his opalescent wings stretched to fill the doorway. Without a pause in their glide, his clawed feet smoothly touched the ground. He began striding closer. His sharp, lethal fangs were bared in an ominous scowl, a beacon of white against his scales.

Darius gave his friend a hard stare, careful to withdraw all emotion from his features. By word or deed, he refused to let any of his men know just how precariously he clung to his control. They would ask questions, questions he did not want to answer. Questions he honestly had no answers for.

"I will not speak with you until you calm down," he said. He crossed his arms over the width of his chest and waited.

Brand drew in a deep breath, then another, and very slowly his dragon form receded, revealing a bronzed chest and human features. His fangs retracted. The cut on his cheek had already healed, a courtesy of his regenerative blood. Darius fingered the scar on his own cheek. He'd acquired the injury from the nymph king years ago during battle and he'd never understood why he'd been left with such a mark.

"You have to do something," Brand repeated more calmly. He claimed the only clothes left on the hooks and tugged them on. "We're ready to kill each other."

Darius had met Brand not long after he'd moved into the palace. They'd both been young, barely more than hatchlings, and both their families had been slain during the human raid. From the beginning, he and Brand had shared a bond. Brand had always laughed and talked with him, made sure he was invited to participate in every dragon activity. While Darius had declined—even then he had kept himself a strict mental distance from others—he'd found companionship with Brand, found someone to listen to and trust.

"Blame your silly game," Darius said with a slight growl, reminded of the previous antics, "not me."

The corners of Brand's lips suddenly stretched to full capacity. "Emotions from you already? I'll take that to mean you want my head on a platter."

"Your head will do…to start." Forcing himself to appear relaxed, he clasped a chair and eased down backward. He rested his forearms against the velvet-trimmed back. "What caused you to transform this time?"

"Boredom and monotony," came his friend's dry tone. "We tried to begin the first round of a tournament, but couldn't stop fighting long enough. We're on the verge of complete madness."

"You deserve to be driven mad after the chaos you caused earlier."

Brand's smile renewed. "*Tsk, tsk, tsk,* Darius. You should be thanking me, not threatening me."

He scowled.

Brows arched, Brand said, "Don't tell me I'm about to win the wager. Not when there is no one here to witness my victory."

His scowl intensified. "Other than the game, what can I do to help ease this boredom?"

"Will you reconsider bringing us women?"

"No," he quickly answered. Grace's lovely face glimmered in his mind, and his lower abdomen contracted tightly. There would be no more women in his palace. Not when such a tiny one as Grace caused this type of reaction in him.

Brand did not seem to notice his disconcertment. "Then let us play our game. Let us try to make you laugh."

"Or rage?"

"Yes, even that. It is long past time someone broke through your barriers."

He shook his head. Someone already had, and he *hated* it. "I'm sorry, but my answer remains the same."

"Every year I watch you grow a little more distant. A little more cold. The game is more for your benefit than it is for ours."

With the fluidity inherent to all dragons, Darius shifted to his feet, causing the chair to glide forward. He did not need this now, not when he struggled so fiercely for control. One grin and he might crumble. One tear and he might fall. One scream and his deepest agonies might be unleashed. Oh, yes. He knew if ever the day came that he lost total control, he would be destroyed in a maelstrom of emotion.

"I am this way for a reason, Brand. Were I to open a door to my emotions, I would not be able to do my duty. Is that something you truly desire?"

Brand tangled a hand roughly through his braids. "You are my friend. While I understand the importance of what you do, I also wish you to find contentment. And to do so, something needs to change in your life."

"No," he said firmly. When Grace had stepped through that portal, his life had changed irrevocably—and not for the better. No, he needed no more change. "I happen to embrace monotony."

Realizing that argument held no sway, Brand changed his tactics. "The men are different from you, then. *I* am different. We need something to occupy our minds."

"My answer is still no."

"We need excitement and challenge," Brand persisted. "We yearn to discover what the vampires are up to, and yet we are forced to stay here and train."

"No."

"No, no, *no*. How I weary of the word."

"Yet you must make peace with it, for it is the only one I can offer you."

Brand stepped to the table, casually running his finger over the surface. "I hate to threaten you, and you know I would not do so if I felt there were any other way," he added quickly. "But if you do not allow us *something*, Darius, chaos will reign supreme in your home. We will continue to fight at the least provocation. We will continue to disrupt the meals. We will continue—"

"You have made your point." Darius saw the truth to his friend's words and sighed. If he did not relent in some way, he would know no peace. "Tell the men I will allow them to finish their wager, if they swear a blood oath to stay away from my chambers." His eyes narrowed and locked on to Brand. "But mark my words. If one—just one man—approaches my private rooms without my express permission, he will spend the next month chained to the bastion."

Brand's chin tilted to the side, and his golden gaze became piercing. Silence thickened around them as curiosity tightened his features. Darius had never barred anyone from his chambers before. His men had always been welcome to come to him with their troubles. That he withdrew that welcome now must seem odd.

He offered no explanation.

Wisely Brand asked no questions. He nodded. "Agreed," he said, giving Darius a friendly slap on the shoulder. "I believe you will see a remarkable change in everyone."

Yes, but would the change be for the better? "Before you reenter the training arena," Darius said, "send a messenger to Javar's holding. I desire a meeting."

"Consider it done." With a happy swagger to his step, Brand strode from the room as quickly as he had entered.

Alone once more, Darius allowed his gaze to focus on the staircase and climb upward toward his rooms. An insidious need to touch Grace's silky skin wove a tangled web through his body, just as potent as if she were sitting in his lap.

Brand had spoken of the men going mad, but it was Darius himself who was in danger of madness. He pushed a hand through his hair. Leaving Grace had not helped him in any way; the image of her atop his bed refused to leave his mind. He realized he was as calm as he would ever be where that woman was concerned. Which meant not calm at all. Best to deal with her now, before his craving for her increased.

Stroking the two medallions he wore, he followed the path his gaze had taken until he stood poised at the doorway. She would give him the answers he wanted, he thought determinedly, and he would act as a Guardian. Not a man, not a beast. But a Guardian.

Resolved, he released the medallions and the doors opened.

CHAPTER FIVE

No HINGES SQUEAKED. In fact, not a single sound emerged. Yet one moment the bedroom doors were closed and the next, the two panels were sliding open.

Grace stood to the left, unseen and hidden by the shadows cast by the thick ivory. When Darius stepped past her, his feet tangled in the sheet—aka trip cord.

He propelled forward with a grunt.

The moment he hit the ground, Grace jumped onto his back, using it as a springboard, and raced into the hall. Her head whipped from side to side as she searched for the right direction. Neither appeared better than the other, so she ran. She didn't get far before strong male hands latched on to her forearms and jerked her to a halt. Suddenly she was heaved onto Darius's shoulder, too shocked to protest as she was carried back to his room. Once there, he slid her down his body. She stilled, feeling the buttery softness of his shirt and the heat of his skin past her clothes. Their bodies were so close she even felt the ripple of his muscles.

Without releasing her, he somehow caused the doors to slam together, blocking her only exit. She watched, her gaze widening. Breath froze in her lungs as failure loomed around her. No. *No!* In a mere two seconds, he'd snatched away her best chance for freedom.

"You will not be leaving this place," he said without a hint of anger, only determination. And regret? "Why are you not in my bed, woman?"

Overwhelmed by her failure, she whispered, "What do you plan to do with me?"

Silence.

"What do you plan to do with me?" she cried.

"I know what I *should* do," he said, his voice now a low growl that vibrated with anger, "but I do not yet know what I *will* do."

"I have friends," she said. "Family. They'll never rest until they find me. Hurting me will only earn you their wrath."

There was a concentrated hesitation, then, "And what if I do not hurt you?" he asked so softly she barely heard him. "What if I only offer you pleasure?"

Had the callused surface of his palms not brushed her forearms, she might have been frightened by his words. Now she was oddly enthralled. Every fantasy she'd ever created rushed through her mind. Naked, writhing bodies—on the floor, against a wall, inside an airplane. Her cheeks fused with heat. *What if I only offer you pleasure?* She didn't answer him. Couldn't.

He answered for her. "No matter what I offer you, there is nothing you or anyone else can do about it." His voice hardened, losing its sensual edge. "You are in my home, in my personal chambers, and I will do whatever I want. No matter what you say."

With such a dire warning ringing in her ears, she snapped from whatever spell he'd woven and called upon her terrorist training from flight school. SING, she inwardly chanted. Solar plexus, instep, nose, groin. Spinning, she elbowed him in the solar plexus, then slammed her foot into his instep. She swung back around and shoved her fist into his cold, unemotional face. Her knuckles collided with his cheek instead of his nose, and she cried out in pain.

He didn't flinch. He didn't even bother to grab her wrist to prevent her from doing it again.

So she did.

She drew back her other arm and let it fly. On impact, she experienced a repeat of the first punch. Throbbing pain for her, smug amusement for him. No, not amusement, she realized. The blue of his eyes was too cold and hollow to hold any type of emotion.

He arched a brow. "Fighting me will only cause *you* hurt."

Her gaze slitted, incredulous, clashing with his. After everything she'd endured these past two days, Grace's temper and frustration erupted full force. "What about you?" She jerked her knee up, hard and fast, gaining a direct hit between his legs. Groin: the last section of her training.

A slight breath whooshed from his lips as he hunched over and squeezed his eyes shut.

She raced to the door and began clawing at the seam. "Open, damn you," she railed at the exit. "Please. Just open."

"You do not look capable of such a deed," Darius said, his voice strained. "But I will not underestimate you again."

She never heard him move, but suddenly he was there, his arms braced next to her temples, his hot breath on her neck. She didn't try to fight him this time. What good would that do? He'd already proved he did not react (much) to physical pain.

"Please," she said. "Just let me go." Her heartbeat thundered in her ears. From fear, she assured herself, not from the sensual strength of his body so close to her own.

"I cannot."

"Yes, you can." She twisted, facing him, and shoved him backward. The impact, though slight, caused him to trip once more on the sheet. He took her down with him and when he hit, he rolled them over and pinned her.

Automatically she reached up to push him away from her. But her fingers caught in his shirt, causing the neckline to gape. Both of the medallions he wore sprang free and one of them plopped against her nose. She gasped. Which one belonged to Alex? The one with the glowing eyes?

What did it matter? she thought then. She'd come here with a medallion, and she was leaving with one.

Determination thudded like a drum inside her chest. To distract him, she screamed with all the power her lungs allowed. She flailed her legs and wrapped her sore hands around his neck, as if she meant to choke him. She hurriedly worked one of the clasps, and when she felt it unlatch, she jerked her hands down and shoved the chain into her pocket. She gave another ear-piercing scream to cover her satisfaction.

"Calm down," he said, his features pinched.

"Bite me." She screamed again.

When she quieted, he said, "I would be most upset if you damaged my ears."

Upset? He would be most upset. Not infuriated, not lost in a rage. Simply mildly upset. Somehow, with this man, that seemed all the more frightening than out-of-control fury. With a deep, shuddering breath, she relaxed into the floor. After all, she had what she wanted, and fighting him did nothing more than press their bodies together, as he was fond of reminding her.

His brows winged up, and he blinked, broadcasting his shock at her easy compliance.

"That easily?" he asked, suspicious.

"I know when I'm beaten."

Darius used her stillness to his advantage and allowed more of his muscled weight to settle atop her. He braced her wrists above her head—something he obviously liked to do, since it was the third time he'd done it to her—causing her back to arch and her breasts to lift for his view.

"You wish for me to bite you?" he asked, dead serious.

Briefly she experienced confusion. Then she realized what he meant. Oh, my God. She *had* told him to bite her. Something dark and hot twisted in her stomach, something she had no business feeling for this man. An image of his straight white teeth sinking into her body and taking a little nibble filled her line of vision. Erotic and sexual; except…

If he were a vampire, she'd just given him an open invitation to make her his next meal.

"I didn't mean it literally," she managed to squeak out. "It's just a figure of speech." With barely a pause, she added, "Please. Get off me." He smelled so good, so masculine, like the sun, the earth and the sea, and she was sucking in great gulps of that scent as if it were the key to her survival. He was beyond dangerous. "Please," she said again.

"Too much do I like where I am."

Those words echoed in her mind with such clarity her body offered a reply: *I like where you are, too.* She ran her teeth over her bottom lip. How did he do this? How did he make her feel strangely captivated and oddly entranced, yet fearful at the same time? He was quite possibly a bloodsucking vampire. He was also so sexy he made her mouth water. Made her ache in places she'd thought dead from disuse. Made her crave and fantasize and hunger.

Get a hold of yourself, Grace. Only an idiot would lust after a man of questionable origins and even more questionable motives.

What did he want from her? She studied his face, but found no hint of his intentions. His features were completely blank. Her gaze probed deeper, taking in the scar that slashed down his cheek, raised and puckered, interrupting the flow of his dark eyebrows. This close, she noticed the slant to his nose, as if it had been broken one too many times.

He was darkly seductive. Dangerous, her mind repeated.

That's it, she realized reproachfully. *That's why I'm so attracted to him. I'm a danger junkie.*

"What did you do to your hands, woman?" he suddenly demanded. His features were no longer blank, but projected a fierceness that was beyond intimidating.

"If I tell you," she said, faltering in the face of that severity, "will you let me go?"

His eyes narrowed, and he brought one of her palms to his mouth. Heated lips seared her flesh before the tip of his tongue flicked out, licking and laving the wounds. Electric currents raced through her arm, and she almost experienced an orgasm right then and there.

"Why are you doing that?" she asked on a breathless moan. Whatever the reason, his actions were utterly suggestive, endearingly sweet, and she gasped at the deliciousness of it. "Stop." But even as she spoke, she prayed he didn't heed her command. Her skin was growing increasingly warm, her nerve-endings increasingly sensitive. A drugging languor floated through her, and God help her, she wanted that tongue to delve further, to explore deeper territory.

"My saliva will heal you," he said, his voice still fierce. But it was a different kind of fierce. More strained, more heated, less angry. "What did you do to your hands?" he asked again.

"I climbed the walls."

He paused. "Why would you do such a thing?"

"I was trying to escape."

"Foolish," he muttered. One of his knees wedged between the juncture of her thighs. The ache in her belly intensified as their legs intertwined.

He exchanged one hand for the other, swirling his tongue along the peaks and hollows, making her aware of all sorts of erotic things. The way his eyes flickered from ice-blue to golden-brown. The way his soft, silky hair fell over his shoulders and tickled her skin.

If he planned to hurt or kill her, surely he wouldn't concern himself with her comfort like this. Surely he would not—

He sucked one of her fingers into his mouth. She moaned and gasped his name. He whorled his tongue around the base. This time, she moaned incoherently and arched up, meshing her nipples into his chest and creating a delicious friction.

"That is better," he said roughly.

Her eyelids fluttered open. His expression taut, he held her hands up for her view. Not a single blemish appeared on the healthy, pink skin.

"But—but—" Confusion overshadowed her pleasure. How was that possible? How was any of this possible? "I don't know what to say."

"Then say nothing."

He could have left her sore and bruised, a punishment for trying to escape, but he hadn't. She didn't understand this man. "Thank you," she said softly.

He nodded, the action stiff. "You are welcome."

"Will you let me up now?" she asked, dreading—anticipating?—his response.

"No." He placed her left palm at her side, but held firm to the right. His fingers continued to caress and trace every line, as if he couldn't stand to break contact. "What did your brother plan to do with the medallion?"

Briefly she considered lying, anything to stop the flood of conflicting desires running rampant. Then, just as briefly, she considered not answering him at all. She knew instinctively, however, that he would not tolerate either from her and that would merely prolong their contact. So she found herself saying, "We've been over this before, and I still don't know. Maybe he wanted to sell it on eBay. Maybe he wanted to keep it for himself, for his private collection."

Darius's brow furrowed. "I don't understand. Explain to me this eBay."

As she expounded on the concept of the online auction, he glowered furiously.

"Why would he do such a thing?" Darius asked, genuinely perplexed. "Selling such an item to a stranger is the epitome of foolishness."

"Where I'm from, people need money to survive. And one way to make money is to sell our possessions."

"We need money here, too, yet we would never barter our most prized possessions. Is your brother too lazy to work for his dinner?"

"I'll have you know he works very hard. And I didn't say he *was* going to sell it. Only that he might. He's an auction addict."

Darius expelled a sigh and finally released her hand, bracing his palms on either side of her head. "If you mean to confuse me, you are doing a fine job. Why would your brother give you the medallion if he had any desire to sell it?"

"I don't know," she said. "Why do you care?"

In stalwart silence, he watched her, looked past her, then watched her again, his dark thoughts churning behind his eyes. Instead of answering her, he said, "You claim to know nothing, Grace, yet you found the mist. You traveled through. You must know something more, something you haven't told me."

"I know I didn't mean to enter your domain." The faintness of her voice drifted between them. "I know I don't want to be hurt. And I know I want to go home. I just want to go home."

When his features hardened dangerously, she replayed her words through her mind. What could she have possibly said to have such an ominous effect on him?

"Why?" he demanded, the single word lashing from him.

She crinkled her forehead and gazed up at him. "Now *you* are confusing *me*."

"Is there a man waiting for you?"

"No." What did that have to do with anything? Unless…surely he wasn't jealous. The prospect amazed her. She was not the kind of woman to inspire any kind of strong emotion in a man. Not lightning-hot lust and certainly not jealousy. "I miss my mom and my aunt, Darius. I miss my brother and my apartment. My furniture. My dad made all of it before he died."

Darius relaxed. "You asked me why I care about the medallion. I do so for *my* home," he said. "I will do anything to protect it, just as you will do anything to return to yours."

"How can my owning the medallion hurt your home?" she asked. "I don't understand."

"Nor do you need to," he replied. "Where is your brother now?"

Her eyes narrowed, and her chin raised in another show of defiance. "I wouldn't tell you even if I knew."

"I respect your loyalty, and even admire it, but it is to your benefit to tell me whether he traveled through the mist or not."

"I told you this before. I don't know."

"This is getting us nowhere," he said. "What does he look like?"

Pure stubbornness melded the blue and green of her eyes together, creating a churning sea of turquoise. Her lips pursed. Darius could tell she had no plans to answer him.

"This way I can know if I have already killed him," he prompted, though he wasn't sure he would recognize any of his victims if he ever saw them again. Killing was second nature to him, and he barely glanced at them anymore.

"Already— Killed him?" She uttered a strangled gasp. "He's a little over six foot. Red hair. Green eyes."

Since Darius had not seen colors before Grace, the description she'd just given meant nothing. "Does he have any distinguishing marks?"

"I—I—" As she struggled to form her reply, a tremor raked her spine and vibrated into him. Her eyes filled with tears. A lone droplet trickled onto her cheek.

His arm muscles constricted as he fought the need to wipe the moisture away. He watched it glide slowly and fall onto her collarbone. Her skin was pale, he noticed, too pale.

The woman was deathly afraid.

The clamor of his conscience—something he'd thought long expired—filled his head. He'd threatened this woman, locked her inside a strange room, and fought her to the ground, yet she had retained her fierce spirit. The concept of her brother's death was breaking her as nothing else had been able.

There was a good chance, a very good chance, he *had* killed her brother. How would she react then? Would those sea-eyes of hers regard him with hatred? Would she vow to spill his blood in vengeance?

"Does he have any distinguishing marks?" Darius asked her again, almost fearing her reply.

"He wears glasses." Her lips and chin trembled. "They're wire-rimmed because he thinks they make him look dig-dignified."

"I know not what these glasses are. Explain."

"Cl-clear, round o-orbs for the eyes." Her trembling had increased so much she had trouble forming her words.

He pushed out a breath he hadn't known he'd been holding. "A man wearing glasses has not entered the mist." He knew this because he would have found the glasses after the head rolled to the ground—and he hadn't. "Your brother is safe." He didn't mention there was a chance Alex could have entered the other portal. Javar's portal.

Grace began to cry in great sobbing howls of relief. "I hadn't wanted to think of the possibility…and when you said…I was so afraid."

Perhaps he should have left her alone just then, but the relief radiating from her acted as an invisible shackle. He couldn't move, didn't want to move. He was jealous that she felt this strongly for another man, no matter that the man was her brother. More than the jealousy, however, he felt possessive. And more than the possessiveness, he felt the need to comfort. He wanted to wrap his arms around her and surround her with his strength, his scent. Wanted her branded by *him*.

How foolish, he thought darkly.

The love she possessed for her brother was the same he had felt for his sisters. He would have fought to the death to protect them. He would have… His lips curled in a snarl, and he banished that line of thought to a hidden corner of his mind.

Grace pressed her lips together but another sob burst free.

"Stop that, woman," he said more harshly than he'd intended. "I forbid you to cry."

She cried harder. Big fat tears rolled down her cheeks, stopping at her chin, then splashing onto her neck. Red splotches branched from the corners of her eyes and spread to her temples.

Hours passed—surely these long, torturous moments could not be mere minutes—until she at last heeded his order and quieted. Shuddering with each breath, she closed her eyes. Her long, dark lashes cast shadowed spikes over the too-red bloom of her cheeks. He held his silence, allowing her this time to gather her composure. If she began crying again, he didn't know what he'd do.

"Is there…anything I can do to help you?" he asked, the words stilted. How long since he'd offered comfort to anyone? He couldn't recall, and wasn't even sure why he'd offered now.

Her eyelids fluttered open. There was no accusation in the watery depths of her gaze. No fear. Only pitying curiosity. "Have you been forced to hurt many people?" she asked. "To save your home, I mean?"

At first, he didn't answer her. He liked that she wanted to believe the best in him, but his honor demanded he warn her, not lock her in delusions about a man he'd never been. Nor would ever be. "Save your pity, Grace. You fool yourself if you think I have ever been forced to do anything. I make my own choices and act of my own free will. Always."

"That doesn't answer my question," she persisted.

He shrugged.

"There are alternatives. You could talk to people, communicate."

She was trying to save him, he realized with no small amount of shock. She knew nothing about him, not his rationale, not his past, not even his beliefs, yet she was trying to save his soul. How…extraordinary.

Women either feared him or wanted him, daring to take a beast into their beds; they never offered him more than that. He'd never wanted more. With Grace, he found himself desirous of all she had to give. She called to the deepest needs inside him. Needs he hadn't even realized he possessed.

Admitting such profound desire, even to himself, was dangerous. Except, he suddenly didn't care. Everything but this moment, this woman, this need, seemed utterly insignificant. It didn't matter that she had passed through the mist. It didn't matter that he had an oath to fulfill.

It didn't matter.

He dropped his gaze to her lips. They were so exotic, so wonderfully inviting. His own ached for hers, a soft press or a tumultuous crush. He'd never kissed before, hadn't cared to try, but right now the need to consume—and to be consumed—by that heady meeting of lips proved stronger than any force he'd ever encountered.

He gave her one warning. Only one. "Stand up or I will kiss you," he told her roughly.

Her mouth dropped opened. "Get off me so I can stand!"

He rose, and she quickly followed. They stood there, two adversaries caught in a frozen moment. The withdrawal of her body from his hadn't lessened his need, however. "I'm going to kiss you," he said. He meant to prepare her, but the words emerged more of a warning.

"You said you wouldn't if I stood," she gasped.

"I changed my mind," he said.

"You can't. Absolutely not."

"Yes."

Her gaze darted from his mouth to his eyes, and she licked her lips just the way *he* wanted to lick them. When she dragged her gaze up again, he met her stare, holding her captive in the crackling embers of his own. Her pupils dilated, black nearly overshadowing the brilliant turquoise hue.

He recaptured her in his arms and dragged her back down to the floor. "Will you give me your mouth?" he asked.

A sizzling pause.

I want this, Grace realized dazedly. *I want him to kiss me.* Whether the fire of his desire had simply burned into her, or the desire was all her own, she wanted to taste him.

Their gazes locked and she sucked in a breath. Such desire. Blistering. Had there ever been a man who had looked at *her,* Grace Carlyle, like this? With such longing in his eyes, as if she was a great treasure to be savored?

The outside world receded, and she saw only this sexy man. Knew only the need to give him something of herself—and take something of him. He was living, breathing sexual gratification, she mused, and more dangerous than a loaded gun, yet as gentle and tender as a bed of clouds. *I truly am a danger junkie,* she thought, loving the contradictions of him. Was he a brute or a lamb—and which did she crave more?

"I shouldn't want to kiss you," she breathed.

"But you do."

"Yes."

"Yes," Darius repeated. Needing no more encouragement, he brushed his lips against hers once, twice. She immediately opened, and his tongue swept inside. She moaned. He moaned. Her arms glided up his chest and locked around his neck. He instinctively deepened the kiss, slipping and sliding and nipping at her mouth just the way he'd imagined. Just the way he wanted, uncaring if he were doing it right.

Their tongues thrust and withdrew, slowly at first, then growing in intensity, becoming as uncivilized as a midnight storm. Becoming wild. Becoming the kind of kiss he'd secretly dreamed of, the kind of kiss that caused the strongest of men to lose all sense of self—and be glad for the loss. Her legs relaxed around him, beckoning him closer, and he fitted himself into her every hollow, hard where she was soft.

"Darius," she said on a raspy pant.

Hearing his name on her lips was sheer bliss.

"Darius," she repeated. "Tastes good."

"Good," he whispered brokenly.

Caught in the same storm, she boldly rubbed herself against the hardness of his erection. Rubbed herself against all of him. Surprise mingled with arousal in her expression, as if she couldn't believe what she was doing but was helpless to stop. "This can't be real," she said. "I mean, you feel too good. *So* good."

"And you taste like—" Darius plunged his tongue deeper inside her mouth. Yes, he tasted her. Truly tasted her. She was sweet and tangy all at once, unfailingly warm. Flavored as delicately as aged wine. Had he ever sampled anything so delicious? "Ambrosia," he said. "You taste like ambrosia."

He buried one hand in her hair, luxuriating in the softness. His other hand traveled down her shoulder, down the slope of her breast, her ribs and over her thigh. She quivered, tightening her legs around his waist. He brought his hand back up and did it all over again. She purred low in her throat.

He wondered what she looked like just then, and wanted to see her eyes as he took his time with her, as he pleasured her in a way he'd never done with another woman. The concept of watching her, *seeing* her take her pleasure, was as foreign as his desire to taste her, but the need was there. He tore himself away from her mouth, breaking the kiss—surely the most difficult task he'd ever performed—and lifted slightly.

His exhalations came shallow and fast, and as he gazed down at her, his jaw clenched. Her eyes were closed, her swollen lips parted. The fiery red of her tresses was an erotically tousled mass around her face. Her cheeks glowed a rosy-pink, and the freckles on her nose seemed darker, more exotic.

She wanted him as desperately as he wanted her. His shaft hardened dangerously with the knowledge. She probably felt the same hopeless fascination and undeniable tug that he did. A tug he didn't understand. His soul was too black, hers too light. They should despise each other. They should have desired distance.

He should have desired her death.

He didn't.

She slowly opened her eyes. The delicate tip of her tongue darted out and traced her lips, leaving a glistening trail of moisture. How soft and fragile she was. How utterly beautiful.

"I'm not ready for you to stop," she said with a seductive smile.

He didn't respond. Couldn't. His vocal cords suddenly seized as something constricted in his chest, something arctic and scorching at the same time. Affection. *I should not have kissed her.* He jerked up and onto his knees, straddling her hips.

How could he have allowed something like this to happen, knowing he had to destroy her?

He was the one who deserved death.

"Darius?" she said questioningly.

Guilt perched heavily on his shoulders, but he fought past it. He always fought past it. He could not allow even guilt in his life if he hoped to survive.

As he continued to watch her, her expression turned to confusion and she gingerly lifted to her elbows. Those long, red curls cascaded down her shoulders in sensual disarray, touching her in all the places he yearned to touch. Her shirt gaped open over one creamy shoulder.

Silence thickened between them. Smiling bitterly, he wet the tips of two fingers and traced the lushness of her lips, letting the healing qualities of his saliva ease the puffiness and erase the evidence of his possession. She surprised him by sucking his fingers into her mouth just as he'd done to her earlier. Feeling the hot tip of her tongue caused his every muscle to bunch in expectation. He hissed in a breath and tugged his fingers away.

"Darius?" she said, her confusion growing.

He'd come here to question her, but the moment he'd seen her, touched her, *tasted* her, those questions had fled. Yes, he'd managed to ask her one or two, but the need to capture a glimmer of her innocent flavor had been so fierce he'd soon forgotten his purpose.

He'd forgotten Javar. He'd forgotten Atlantis.

He would not forget again.

If only he could prove her duplicitous, he could kill her now without a qualm, then rip her image from his mind. As it was, he wasn't sure he could force himself to even chip one of her pink oval-shaped nails. The thought unnerved him, battered against him, and filled him with the urge to howl at the gods. Failure to act against her would mean breaking his vow and surrendering his honor. But hurting her would mean obliterating the last shreds of his humanity.

Gods, what was he going to do?

He felt shredded as he lunged to his feet. A cold sweat popped on to his brow, and it required all of his strength to spin and stalk to the door. There, he paused. "Do not attempt to escape again," he said, not glancing back at her. If he faced her, he might lose the strength required to leave her. "You will not like what happens if you do."

"Where are you going? When will you be back?"

"Remember what I said." The thick ivory opened for him, and he stepped into his bathing room. Then the door sealed automatically, not emitting a single noise as it blocked her dangerous beauty from his view.

Grace sat where she was, shaking with…hurt? He'd wanted her, hadn't he? If so, why had he left her reeling from the intensity of his kiss?

Why had he left her at all?

He'd walked blithely away, almost callously, as if they'd done nothing more than discuss their least favorite disease. She laughed humorlessly.

Had he merely toyed with her? While she panted and ached for him, while she bathed in the decadence, the wildness and the exquisite need, had he merely sought to control her? To gain the answers he seemed to think she possessed?

Perhaps it was best that he'd left, she thought furiously. He was a confessed assassin, but if he'd stayed, she would have stripped herself naked, stripped him naked, then made love to him right here on the floor.

For that one moment in his arms, she'd finally felt whole and she hadn't wanted the feeling to end.

This hunger he awakened inside her…it was too intense to be real, but too real to be denied.

Beneath his cold, untouchable mask, she'd thought she had seen a fire blazing inside him, a tender fire that licked sweetly rather than devoured needlessly. When he'd gazed down at her so carnally and said, "I want to kiss you," she'd been so sure the fire was there, simmering under the surface of his skin.

Her long repressed hormones cried out whenever he was near, assuring her that any intimate contact with him would be wild and wicked. The kind she'd fantasized about for years now. The kind she read about in romance novels, then lay in bed, wishing a man was beside her.

Enough! You need to find a way out of here. Forget about Darius and his kisses.

Though her body protested something so sacrilegious, forgetting such an earth-shattering experience, Grace pushed the kiss to the back of her mind then dug the medallion from her pocket and anchored it around her neck, where it belonged. *Ha! Take that, Darius.*

She vaulted to her feet and spun in a circle, hoping that by searching the chamber this second time, she'd find a way out. A hidden latch, a sensor, *something.* When she saw only the same jagged walls, with no break in the pattern, she cursed under her breath. How did Darius enter and exit without so much as a word or touch?

Magic, most likely.

She blinked in surprise at the ease with which she entertained such a concept. Magic. Yesterday she would have committed anyone who claimed magic spells were real to a psych ward. Now, she knew better. She could speak a language she'd never learned.

Not possessing any magic of her own, she decided to ram into the door with her shoulder. She prayed she didn't break a bone as she girded herself for impact.

One breath, two. She rushed forward.

She never hit.

The door slid right open.

She nearly tripped over her own feet but managed to slow her momentum. When she stopped, she glared over at the door. If she didn't know better, she'd swear it was alive and purposefully tormenting her. There had been no reason for it to open this time. No reason except the medallion... Her eyes widened and she fingered the warm, ridged alloy at her neck. Of course. It had to be some sort of passkey, like a motion detector. That explained why Darius hadn't wanted her to have it.

I can escape, she thought excitedly. She surveyed her new surroundings. She wasn't in the hallway she'd expected. She was in some type of bathing room. There was a lavender chaise longue piled high with beaded, satin pillows; a large glistening pool rested inside a stone ledge. Towering, twisted columns. Multiple layers of sheer fabric hung from the ceiling. A decorator's dream.

In each of the three corners was an archway leading off somewhere. Grace debated which direction to take. Sucking in a deep breath, she raced through the center route. Her legs ate up the distance as she pumped her arms. The walls consisted of one jewel stacked upon another. From ruby to sapphire, topaz to emerald, the gems were interspersed with weblike gold filigree.

There were enough riches in this one little hallway to feed an entire country. Even the least avaricious of people would have trouble resisting such allure. That was exactly what Darius guarded against, she realized, the greed of modern day society. Exactly why he killed.

With all of this obvious wealth, she expected servants or guards, but she remained alone as she ran and ran and ran. A light at the end of the hallway caught her eye—and no, she didn't miss the irony of that. Huffing from exertion, she headed straight into the light. She may not have an exciting life to get back to, but at least she had a life. She had her mother, her aunt Sophie and Alex. Here she had only fear.

And Darius's kisses.

She scowled, not liking the heady thrill she received from the remembrance of his lips against hers, of his tongue invading her mouth oh, so sweetly. Of his body pressing into hers.

Lost yet again in the memory of such a soul-searing kiss, she didn't hear the frenzied male voices until it was too late. A table of weapons whizzed past before Grace spurted to a halt. Sand flicked around her ankles. Her mouth dropped open, as did the pit of her stomach.

Oh, my God.

She'd escaped Darius only to throw herself at six other warriors just like him.

CHAPTER SIX

GRACE STOOD at the edge of a huge arena of white stone and marble that resembled a restored Roman coliseum. Only the ceiling marred the illusion, boasting the same sea-covered crystal dome that comprised the rest of the…building? Castle?

Wide and long, the arena spanned the length of a football field. The air was scented with sweat and dirt, courtesy of the six men brandishing swords and basically trying to annihilate each other. Their grunts and groans blended with the cringe-worthy clang of metal. They had yet to notice her.

Her heart thudded in her chest, and she whipped around, intent on running back down the corridor. When she spied yet *another* warrior, this one just entering the far end, she scooted to the side, out of sight. Had he seen her? She didn't know; she only knew the nearest exit was blocked. *The nearest exit was blocked!*

"Calm down," she whispered. She'd wait two minutes. Surely the hallway would be clear by then; surely for such a short amount of time she could stay right here and remain unnoticed. Then she'd escape. Simple. Easy.

Please let it be simple and easy.

"Who taught you to fight, Kendrick?" one man snarled. He was the tallest man present, with broad shoulders and ropelike muscles. His pale hair was pulled back in a low ponytail, and the long length of it slapped his cheek as he shoved his opponent to the ground. "Your sister?"

The one called Kendrick jumped to his feet, sword raised in front of him. He wore the same black leather pants and black shirt as the others. He was obviously the youngest. "Perhaps it was *your* sister," he growled. "After I tumbled her, of course."

Grace's jaw dropped as green scales momentarily appeared on the first man's face. When she blinked, they were gone.

The tall blonde sheathed his sword and held out his hands. He motioned for Kendrick to approach him. "If I actually had a sister, I would kill you where you stand. Since I do not, I'm merely going to beat you senseless."

A man stepped between the two combatants. He had brown hair and surprisingly sad features. He was unarmed. "That's enough," he said. "We are friends here. Not enemies."

"Shut up, Renard." A boy only slightly older than Kendrick jumped into the argument. He pointed the tip of his sword at the sad one's chest. Wet strands of brown hair clung to his temples and framed the dragon tattoo that stretched up from his jawline. "It's time you and all the other *lucifaeres* learned you're not infallible."

Renard's golden eyes narrowed. "Remove the weapon, little hatchling, or I will gut you where you stand."

The "little hatchling's" face paled, and he did as commanded.

Grace inched backward a step. *Breathe,* she commanded herself. *Just keep breathing.* They were going to kill each other. Good news: If they were dead, they couldn't stop her from escaping.

"Smart move," another male said. This one had strawberry-blond hair and a breathtakingly beautiful face, which thoroughly contrasted with the fact that he was polishing a two-pronged hatchet. Dry amusement gleamed in his golden eyes. "Renard has killed men for less. I guess it helps that he knows exactly where to cut them, where to make them bleed and suffer for days at a time before finally, mercifully dying."

At his words, cold sweat beaded on Grace's forehead. She managed another inch backward.

"He's only trying to scare you," one of the younger boys gritted out. "Don't listen to him."

"I hope you kill each other." The heated phrase came from a black-haired warrior who slammed his weapon into the ground. "Gods know I'm tired of listening to all of your whining."

"Whining?" someone said. "That's rich coming from you, Tagart."

Kendrick chose that moment to launch himself at the large blonde. With a howl, the two men fell to the ground, fists flying. Every other man present paused only a moment before throwing himself into the fray. Oddly enough, every one of them seemed to be smiling.

Grace cast a quick glance to the hall. Empty. Relief threatened to topple her. She kept her eyes on the combatants and moved another inch backward…then another…then another.

And backed herself right into the table of weapons.

In a sudden symphony of disharmony, the different metals clanged together and tottered to the floor.

Then…silence.

All six men stopped, whirled and faced her. In the space of a few seconds, their bloody and bruised expressions registered shock, then happiness, then wicked hunger. Her breath snagged in her throat. She scrambled behind the table, specks of dirt flying about her shoes. A thin piece of wood would not stop these men, she knew, but she garnered a little courage with a barrier between them. She tried to lift a blade but it was too heavy.

A solid wall suddenly crowded her from behind. A very much alive, solid wall.

"Like to play with a man's sword, do you?"

Strong male arms wound around her waist—and they weren't Darius's. This man's skin was darker, his hands not quite as thick. But more than that, he didn't cause the same wave of arousal that Darius stirred in her. This man's embrace caused only fear.

"Remove your hands this instant," she said calmly, mentally applauding herself. "Otherwise you'll regret it."

"Regret it, or keep loving it?"

"Who do you have there, Brand?" one of the warriors asked.

"Give me a moment to find out," her captor answered. His rough voice drew closer to her ear, becoming a suggestive rumble. "What are you doing here, hmm?" he asked. "Women are not allowed in this palace, much less the training arena."

She gulped. "I—I—Darius is—"

He tensed against her. "Darius sent you?"

"Yes," she answered, praying such an admission would scare the man into freeing her. "Yes, he did."

A chuckle rumbled from him. "So he heeded my advice, after all. To keep us from teasing him, our leader sent us a whore. I never expected that. What's more, I never expected him to act so quickly."

Her mind only registered one portion of his speech. A whore? Whore! If they thought she was paid to have sex with them, they'd most likely see any resistance on her part as a game. She shuddered.

"Excited already, little whore?" He chuckled again. "Me, too."

Applying the same technique she'd used on Darius, she jabbed her foot atop her captor's instep, then rammed her elbow into his stomach. He *umphed* and loosened his hold. She twisted, jerked back her fist and let it fly. Her knuckles collided with his jaw. On impact, his chin snapped to the side, whipping his sandy-colored braids across his cheek. He howled and released her.

Free now, she attempted to run. The other warriors

had already encircled her, however, halting any progress. Her heart stopped beating. Their bloodlust seemed to have deserted them entirely—leaving only lust.

One of them pointed at Brand. "I guess she doesn't like you, Brand." He laughed.

"I'm willing to bet she'll like me."

"None of us like you, Madox. Why would she?"

"Why don't you send her over here to me? I know how to treat a woman."

"Yes, but do you know how to eat one?"

They erupted in laughter.

Eat her? Good God. They were cannibals. They wanted her to whore for them and then become their evening snack. Worse and worse. A tremor shook her, trekking down her spine, then spreading over the rest of her body. Death by human banquet. No, thank you.

Brand, the one who had grabbed her, rubbed his jaw and smiled at her with genuine amusement. "Did you bring any friends, little whore? I do not think I want to share you with the others."

As he spoke, "the others" began tightening the circle around her. She felt like a slab of beef at a barbecue for the starving. Literally. All they needed to make the meal complete was a knife, a fork and an extra large bottle of easy-squeeze ketchup.

"I want her first," the warrior with the thickest shoulders said.

"You can't have her first. You owe me a favor, and I'm collecting. She's mine. You can have her when I'm done."

"Both of you can shut up," the most beautiful of the group said—the one who'd polished his hatchet. "I have a feeling the little whore will want me first. Women like this face of mine."

"No, I don't and no, you can't have me first," Grace announced. "No one can have me. I am not a whore!"

The man with the tattoo on his jaw grinned at her suggestively. "If you don't want to be our bedmate, you can be our meal."

She gasped, moving in circles to avoid their out-stretched hands. *Threaten them, scare them.* "I taste sour," she rushed out. "I've been known to cause major heartburn."

Their grins widened.

"Acid reflux is serious. It can cause cancer of the esophagus. It can erode your stomach lining!"

Closer, closer they came.

"I belong to Darius!" she rushed out next, grasping at any frenzied thought her mind produced.

Each of them ground to a halt.

"What did you say?" Brand asked, giving her a blistering frown.

She gulped. Perhaps claiming Darius as her lover hadn't been such a good idea. He could have a wife—why did she suddenly want to destroy something?—and these men could be said wife's brothers. "I, uh, said I belong to Darius?" The words flowed out as more of a question than a statement.

"That's impossible." Brand's frown became a vehement scowl, and his gaze bored into her, in-specting, taking her measure for a different scale than he'd previously used. "Our king would not claim a woman such as you for his own."

King? A woman such as her? Did they think she was good enough to eat for dinner, good enough to whore for them, but not good enough to belong to their precious leader, Darius? Well, that offended her on every level.

She couldn't be any more irrational, she knew, and blamed her overwrought emotions. They'd run the gamut today and were no longer hers to command. She'd always been emotional, but usually controlled her impulses.

"Is he married?" she demanded.

"No."

"Then yes," she said, not taking the time to analyze her relief, "he would welcome a woman such as me. In fact, he's expecting me back. I'd better be going. You know how upset he gets when someone's late." Nervous laugh.

Brand didn't let her pass. He continued to study her with unnerving intensity. What was he searching for? And what did he see?

Suddenly he grinned, a grin that spread and lit his entire face. He was extremely handsome, but he wasn't Darius. "I believe she speaks the truth, men," he said. "Look at the love mark on her neck."

Quick as a snap, Grace brought her hand up to her neck. Her cheeks warmed. Had Darius given her a hickey? She was struck first by shock, then by an unexpected, unwanted and ridiculous surge of pleasure. She'd never had a hickey before.

What's wrong with me? Jolting into motion, Grace shoved her way past Brand, past the others. They let her go without protest. She sprinted down the hallway, fully expecting them to follow. She heard no footsteps, and a quick glance behind her showed she was alone. When she reached the fork inside the bathing area, she trudged around the opening on the left. A salty breeze hit her in the face. She prayed she'd made the right decision this time.

She hadn't.

At the end, she found herself in a large dining hall. Darius was there, sitting at an enormous table, his eyes focused on the far wall of windows as if he were in deep thought. A heavy air of sadness enveloped him. He looked so lost and alone. Grace felt herself freezing, felt her muscles locking in place.

He must have sensed her, or smelled her, or *something,* because his gaze abruptly leveled on her, widening with puzzlement, then narrowing with ire. "Grace."

"Stay where you are," she said.

He growled low in his throat and sprang up, a panther ready to strike. And like a panther, he leapt over the table, coming straight toward her. She glanced around wildly. A side-table rested next to her, decorated with a multitude of breakable items. She swiped them to the ground, causing vases and bowls to shatter and sprinkle glass in every direction. Perhaps that would slow him, perhaps not. Either way, she pivoted on her heel and bolted.

Arms pumping frantically, shoes thumping into the

ebony, she snaked the corner and rushed through the final hallway. She didn't have to glance back to know Darius was closing in on her. His footsteps resonated in her ears. His fury bored intense, determined flames into her back.

At the end of the corridor, she spied a downward spiraling staircase. She quickened her speed. How close was she to victory? How close to failure?

"Get back here, Grace," he called.

Her only response was the shallowness of her breathing.

"I'll come after you. I'll not rest until I find you."

"I'm tired of your threats," she growled, throwing the words over her shoulder.

"No more threatening," he promised.

"Doesn't matter." Faster and faster, she pounded down the stairs.

"You don't understand."

At the bottom of the last step, she spied the opening to a cave. And there, just ahead, the mist swirled, calling to her, beckoning. *Home,* her mind shouted. *Almost home.*

"Grace!"

With one backward glance in his direction, she hurled herself into the fog.

Instantly her world spun out of control, and she lost the solid anchor beneath her feet. Dizziness assaulted her; nausea churned arduously in her stomach. Round and round she plunged and spun, so jerkily, so erratically the dragon medallion tore from her neck.

Screeching, she reached out and tried to scoop the chain into her hands.

"Nooo," she cried when it danced out of reach. But in the next instant, she forgot all about the necklace. Stars winked in every direction, so bright and blinding she squeezed her eyelids closed. Grace flailed her arms and legs; she was more scared this time than before. What if she landed in a place more terrifying than the last? What if she didn't land at all, but remained in this enigmatic pit of nonexistence?

Loud screams resounded, piercing her ears, but one stood out from the others: a deep male voice that continually bellowed her name.

CHAPTER SEVEN

ONCE SHE REGAINED her sense of stability, Grace crawled through the cave. Warm, humid air brushed her skin, thawing her inside and out. Following flashes of light, she soon emerged from the rocky exit. Familiar sounds of the Amazon welcomed her: the screech of howler monkeys, the incessant drone of insects, the hurried rush of a river. Utterly relieved, she jackknifed to her feet. Her knees almost gave out, but she forced herself to move forward, to put distance between this world and the other.

As she ran, the backdrop of sounds tapered to quiet. Sunlight faded, leaving a horrendous darkness. Then, rain burst from the sky, pelting and soaking her. Under the weight of the water and darkness, she was forced to seek shelter beneath a nearby bush. *Hurry up, hurry up, hurry up.*

Finally the rain ended and she popped up, once again dashing through the forest. Gnarled tree limbs reached out, clawing at her face, slapping at her arms and legs, splashing remaining raindrops into her eyes. She wiped them away and kept moving, never breaking stride.

Shards of sunlight gradually returned, winking in and out between clouds and foliage, illuminating a treacherous path of trees, dirt and rocks. Twigs snapped beneath her boots. Every few steps she tossed a fearful glance over her shoulder. Looking, always looking, fearing the worst.

I'll come after you, Darius had said. *I'll not rest until I find you.*

She shot another look over her shoulder…and slammed into a male chest. Grace flew backward, landing on her back with a thump. The man she hit was barely taller than she was and flew backward, as well, remaining supine, gasping for breath. She came up swinging. She'd escaped a horde of warriors, and she wasn't going to be captured or assaulted now.

"Whoa, there," another man said, stepping over his fallen comrade and holding up his dirt-smudged, empty palms. Droplets of water sprinkled from his baseball cap. "Calm down. We won't hurt you."

English. He was speaking English. Like the man lying on the jungle floor, this one was of average height with brown hair, brown eyes and tanned skin. He was thin, not corded with muscles and he wore a beige canvas shirt. The Argonaut logo was stitched over the left breast, an ancient ship with two spears erected on either side. The name Jason perched above the ship.

Jason of the Argonauts, she thought with a humorless, inward laugh.

Alex worked for Argonauts. She rolled the name

Jason through her mind, wondering if Alex had ever spoken of him, but she found no reference. It didn't matter. He worked with her brother and that was good enough.

The cavalry is here.

"Thank God," she breathed.

"Get up, Mitch," Jason said to the fallen man. "The woman isn't hurt, and it doesn't speak well of you if you are." To her he offered a canteen of water. "Take a drink. Slowly. You look like you need it."

She grabbed the canteen eagerly and gulped down all that her stomach could hold. The coolness. The sweetness. Nothing had ever tasted so good. Except for Darius, her mind whispered. Tasting him was an experience with no equal.

"Slow down," Jason said, reaching for the flask. "You'll make yourself sick."

She wanted to snarl and snap at him, but allowed him to reclaim his property. Water dribbled down her chin, and she wiped it away with the back of her hand. "Thank you," she panted. "Now let's get the hell out of here."

"Wait a minute," he said, closing the distance between them. He grasped her wrist and placed two fingers over her pulse. "First we need to know who you are and what you're doing here. Besides that, you're clearly nearing exhaustion. You need to rest."

"I'll rest later. Explain about myself later." She hadn't seen Darius exit the mist, hadn't heard him, but she wasn't taking any chances. He could kill both of these men with a mere snap of his fingers.

Jason must have caught her desperation, because she watched with widening eyes as he withdrew a 9mm Glock. Alex always carried a weapon when he went on expeditions, so the sight of it shouldn't have bothered her, but it did.

"Is there someone after you?" He didn't spare her a glance. He was too busy scanning the wooded area behind her.

"I don't know," she answered, gaze darting through the trees. What she wouldn't do for her own weapon right now. "I don't know."

"How can you not know?" he demanded. Then he softened his tone, and added, "Clearly you're spooked. If you *were* being followed, what would we be dealing with? A tribesman? An animal?"

"Tr-tribesman." Her voice barely rose above a whisper. "Is there anyone out there?"

"Not that I can see. Robert," he shouted, gaze boring into the trees.

"Yeah," came a distant, rough voice. She couldn't see the one who had uttered the response and figured he was hidden in the thick stumps and leaves.

"Robert is one of our guards," Jason explained to her. To Robert he called, "See any natives out there?"

"No, sir."

"You sure?"

"One hundred percent."

After Jason put on the gun's safety, he anchored the weapon in the waist of his jeans. "No one's after you," he told Grace. "You can relax."

"But—"

"Even if there were someone out there, we've got scouts all around us and they'd never make it anywhere near you."

So Darius *hadn't* followed her. Why hadn't Darius followed her? The question echoed through her mind, plaguing her, confusing her. "You're sure there's not a large, half-dressed man out there?" she asked. "With a sword?"

"A sword?" Dark intensity filled Jason's eyes, and he studied her. His body seemed to loom around her, bigger than she'd thought. "A man with a sword was chasing you?"

"Sword, spear, they're all the same, right?" she lied, not sure why she did so.

Jason relaxed. "No one's out there but my men," he said confidently. "The tribes out here won't bother us."

This didn't make sense. Darius had been so intent on catching her. Why hadn't he followed her? She was torn between fear and—surely not—disappointment.

Her thoughts scattered as a wave of dizziness swept through her. She swayed and scrubbed a hand across her forehead.

"How long have you been out here?" Jason asked. He wrapped a parka around her shoulders. "You might have been bitten by a diseased mosquito. You're shaky and flushed, and I'm willing to bet you've got a fever."

Malaria? He thought she had malaria? She laughed humorlessly, fighting the knot twisting her stomach. She was tired and weak, but she knew she didn't have malaria. Before flying into Brazil, she'd taken medication to prevent the illness.

"I'm not sick," she said.

"Then why— You're scared of us," he said. He grinned. "You don't have anything to fear from us. Like you, we're Americans. Hardly dangerous."

Another wave of dizziness overtook her. She clutched the parka closer to her chest, drawing on its warmth as she recovered her equilibrium. "You work for Argonauts, right?" she asked weakly.

"That's right," he said, losing his smile. "How did you know?"

"My brother works there, too. Alex Carlyle. Is he here with you?"

"Alex?" came another male voice. "Alex Carlyle?"

Grace turned her attention to…what was his name? Mitch, she recalled. "Yes."

"You're Alex's sister?" Mitch asked.

"That's right. Where is he?"

Mitch was older than Jason, with salt and pepper hair and slightly weathered features. Lines of tension branched from his eyes. "Why are you here?" he asked.

"Answer me first. Where's my brother?"

The two men exchanged a glance, and Mitch shifted uncomfortably on his feet. When she returned her attention to Jason, he arched one of his brows. He appeared calm and casual, but there was a speculative gleam in his eyes.

"Do you have any identification?" he asked.

She blinked at him and spread her arms wide. "Do I look like I have identification?"

His gaze roamed over her, lingering on her breasts and thighs, barely visible under the camouflage slicker. "No," he said. "You don't."

Unease stole through her. She was a lone woman, days away from civilization, in the company of men she didn't know. *They're Argonauts,* she reminded herself. *They work with Alex. You're fine.* Hands shaky, she pushed wet hair back from her face. "Where's my brother?"

Mitch sighed and wiped a trickle of rain from his brow. "To be honest, we don't know. That's why we're here. We want to find him."

"Have *you* seen him?" Jason asked.

Disappointed, worried, Grace rubbed her eyes. Clouds were beginning to fill her vision. "No. I haven't," she said. "I haven't heard from him in a while."

"Is that why you're here? Looking for him?"

She nodded, then pressed her fingertips to her temple. The simple action had caused a sharp, unabating ache. What was wrong with her? Even as she wondered, the pain in her temples knifed to her abdomen. She moaned. The next thing she knew, she was hunched over vomiting, every fiber of her being clenched in rebellion.

Jason and Mitch leapt away from her as if she were nuclear waste. When she at last finished, she wiped her mouth with her palm and closed her eyes.

Mitch skirted around and handed her another canteen of water. He remained a safe distance away.

"Are you all right?" he asked.

Stomach still churning, she sipped. "No. Yes," she answered. "I don't know." Where the hell was her brother? "Were you part of Alex's team?"

"No, but we do work with him. Unfortunately, like you, we haven't heard from him in a while. He simply stopped checking in." Jason paused. "What's your name?"

"Grace. Did you just arrive in Brazil?"

"A couple of days ago."

She hated her next question, but she *had* to ask. "Do you suspect foul play?"

"Not yet," Mitch answered. He cleared his throat. "We found one of Alex's men. He was dehydrated pretty badly, but said Alex had left him to follow another lead. The man's at our boat now, hooked to an IV."

"Where did this other lead take him?" she asked.

"We don't know." His gaze skidded away from her. "Do you know what Alex was looking for? His teammate babbled about, uh, Atlantis."

"Atlantis?" She feigned surprise. Yes, this man worked with Alex. Judging by his words, however, he hadn't known Alex's agenda. That meant her brother hadn't wanted him to know, and Grace wasn't going to be the one to tell him. Besides, how did she explain something so unbelievable? "I thought he was trying to prove the legend about the female warriors. You know, the Amazons."

He nodded, satisfied with that. "How long have you been out here?"

"Since Monday." Two miserable days that felt like an eternity.

"Last Monday?" Jason asked, rejoining the conversation. "You've survived out here—on your own—for seven days?"

"Seven days? No, I've only been here for two."

"Today is Monday, June 12."

Holding back her gasp, Grace counted the days. She'd entered the jungle on the fifth. She'd spent two days wandering through the interior of the rain forest before traveling through the mist. Today should be the seventh. "You said today is the twelfth?" she asked him.

"That's right."

My God, she'd lost five days. How was that possible? What if— No. She immediately cut off the thought.

The possibility continued to flood her, however.

She pushed out a breath. If it weren't for those missing days, she wouldn't entertain the idea at all. But…what if everything she'd just endured was merely a figment of her imagination? Like a mirage in a desert? What were the chances of there being a man who could teach her a new language with a magic spell? Or lick her wounds and heal her?

Or kiss her and make her want to weep from the beauty of it?

Unconsciously she reached for the medallion at her neck. Her fingers met only skin and cotton, and she frowned. She'd lost it in the mist. Hadn't she? She just didn't know, because in all actuality she could have lost it anywhere in this godforsaken jungle.

Her confusion grew, the truth dancing just beyond her grasp. Later, she decided. She'd worry about sorting truth from fiction later. After she'd had a shower and eaten a good meal.

There was no way to explain her suspicions to these men without sounding totally and completely insane, so she didn't even try. "Yes, last Monday," she said weakly.

"And you've been alone the entire time?" Jason asked skeptically.

"No, I had a guide. He abandoned me."

That seemed to pacify him, and he relaxed his stance. "Did you see Alex at all?" He patted her shoulder in a gesture meant to comfort her.

She pretended to stumble backward a step, dislodging his hand. She didn't want to be patronized or coddled. She just wanted to find Alex. When she'd first entered the Amazon, she hadn't worried about him, hadn't worried that he might be lost or hurt somewhere. Or worse. He was smart and resourceful, and had traversed jungles like this before, so she'd just assumed he was not in any real danger.

"I wish I had seen him," she said. "I'm concerned about him."

"Do you know anywhere he might have gone?" Mitch asked. "Anything about that lead?"

"No. Wouldn't his teammate know?"

"Not necessarily." Jason sighed, a pronounced sigh that revealed a hint of too-white teeth. "All right," he said. "I need to stay here and continue searching, but I'm going to have Patrick—that's another member of our crew—"

Patrick stepped from the shadows in a swath of camouflage, holding a semiautomatic. A startled jolt sped through her at the sight of the man and his gun. He ignored her upset and tipped his chin to her by way of introduction.

"He won't hurt you," Jason continued. "I'm going to have Patrick get you to our boat. It's loaded with medical supplies. I want you hooked to an IV ASAP."

"No," she said after a moment's thought. Alex might still be in the jungle, alone and hungry. He might need her; he'd always been there for her, through the years of their father's cancer, and she wanted to be there for him. "I'll stay with you and help you look for him."

"I'm afraid that's impossible."

"Why?"

"If you're hurt, or worse, it's my ass in a sling. Let Patrick take you to the boat," he cajoled. "It's docked on the river and not far from here, about an hour's hike."

He didn't want her help here, fine. It would be better to spread out the search, anyway. "I'll go into town and—"

"You're two days from civilization. You'd never make it alone. And I'm not sending any of my men into town right now. I need them here."

"Then I'll stay here. I can help," she said stubbornly. She would *not* be thwarted.

"To be honest, you'd be more of a hindrance. You're clearly near collapse, and we'd waste precious time having to carry you."

Though she didn't like it, she understood his logic. Without strength and energy, she would be a burden. Still, helplessness bombarded her because she desperately wanted to do something to aid her brother. Perhaps she'd question the man on the boat, the one who had spent time with him.

She gave Mitch and Jason a barely perceptible nod. "I'll go to the boat."

"Thank you," Jason said.

"We'll keep you apprised of our progress," Mitch added. "I promise."

"If you haven't found him in a day or two," she warned, "I'm coming back in here."

Jason lifted his shoulders in a casual shrug. "I'll give you a piece of advice, Grace. Go home when you've regained your strength. Alex may already be there, worried about *you*."

Her back straightened, and she leveled him with a frown. "What do you mean?"

"If he's anything like me and his lead fell through, first place he'd go was home. To regroup, see his loved ones."

That made sense. "Anyone check to see if he bought a plane ticket?"

"We have people at the airport now, searching, but don't have any answers yet," Mitch said, shifting on his feet. "Because this is the last place he was seen, we're to stay here and search until the office hears from him."

Could Alex be home? The concept was so welcome after everything she'd been through that she latched on to it with a vengeance. She turned to Patrick. "I'm ready. Take me to the boat."

CHAPTER EIGHT

ONCE AGAIN seeing only black-and-white, Darius flattened his palms above his head, against the rocky cavern wall. He stared into the swirling mist. She'd escaped. Grace had actually escaped. Everything inside him urged him to vault into her world and hunt her down. *Now.* However, his reasons were not what they should have been. It was the beast inside him that craved her nearness—not the Guardian.

Teeth gnashing together, he remained in place. No matter his desires, entering the surface world was not an option. Not until he appointed a temporary Guardian. Darius uttered a brutal curse into the mist, hating that he must wait. Yet beneath his impatience was an undeniable pang of relief. Grace would live a while longer, and he *would* see her again, no matter where she went, no matter how many days passed.

He dropped one of his hands and clasped his medallion from beneath his shirt. When he felt only one, he stilled. Frowning, he reached inside his pocket, encountering only the buttery soft glide of leather. His breath became as chilled and frosted as the mist, and dark fury pounded through him. Not only had Grace escaped him, and quite easily, too, but she had also stolen the Ra-Dracus. His hands fisted so tightly his bones threatened to grind to powder.

The woman had to be found. Soon.

With one last glance at the mist, he stole out of the doomed cave and up into the palace. Seven of his warriors were waiting for him in the dining hall.

They stood united, each of their arms crossed, each of their legs braced apart. The stance for war. In the center was Brand. His lips were thinned in displeasure, and his brow was stern. There was a mischievous gleam in his eyes that didn't quite match the rest of his expression.

"Do you have something to tell us, Darius?" his first in command said.

Darius paused midstep, then he, too, assumed a prebattle position. His men had never waylaid him like this, and he cursed himself for allowing their game. "No," he said. "I have nothing to tell you."

"Well, *I* have something to tell *you*," Zaeven growled.

Madox placed a warning hand on the young dragon's shoulder. "That tone will get you nothing but a beating."

Zaeven mashed his lips together in silence.

"I do not have time to play your silly game right now."

"Game?" Renard said, exasperated. "You think we're playing a game?"

"What else would you be doing here if not trying

to win your wager? I told you to stay inside the practice arena for the rest of the day. That is where I expect you to be." Darius pivoted and strode toward the hallway.

"We know about the woman," Tagart called, stepping forward. A scowl marred the clean lines of his features.

Darius paused abruptly and spun to face them. He schooled his features to reveal only mild curiosity. "Which woman is that?" he asked with false casualness.

"You mean there is more than one?" Zaeven jumped in front of Tagart. His features lost their steely edge.

"Shut up," Brand told the boy. He refocused on Darius. His next words lashed out as sharply as a sword. "I'll ask you again. Do you have anything to tell us?"

"No." Darius's tone was absolute.

Tagart's scowl darkened with a flash of scales. "How is it fair that you are allowed to have a woman here and we are not?"

Brittan leaned against the far wall. He crossed his feet at the ankles and grinned with wry humor. The infuriating man found amusement in every situation. "I say we share the woman like the nice little fire lizards we are."

"There is no woman," Darius announced.

Their protests erupted immediately. "We saw her, Darius."

"Brand touched her."

"We even fought over who would have her first."

Silence. Thick, cold silence.

Very slowly, very evenly, Darius roamed his gaze over every man present. "What do you mean Brand touched her?"

The question elicited different reactions. Brittan chuckled. The younger dragons paled, and Madox and Renard shook their heads. Tagart stormed from the room, muttering, "I've had enough of this."

Brand—the gods curse him—rolled his eyes.

"You're missing the point," Brand said. "For years we have followed your orders and your rules without dispute. You said women were not allowed, and so we have always forgone pleasures of the flesh while residing in the palace. For us to discover that you have a whore hidden in your chambers for your own personal use makes a mockery of your rules."

"She is not a whore," he growled. Instead of offering an explanation, he repeated his previous question. "What did they mean you touched her?"

His friend pushed out an exasperated sigh and threw up his hands. "That's it? That's all you have to say?"

"Did you touch her?"

"She backed into a table, and I helped right her. Now will you concentrate?"

Darius relaxed…until Madox muttered, "Yes, but did you have to 'help' her for so long, Brand?"

With surprise his lips thinned.

With disbelief his jaw tightened.

With fury his nostrils heated with sparks of fire.

Darius recognized the emotions and did not even try to mute them. All three hammered through him, hot and hungry, nearly consuming him. He didn't want any man save himself touching Grace. Ever. He didn't stop to examine the absurdity of his possessiveness. He just knew it was there. He didn't like it, but it was there all the same.

"Did you hurt her?" he demanded.

"No," Brand said, recrossing his arms over his chest. "Of course not. I'm insulted that you even have to ask."

"You will not touch her again. Not any of you. Do you understand?" His piercing gaze circled the group.

Each man wore his own expression of shock during the ensuing silence. Then, as if a dam had broken, they hurdled rapid-fire questions at him.

"What is she to you? She wore your mark on her neck."

"Where is she?"

"What's her name?"

"How long has she been here?"

"When can we see her again?"

He ground his teeth together.

"You have to tell us something," Madox snapped. *Or there will be a revolt,* rang in the air unsaid.

Darius tilted his head to the left, felt the bones pop, then tilted his head to the right, felt the bones pop. Control. He needed control. "She only just arrived," he said, offering them a bit of information to pacify them. He liked and respected all of his men. They'd been together for hundreds of years, but right now they were nearly more than his precarious discipline could withstand. "She has already left."

Several moans of disappointment harmonized, from the deep baritones of the elders, to the crackling timbres of the young.

"Can you bring her back?" Zaeven asked eagerly. "I liked her. I've never seen hair that color before."

"She will not be returning, no." A sharp pang of disappointment caught him off guard. He wanted to see her again—and he would—but he wasn't supposed to desire her here, in his home, lighting the room with her very presence. He wasn't supposed to look forward to their encounter, to sparring with her or touching her. Neither was he supposed to mourn her loss.

It wasn't the woman herself he wanted, he assured himself. Merely her ability to regenerate his senses. Senses he'd once *fought* to destroy.

"There has to be a way we can bring her back," Zaeven said.

They didn't know that she was a traveler and must die, and he didn't tell them. They had never understood his oath, so how could he explain this most loathsome task of all?

"Brand," he barked. "I need to speak with you privately."

"We aren't finished with this conversation." A muscle ticked in Madox's temple. "You have not yet explained your actions."

"Nor will I. The woman was not my lover and was

not here to see to my personal pleasure. That is all you need to know." He pivoted on his heel. "This way, Brand."

Without another word or even a backward glance to ensure his friend followed, Darius strode to his chambers. He sank stiffly onto the outer lounge and jerked his hands behind his head.

How had his life become so chaotic in only a few short hours? His men were near revolt. A woman had bested him—not once but twice. And though he'd had sufficient time, he had failed to do his duty. His hands curled into fists.

Now he had to leave all that he knew and travel to the surface.

He despised chaos, despised change, yet the moment he'd encountered Grace he'd all but welcomed both with open arms.

Brand stepped inside and stopped when he reached the edge of the bathing pool. Darius knew that if he could see colors right now, Brand's eyes would be a deep, dark gold filled with bafflement. "What is going on?" his friend asked. "You are acting so unlike yourself."

"I need your help."

"Then it is yours."

"I must journey to the surface and—"

"What!" Brand's exclamation rang in his ears, followed quickly by a heavy pause. "Please repeat what you just said. I'm sure I misheard."

"Your hearing is excellent. I must journey to the surface."

Brand frowned. "Leaving Atlantis is forbidden. You know the gods bound us to this place. If we leave, we weaken and die."

"I will not be gone more than a single day."

"And if that is too long?"

"I would go still. There has been a…slight complication. The woman was my prisoner. She escaped." The confession tasted foul in his mouth. "I must find her."

Brand absorbed that information and shook his head. "Do you mean you let her go?"

"No."

"Surely she did not escape on her own."

"Yes, she did." His jaw clenched.

"So you did not let her go?" Brand persisted, obviously stymied by the concept of his leader's failure. "She managed to outwit you?"

"How many ways would you have me say it? I locked her up, but she found a way out." *Because she slipped the medallion from my neck when I was distracted by the feel of her body under mine,* he silently added.

Slowly Brand grinned. "That is amazing. I'm willing to bet that woman is like a wild demon in bed and—" His words ground to a halt when he noticed Darius's thunderous glower. He cleared his throat. "Why did you have her locked away?"

"She is a traveler."

His grin faded, and his eyes lost all sparks of merriment. "She must die. Even a woman can lead an army to us."

"I know." Darius sighed.

Brand's tone became stark. "What do you need me to do?"

"Guard the mist while I am gone."

"But I am not truly a Guardian. The coldness of the cave will weaken me."

"Only temporarily." Darius sent his gaze to the domed ceiling. The seawater that encompassed their great city churned as fiercely as his need to see Grace. The temptress, the tormentor. The innocent, the guilty. Just what was she? Waves crashed turbulently against the crystal, swishing and swirling, driving away all sea life. Just as quickly as one wave appeared, another took its place, leaving a splattering of foam on each individual prism. Was this an omen, perhaps, of his coming days? Days of storms and turmoil?

He heaved another sigh. "What say you, Brand? Will you remain in the cave and destroy any human who passes through the portal, be they man or woman, adult or child?"

With only a brief hesitation, Brand nodded. "I will guard the mist while you are gone. You have my word of honor."

"Thank you." He trusted Brand completely with this task. Only a man who had lost loved ones to a traveler truly understood the importance of the Guardian. Brand would let no one through.

Brand inclined his head in acknowledgment. "What am I to tell the others?"

"The truth. Or nothing at all. That is up to you."

"Very well. I will leave you now so that you may prepare for your journey."

Darius nodded and wondered if there was any way to actually prepare himself for another encounter with Grace.

THE MESSENGER he sent to Javar's holding returned as the sounds of the day began to fade. Darius was submerged from the waist down in his bathing pool, gazing out at the breathtaking view of ocean beyond the window he'd bared only an hour ago. Its viewing had become a nightly ritual, granting him some measure of tranquillity. He motioned for the young dragon to share his news.

Standing at the edge of the pool and shifting nervously from foot to foot, Grayley said, "I'm sorry, but I was unable to deliver your message. Does that," he gulped, "make you want to yell at me?"

Darius's eyes narrowed, and his hand stilled over the warmth of the water. "Did you purposely act against my orders merely to win your game?"

"No, no," the boy rushed out, game forgotten. "I swear. The guards refused my entrance."

"Guards? What guards?"

"The guards who told me to leave. The guards who said I was not wanted there."

"And Javar?"

"Refused to speak with me, as well."

"Did he tell you this himself?"

"No. The guards informed me of his refusal."

Darius frowned. This made no sense. Why would

Javar refuse a messenger entrance? That was their usual way of communication, and neither of them had ever refused the other. Besides, why would a dragon refuse another dragon?

"There is something else," the dragon said, hesitating. "The guards…they were wholly human and carried strange metal objects like weapons."

Human. Strange metal objects… He jolted to his feet, sloshing water over the rim of the pool, then stalked naked to his desk and withdrew a sheet of paper and writing ink. He gave both to Grayley. "Draw the weapon for me."

What the young warrior drew appeared larger than what Grace had carried, yet was roughly the same design. Darius absorbed that information, mulled it over, then came to a decision. "Gather my men in the dining hall. After that, I wish you to find the unit on patrol in the Outer City. Vorik is acting as leader. Tell him I want him and the others surrounding Javar's palace, unseen, detaining any who enter or leave."

"As you command." The young dragon bowed and rushed to do as he was bid.

Darius dried himself with the nearest robe before jerking on a pair of pants. What a mess this was becoming. He'd thought Javar alive, and had hoped his tutor had merely lost his medallion. Now that seemed implausible.

What were humans doing inside his tutor's palace? Humans. Plural. More than one. Perhaps an army. Frustrated, Darius shoved a hand through his hair. Grace's arrival was no coincidence. The answer lay with her and her brother. He was sure of it. Finding her, he realized, was no longer a luxury. Finding her was a necessity.

His warriors awaited him inside the dining hall. They sat at the table, silent, unsure of his intentions. He positioned himself at the head. Before they could think to begin their game, he said, "You wanted something to do, and now I am giving it to you. I want you to prepare for war."

"War?" they all gasped, though there was an undercurrent of excitement in every voice.

"You are letting us declare war upon the vampires?" Madox asked.

"No. Humans have overtaken Javar's palace, and they carry strange weapons. I do not yet know if they have killed the dragons inside, nor do I know what they are planning. But I have sent Grayley to the Outer City where he is to inform Vorik's unit to surround the palace. Tomorrow's eve, you will join them."

"Tomorrow?" Madox pounded a fist into the table. "We should act today. Now. This instant. If there is a chance the dragons are alive, we must do what we can to save them."

Darius arched a brow. "What good are you to them if you are dead? We do not know what kind of weapons these humans wield. We do not know how to protect ourselves from them."

"He's right," Renard said, leaning forward. "We must discover what these weapons do."

"I will be traveling to the surface," Darius said. "I will learn what I can."

"The surface?" Zaeven gasped.

"You cannot," Madox growled.

"Lucky bastard," Brittan said with a wry smile.

"Go now," Darius told them. "Sharpen your weapons and prepare your minds. Brand, your new duties will begin immediately."

His friend opened his mouth to question him, but changed his mind. He nodded in understanding.

Chairs skidded as they rushed to obey; then the shuffle of their footsteps sounded.

Darius shut himself in his personal chambers. With Brand now guarding the mist, he closed his eyes and pictured Javar's palace. Within seconds, he stood inside the very walls he imagined. Except, these walls were barren, devoid of any type of jewel or decoration. He frowned.

A billowing mist stretched to the prismed ceiling, and as he floated into the next room, he noticed what looked to be ice crystals scattered across the floor. Those crystals produced the mist. He bent down and smoothed his palm over a few shards, wishing he could hold them in his hand and feel their coolness. Why weren't they melting? His frown deepened, and he straightened. Unlike the emptiness of the first room, human men abounded in this one. No one saw him, for he was like the mist. There, but not there. Able to observe, but unable to touch.

Some of the occupants were striding in and out, holding weapons just as Grayley described. Attached to their backs were strange, round containers with a single tube that stretched from the top. The men who weren't holding weapons were holding spikes crafted by Hephaestus himself. They jammed those spikes into the wall and pried at the jewels. Where had these humans acquired tools of the gods?

Had he been a man who allowed emotions to rule him, Darius would have morphed into dragon form. Prongs of fury simmered to life just beneath his skin. He watched a female vampire glide casually inside the room and lick her lips as her gaze caressed the humans. A trickle of blood fell from her chin, testament of a recent feeding. She stopped to speak with a human.

"Tell your leader we've done all that was required of us," she said in the human language, trailing a finger over his now pale cheek. "We are ready for our reward."

The man shifted nervously, but nodded. "We're almost ready to venture further."

"Do not take too long. We might decide to turn our appetites to you." With one last lick of her lips, which sent the man rearing backward in fear, she left as casually as she'd entered. Her white gown flowed behind her in sensuous waves.

Darius watched in shock. Vampires and humans aiding one another? Inconceivable. Perplexed, he moved his gaze over the rest of the chamber. Sections of the walls and floor were blackened from fire. In a far corner lay the broken, dead body of a dragon. Veran, one of Javar's fiercest soldiers.

A white film covered him from head to toe. He bore several injuries, yet there was no blood around him.

What type of weapon could destroy such a strong creature? Vampires were strong, yes. Humans were resourceful, yes. But that wasn't enough to capture an entire dragon palace. His fury increased. Darius found himself reaching for one of the humans, intent on curling his fingers around the bastard's vulnerable neck, but his hands drifted through the man like mist.

Now more than before he knew he could not send his own army here until he learned just how to combat these men and their weapons.

Darius searched the rest of the palace. He did not find a sign of Javar or any more of his men. Had the rest met the same fate as Veran? Or had they merely abandoned this place? Left unsure, he whisked himself back inside his own chamber. Answers. He wanted answers. Answers he suspected lay with Grace. If he hoped to gain what he wanted from her, he needed to be focused, distant. Utterly unfeeling.

Heartless.

He only wished he did not feel so alive each time he thought of her. So vital.

Well, he *would* remove the sight of her from his mind. All of that glorious hair tumbling down her shoulders. Eyes more vibrant than the sea. He would even remove the sound of her voice from his ears. That sweet voice entreating him to continue their kiss.

Instead of forcing her from his thoughts, he only managed to strengthen her hold.

He easily saw himself carrying her to his bed, laying her down and stripping the clothes from her body. He imagined himself parting her sweet thighs, luxuriating in the softness of her skin, then sliding deeply inside her. He could see her head thrashing from side to side. Could almost hear her moans of rapture.

Desire became a heady essence in his veins, and his cock strained to an unbearable thickness. He growled from the pain of it. Jaw clenched, he removed the medallion from his neck and held it in his palm. "Show me Grace Carlyle," he commanded.

The twin dragons glowed incandescent with energy. Power whirled inside them, mighty, burgeoning, and when it became too much for them to bear, blood-red beams shot from their eyes, creating a circle of light. Inside the light, air crackled and thickened.

Grace's image formed in the center.

In that instant, his senses came to life. He still didn't understand how a simple glance at her could undo centuries of safeguards. She lay in a small bed, and he studied her. Her eyes were closed; her cheeks were pale, making the freckles scattered across her dirt-smudged nose and forehead appear darker. Her carmine curls were wound atop her head, all but a few loose tendrils framing her temples.

She wore the same dirty shirt, and some sort of small, clear tube protruded from her arm, partially covered by the thin white sheet draping her from the chest down. Two male humans approached her bed.

Darius scowled as his possessiveness resurfaced.

"Looks like the morphine is working," the man with dark hair said, his voice a smooth baritone.

"Not just morphine. I gave her three different sedatives. She'll be out for hours."

"What are we going to do with her?"

"Whatever she wants us to do." He chuckled. "We're to play the gracious host."

"We should just kill her and be done with it."

"We don't need the attention her disappearance would bring—not when her brother is already missing."

"She won't stop searching for Alex. That much is obvious."

"She can search all she wants. She'll never find him."

The dark-headed one reached out and trailed his fingers over Grace's cheek. She didn't awaken, but mumbled something unintelligible under her breath. "She's pretty," he said.

A low, menacing snarl rose in Darius's throat.

"She's too fat," the other said.

"Not fat, just not anorexic. She's soft in all the right places."

"Well, keep your hands to yourself. Women know when their bodies have been used, and we don't need her bitching about it. The boss wouldn't like it." With a disgusted shake of his head, he added, "Come on. We've got work to do."

The two humans walked away—which saved their lives. Grace's image began to fade. With much regret Darius hung the chain back around his neck.

Soon. Soon he would be with her again.

CHAPTER NINE

"HOME," Grace sighed as she tossed her keys and purse on the small table beside her front door. She padded to her bedroom, the sound of honking cars filling her ears. Sunlight burst directly into her line of vision from the open blinds, too bright, too cheery.

She was not in a good mood.

She'd spent the past week with the Argonauts. While they had been perfectly solicitous of her, they had failed to find any clue as to her brother's whereabouts. Neither had she. Every day she'd called his cell phone. Every day she'd called his apartment. He never answered. She'd had no luck tracking down what flight he'd taken out of Brazil. *If* he'd taken one. The federal police had been no help.

She finally caught the red-eye and here she was, though she didn't know what she was going to do. File a missing person's report here like she'd done there? Hire a P.I.? Uttering another sigh, she picked up the cordless phone perched on the edge of her desk. Three new voice mails, all of them from her mom. Grace dialed her brother's number. One ring, two. Three, four, five. The answering machine picked up.

She called his cell. Straight to voice mail.

She hung up and punched in her mother's number.

"Hello," her mom answered.

"Hey, Mom."

"Grace Elizabeth Carlyle. My caller ID says you're calling from home." Accusation layered her voice.

Grace pictured her sitting at the kitchen counter, one hand on her hip while she glared at the red checkered curtains hanging over the window.

"I flew home last night."

"I didn't realize Brazil had yet to embrace modern technology."

"What are you talking about?"

"Phones, Grace. I didn't realize there were no phones in Brazil."

She rolled her eyes. "I left you messages." She had purposely called when her mom wouldn't answer.

Ignoring her, her mom said, "Not once did I get to talk to my only daughter. Not once. You know how your aunt worries."

"Is that Gracie?" a second female said in the background. Her "worried" aunt Sophie was probably standing over her mom's shoulder, grinning from ear to ear.

The two sisters had lived together for the last five years. They were polar opposites, but managed to complement each other in a strange sort of way. Her mom was schedule-oriented and thrived on fixing other people's problems. Sophie was a free spirit who *caused* problems.

"Yes, it's Grace," her mom said. "She's calling to tell us she's alive and well and not being held hostage in the jungle like you feared."

"Like *I* feared?" Sophie laughed. "Ha!"

"How are you feeling, Mom?" Her mom's health had been dismal lately. Weight loss. Fatigue. They didn't know exactly what the cause was.

"Fine. Just fine."

"Let me talk to her," Sophie said. Slight pause, crackling static, then, "Did you get lucky?"

"I don't want to hear this," her mom groaned in the background.

Automatically Grace opened her mouth to say yes, she'd made out with a sexy, tattooed warrior and had nearly given him everything a woman could possibly give a man. Then she clamped her mouth closed. Dreams, or mirages, or whatever Darius had been, did not count in Sophie's estimation.

Over the past week, she'd mulled over her experience in Atlantis. She always came back to the same conclusion. None of it had been real. Couldn't possibly have been real.

"No," she said, careful to keep the disappointment from her voice. "I didn't."

"Did you wear the outfit I bought for you?"

The leopard-print spandex skirt with matching low-cut, too tight shirt? "I didn't have a chance."

"Men go crazy for that sort of thing, Gracie honey. They're like fish. You have to hook them with the proper bait, then reel them in."

Her mom reclaimed the phone with a muttered,

"I will not allow you to give my daughter lessons on seduction." Then to Grace she said, "How's Alex doing? Is he eating enough? He never eats enough when he goes on these expeditions of his."

With each word, dread uncurled inside of Grace. "So you haven't talked to him?" she asked, hoping her fear and uncertainty were masked. "He hasn't called you?"

"Well, no," her mother said. "Is he back? He's back, isn't he, and just didn't call?"

"No, I just—" Just what? Don't know if he's eating enough because no one's heard from him in several weeks?

"What's going on, Grace?" Worry tinged her mom's tone. "You took this trip specifically to see your brother. Why don't you know how he is?"

"Does this have anything to do with the man who called us?" Sophie asked, her voice clear enough that Grace knew she was still standing over her mom's shoulder.

"What man?" she demanded. "When?"

"Someone called for Alex about a week ago," her mom said. "Asked if we'd heard from him, if we knew where he was. Grace, what's going on? You're worrying me."

To tell the truth, or not tell the truth… She loved her mom and hated to cause her any worry. Yet, as Alex's mother, Gretchen had a right to know that her son was missing. The worry might make her sicker, though. She'd tell her, Grace decided then, but not now, and not over the phone. She'd wait a few days and see if she learned anything new. No reason to cause her mom anxiety until absolutely necessary.

"You know how Alex likes those doughnuts," she said, evading. And not lying. "I can say with one hundred percent surety that he's not eating right." He never did.

"So he's okay?" her mom asked, relieved.

"I'd tell you if anything was wrong, wouldn't I?" Again, evading and not lying, since she'd posed the words as a question.

"You've always told the truth," her mom said proudly, then *tsked* under her tongue. "I swear, your brother is a walking advertisement for heart disease. Maybe I'll send him some soy muffins. I can FedEx them. Does FedEx deliver to Brazil?"

"Not in the heart of the jungle."

"I'll send him a Cindy Crawford workout DVD," Sophie called.

"I doubt his tent has an electrical outlet."

"He has to go to his hotel room sometime," her mom said.

Grace rubbed her temple. "I hate to do this, but I've got to let you go."

"What! Why? You haven't told me about your trip. Did you do any shopping? Did you visit with the natives? I hear they walk around…" She paused and uttered a scandalized gasp, "Naked."

"Unfortunately I didn't see them. Which is too bad, since I'd promised to take pictures for Aunt Sophie."

"Speaking of Sophie, she's wondering if you brought her a souvenir."

"I was not," her aunt said.

"I'll come by in a few days and give you all the details. Promise."

"But—"

"Bye. Love you." Grace gently placed the receiver in its cradle and cringed. Oh, she was going to be punished for that one. A never-ending lecture, followed by a reminder every time her mother needed a favor. "Do you remember the time you hung up on me? I cried for days."

Rolling her eyes, Grace punched in one last number. Her friend Meg was head of reservations for a major airline, so she had Meg check all databases for Alex's name. He wasn't listed, but that didn't mean anything. He could have flown private.

Not about to give up, Grace stuffed her keys, wallet and a can of Mace into her favorite backpack. She caught a subway to the Upper East Side. She *needed* to find her brother, or at least find proof that he was okay. He'd always been there for her as a child. He was the one who bandaged her cuts and bruises. He was the one who held and comforted her when their dad died. They both traveled extensively, but they always managed to make time for each other.

Please, please let Alex be home, she inwardly recited, a mantra in rhythm to the rocking of the car against the rails. If he was home, they could spend the rest of the day together. Maybe have dinner at Joe Shanghai in Chinatown, a favorite restaurant of theirs.

Soon she was strolling past the security desk at

Alex's apartment building. He'd lived in the ritzy building only a short time. Despite her few visits, the doorman must have recognized her because he let her pass without a hitch. After a short elevator ride, she found herself knocking on Alex's door. When he didn't answer, she used her key and let herself inside. Only three steps in, she paused with a gasp. Papers were scattered across the thick, wool carpet.

Either someone had broken in, or her brother the neat freak had left in a hurry. "Alex," she called, remaining in the foyer.

No response.

"Alex," she called again, this time louder, more desperate.

Not even the shuffle of footsteps or the hum of a fan greeted her.

Though she knew she shouldn't, knew she should call for help first, Grace withdrew her Mace, holding the can out as she inspected every inch of the spacious apartment. Her need to know Alex's whereabouts completely obliterated any sense of caution.

There was no intruder lying in wait for her, but there was no sign of her brother, either. She walked to the living room and lifted a framed photograph of her and Alex, smiling and standing in Central Park, the sun glistening around them. Her aunt had taken the picture several months ago when they'd all decided to jog around the park. Two minutes into their run, Sophie had panted that she was too tired to continue. So they'd taken a break and snapped the picture. The memory made her ache.

Disheartened, Grace locked up and leaned her back against the door. She had no idea what to do next or— A man strolled past. "Excuse me," she called, an idea forming. She flashed him a quick, I'm-a-sweet-Southern-girl smile that proclaimed you-can-tell-me-anything. She only hoped it worked. "You live in this building, right?"

He nodded wearily. "Why?"

"Do you know Alex Carlyle?"

"Yes." Again, he asked, "Why?"

"He's my brother. I'm looking for him and was wondering if you'd seen him."

Her words relaxed him, and he gave her a half smile. He even held out his hand to shake. "You're Grace," he said. "The picture Alex has of you in his office is of a little girl. I thought you were younger."

"At the office?" Grace asked. "You work for Argonauts?"

"Nearly everyone here does. They own the building." He paused, his smile fading to a frown. "Unfortunately I haven't seen your brother in weeks. He hasn't been home, or even to work."

"Do you know anyone he might have contacted?"

"Well, Melva in 402 has been picking up his mail...I saw her this morning. She's rent controlled," he whispered, as if it were a shameful secret. "Argonauts can't get rid of her. Not legally at least."

Grace gave him her biggest, brightest smile. "Thank you," she said, taking off. Her first break. Another elevator ride and she was hammering on Melva's door.

"Coming. I'm coming," a craggy voice called. Moments later, the door swung open. Melva was thin, wrinkled and wrapped in a fluffy white bathrobe. She held herself up with a walker. The only difference between her and every other great-grandma across the country was that she wore a diamond choker and sapphire earrings.

"Can I help you?" she asked, her rough voice testament to years of smoking.

"I'm Grace Carlyle. I'm looking for my brother and wondered if he'd contacted you recently."

Melva's wrinkled gaze studied her. "Sister, eh? That slyboots never mentioned a sister. I'll have to see some ID."

Grace slid a photo ID from her wallet and allowed Melva to glance at the picture. The old woman nodded in satisfaction. "I haven't seen Alex for a while now. I have his mail, though. It's been piling up in his box. He asked me to collect it for him, but I was under the impression he would return last week."

"If it wouldn't be too much trouble, I'd like to take his mail with me."

"Give me a second. I'm still recovering from hip surgery and it takes me a bit longer to get around." She slowly turned, her diamonds twinkling in the light, and disappeared beyond the foyer. When she returned, she wore a fanny pack stuffed with different sized and colored envelopes. "Here you go." She braced one hand on the walker and handed Grace the letters with the other.

"Thank you so much." Grace quickly riffled through the contents. When nothing jumped out at her, she crammed them in her backpack. She'd go through them more thoroughly when she returned home. "Do you need help getting back inside?"

"Oh, no." Melva waved her off. "I'll be fine."

Spirits buoyed, Grace bounded outside. But her good mood didn't last. All too soon she felt an ominous gaze slicing into her back, observant, penetrating. The sensation unnerved her, and she glanced over her shoulder. Nothing appeared out of the ordinary. After everything that had happened with Alex, however, she didn't try to convince herself that her imagination was playing games. She increased her pace and slipped one hand inside her backpack, wrapping her fingers around her Mace.

Instead of going straight home, she stopped in a coffee shop, a souvenir shop and a bakery, trying to lose herself in the crowds. By the time she felt safe, the sun was beginning its descent. She reached her apartment building as darkness fell completely. She gathered her own mail, then bolted herself inside her little efficiency. *What have I gotten myself into?* she wondered, securing all of the window locks. A thirst for danger seemed so silly now.

Exhausted both mentally and physically, she tossed her backpack onto her nightstand and sank into the chair at her desk. She booted up her computer and checked her e-mail. When she saw one was from Alex's return address, dated yesterday morning, she broke into a huge smile and eagerly pressed Open.

Hey Grace,
I'm fine. I've got a lead elsewhere and had to follow it. Sorry for the note, but there wasn't time to call. I'll probably be out of touch for a while.
Love,
Alex

As she read, her smile faded. She should have been relieved by the note. This was, after all, what she'd wanted. Contact with Alex. But if there'd been no time to call, how had there been time to type a note?

With that question floating in her mind, she stripped to her tank and panties, poured herself a glass of wine and sprawled across her bed. She meticulously sorted through Alex's mail. Junk mostly, with a few cards and bills thrown into the mix. She checked her own. Her eyes widened then subsequently narrowed when she came to a postcard from her dad. *Her dad!* A man who had died many years ago after a long battle with lymphoma. Confused, she shook her head and read it again.

Gracie Lacie,
Can't come to see you as planned. I've been detained. I'll contact you. Don't worry. I'll be fine.
Yours,
Dad

This was Alex's handwriting and had to be some sort of code. But what did it mean, other than someone had sent her a false e-mail? Perhaps the same person who had "detained" Alex. Why had he been detained? And for how long?

Where was he now?

She studied the postmark. Sent from Florida, one week ago. A lot could have happened in a week. Alex said not to worry about him, but she couldn't help herself. She *was* worried. None of this made sense. Why Florida? The lead? Should she travel there?

Well, she certainly couldn't go tonight. She wouldn't do anyone any good in this condition. Moonlight had settled comfortably inside her bedroom, and the scent of unlit apple cinnamon candles filled the air, exhausting her further. Grace drew in a shaky breath and set the mail aside. She closed her eyes and leaned against the mountain of pillows behind her, wondering what to do next. If only Darius were here…

He's not real, she reminded herself. Unbidden, his image floated to the forefront of her mind. With his harshly angled face, he radiated rawness and sheer male virility.

She should have known the moment she first saw him that he was a figment of her deepest fantasies. Real men were nothing like him. Real men lacked the savageness, the fierceness and didn't taste like fire, passion and excitement when they kissed her.

Real men didn't chase her down and threaten to hurt her, then tenderly caress her in the next heart-beat of time.

A shiver of remembrance swept through her, until she recalled one last fact about him. Real men didn't blithely admit to being an assassin.

His confession had startled her, made her feel unexpected sorrow for him because even though he'd claimed he made his own choices, that he was never *forced* to kill, she'd glimpsed flickers of agonizing despair in his eyes. She'd glimpsed endless torment. And at that moment, his eyes had been without any shred of hope.

No man should be without hope.

Grace rolled to her side, taking a pillow with her. *Forget about Darius and get some rest.* Nothing mattered but Alex. Perhaps the key to finding him would come to her after a good night's sleep.

But how could she have known that key would come in a six foot five, two-hundred-and-fifty-pound package?

CHAPTER TEN

DARIUS STOOD at the edge of the bed, staring down at Grace.

She was surrounded by a multitude of colors. A pink satin sheet beneath her, a waterfall of red curls around her shoulders and an emerald blanket draped over her. The sight was intoxicating. She looked more relaxed than she had in his vision. Sleeping peacefully, languidly, her expression was soft and innocent. The moment he'd first seen her, his only thoughts had been of joining her. How he longed to reach out and stroke the pale delicacy of her skin. How he longed to comb his fingers into the silky cloud of her hair.

Perhaps he should fulfill his oath here and now, he mused, simply to end this strange fascination he had with her. But he knew he wouldn't. He was too much a man of strategy. He liked all facts before him, and much still remained a mystery. He needed to know more about these surface dwellers and their weapons. Only then would his army be able to storm Javar's palace and conquer everyone inside.

Darius had spent several hours searching for

Grace, following magical wafts from the spell of understanding. Since no Atlantean could survive outside of Atlantis for long, he should have been filled with a sense of urgency now that he'd found her.

He wasn't.

He lingered.

His breath ragged, Darius continued to drink in the sight of his tormentor. She wore a thin white shirt, leaving her shoulders bare and glistening in the moonlight. Leaving her full breasts clearly outlined. Her nipples formed shadowed circles he longed to trace with his tongue. He watched the rise and fall of her chest, watched the life that radiated from her. The longer he studied her, the more starved and desperate he felt for her. What would her heartbeat feel like under his palms? Steady and gentle? Or hurried and erratic? His blood sang with vitality, rushing to his cock and hardening him painfully.

I do not want to hurt this woman, he thought. *I want to relish every moment in her presence.* He shook his head against such dishonorable thoughts.

He had lived so long by his oath of death and destruction that he knew not what to make of these newly acquired desires—desires that had not muted with the distance between them.

Desires such as these could drive a man from his chosen path, push him and beat him down until he collapsed from regret.

Grace muttered something under her breath, then gently, delightfully moaned. What did she dream of?

He would be lying if he denied that he wished her to dream of him. She fascinated him in so many ways. Her resourcefulness. Her bravery in challenging him as few men had ever dared. Her defiance.

What would she do if he lay down beside her on the bed? If he stripped the clothes from her body and tasted every inch of her honey-smooth skin—lingering, savoring, sinking deeply into the hot moistness between her thighs? Sliding, slipping, slowly pumping?

He tore his gaze from her. *Gird yourself against her. Distance yourself from the situation. Stay sane. Sure.* This woman posed a greater threat than any army. She had plunged through the mist and completely destroyed his sense of order. She had violated his innermost thoughts, ignored his commands and lured him to dishonor with her beauty.

And yet she still lived. Perhaps he should bed her, forget her like his other lovers.

Yes. Take her like you took the others: primitive, savage and quick. A fine plan. But... With *this* woman, Darius desired something slow and easy. Something gentle. Like their kiss.

If he didn't lure his mind away from her, he would do something foolish.

As he observed the rest of the room, he saw floral curtains hanging over both windows, each a symphony of colors. Pink, yellow, blue, purple... A rainbow. A mirror consumed one wall, while flowers and vines were painted on another. Green leaves and purple grapes bloomed in feigned sunlight. Grace was a woman who enjoyed the sensuality of life. Things he, too, enjoyed of late.

Grace, Grace, Grace. His mind chanted her name. If he could have one more taste of her, perhaps he could forget her without bedding her. A bedding would be too intimate, he decided. A kiss would be enough to satisfy him, but not enough to ruin him.

Liar. The last kiss left you raw. You can allow nothing. Still. He found himself approaching the side of the bed. Compelled by a force greater than himself, he leaned down and inhaled her exotic fragrance. His eyes closed as he relished the carnal sweetness of her. Lost in her dreams, she instinctively tried to mold herself against him.

He knew, though, that if she'd awoken just then she would have fought him. If she fought him, he would cave. Not knowing what else to do, he uttered a temporary peace spell that would keep her relaxed for the first few moments after she woke.

When he finished, he straightened. "Grace," he said softly. "Awaken." He would question her. Nothing more.

"Hmm," she muttered. Her eyes remained blissfully closed as she shifted, causing the pale pink and emerald linens enfolding her to wrinkle and bunch.

"Grace," he said again. "We must talk."

Slowly her eyelids fluttered open. She offered him a drowsy sweet smile. "Darius?" she asked breathlessly.

At the sound of his name on her lips, his mouth went dry, and he found himself unable to reply.

"You're here." Her smile widening, she stretched her arms over her head and purred low in her throat. "Am I dreaming?" She considered her words, and her brow wrinkled. "This doesn't feel like a dream."

"No dream," he said, the words ragged. The color of her eyes was far more beautiful than any other color he'd ever encountered.

"So you're real?" she asked, not the least afraid of him.

He nodded, knowing the peace spell was responsible for her languor. It was irrational, he knew, but he wished he himself had caused such a reception, not his powers.

"What are you doing here?"

"I have more questions for you."

"I'm glad you came," she said.

"I need the medallion, Grace. Where is it?"

She watched him for a long, slumberous moment, then eased up and wound her arms around his neck, crushing her breasts into his chest. She tugged him closer until they were nose to nose. "Questions later," she said. "Kiss now."

His nostrils flared at her demand—but not in anger. A traitorous fire licked through him. He'd meant to relax her, not arouse her. Gods, he'd cast the peace spell to *avoid* touching her, yet here she was demanding that he do so! "Release me," he said softly, knowing he could pull himself away if only he could find the will.

"I don't want to." Her fingers toyed with the hair at the base of his neck, and her eyes beseeched him.

"Every night I've dreamt of our kiss. It's the only thing I've ever done that made me feel complete, and I want more." She frowned slightly. "I don't know why I just told you that. I— Why am I not afraid of you?"

I deserve a beating, he berated himself, but he lowered his head anyway. Her admission lured him as surely as a chain around his neck. He was helpless against her allure. Any moment the aura of peace around her would wither, and she would jerk away from him. Until then... "Open," he told her. And he didn't care what type of man this made him. Dishonorable, so be it.

She immediately obeyed. His tongue swept inside, swirling and searching. His rough moan blended with her airy sigh. She was a mélange of flavors: warm, delicious, mesmerizing. It was a taste he'd experienced only once before, the first time they kissed. He wanted to experience that sweetness again and again.

She clutched at his shirt, then kneaded his neck, opening herself up, silently demanding he hold nothing back. He was humbled that she responded to him so openly, so uninhibitedly and so quickly. A deep-seated yearning to let her goodness seep into him blossomed and heightened. How desperately he wanted to press deeply inside her, over and over, and take her in every position imaginable until this hunger for her vanished.

He eased himself on top of her, allowing them both to lie in her bed as he'd imagined doing moments before. He gently rolled them to their sides.

Had she been coaxing him to his death, he gladly would have followed. The full lushness of her breasts cushioned his chest. Besides the thin shirt, she wore a small patch of lace between her thighs. She was the most erotic little creature, and he resented the minimal barriers preventing complete skin to skin contact.

She settled one leg over his waist, cradling him intimately, and he sank deeper into the apex of her legs. He hissed in a breath at the exquisite pleasure. He knew he should shove her away, knew he should begin the questioning. He did not have much time, for he already felt the weakening effects of leaving Atlantis.

But he could not stop. Was helpless. Desperate for her.

He had to have this woman.

His lust for her was dangerous, forbidden, but time slipped outside of reality, and Darius allowed himself to *feel* instead of think. As he did so, the very things he'd always despised became his greatest allies. Tenderness. Passion. Greed. Warm, female flesh tantalized him. Her sweet, feminine scent drugged him. Smooth and perfect. A sheen of sweat covered his brow.

As if she read his mind and discerned his needs, she sucked on his tongue, nibbled on his lips, and slanted her mouth for greater penetration. She taught him the way of it, consuming him bit by enticing bit. And he let her do it. He would have begged her to continue if necessary.

He trailed one hand over her body, tracing the velvety texture of her skin, first along the column of her spine, then over the roundness of her bottom. She moaned, and he slid his fingers between her legs, allowing them to travel up and over her panties, her moist heat, then under her shirt.

"I love the feel of your hands," she gasped when his fingertips grazed her nipple. He circled the hard bud with the tip of his finger. "So good."

She'd said as much to him before and still he relished the words. They made his every nerve dance and clamor to please her. He licked her neck and rubbed against her, nestling his erection in the pulsing heart of her desire. Their gasps blended, his strained, hers hoarse. Which only made it clear they both needed more.

"I want you naked," he said raggedly.

"Yes, yes."

Impatient to see her, he tore the folds of her shirt in two. She didn't flinch from his action; instead she arched her back, offering herself to him. Silently telling him to do with her what he would. Her breasts sprang free, revealing two rosy nipples, both pebbled and wanting. In the moonlight, her slightly rounded stomach glowed like fresh cream, and a small, silver jewel winked from her navel. He paused and fingered the stone.

"What is this?" he asked.

She wet her lips. "A belly-button ring."

He'd never heard of such a thing, but praise be the gods for its creation. The eroticism of seeing a jewel nestled in the hollow of her stomach nearly felled him. His muscles taut, he bent his head and flicked his tongue over the little bud. She gasped and shivered. His body jerked in response.

"I shouldn't have done it," she said, gripping his shoulders, urging him on with the sting of her nails. "I'm not skinny enough."

"You are the most beautiful sight I have ever beheld."

Her heavy-lidded gaze met his. She opened her mouth to protest, then cupped his jaw and compelled his lips to hers. He slanted his chin, taking more of her, sinking into her. As his fingertips continued to caress the jewel, he trailed kisses along her shoulder and neck, then moved to her breasts. Biting her lip, moaning, she bowed toward him, letting him suck her nipples deeply, hungrily. He wanted to taste all of her at the same time: her stomach, her nipples, the core of her.

"Darius?" she said, her tone thick and drugged with arousal.

"Hmm?" Though his body urged him to finish what they'd started, he continued to savor. Continued to feast on her.

"I want to possess you, body and soul."

He stilled, gazing down at her and thinking he must have misheard. No woman had ever said such a thing to him before. Perhaps he'd left them too quickly. Or perhaps they'd been as unconcerned with him as he was with them. "Tell me what you wish to do to me." His voice emerged hoarse, choked.

"I want to give you pleasure." Her eyes were like turquoise flames. "So much pleasure."

"How?"

"By kissing you like you're kissing me. By touching you like you're touching me."

"Where?" He couldn't stop the questions. He needed the words.

"Everywhere."

"Here?" He skimmed his hand inside her panties, felt the softness of her hair, and dove two fingers inside her silky wetness.

"God, yes!" she screamed. Her eyes closed, and she moved her hips with his fingers. She moaned, "That feels…that makes me… Ohmygod."

"Do you want to touch me like this, sweet Grace. Between my legs?"

"Yes. Oh, yes." Grace uttered a ragged exhalation and coasted her hands under his shirt and across the bold, black tattoos on his chest. The tips of his nipples speared into her palms as a deep thrum of pleasure rocked her entire body.

His fingers were stretching her, but oh, Lord, the pleasure. Darius's thumb found and circled her clitoris. Lost in the magic of sensation, she gripped his forearms and let herself be swept away. So close… almost there.

"Seeing you like this," he whispered, "touching you like this gives me more pleasure than I deserve."

He crushed his lips to hers in a deep, open-mouthed kiss that stole the breath from her lungs. He was kissing her the way a man kissed a woman right before sinking into her body. Kissing her the way she needed to be kissed. Her knees squeezed his waist, and she gripped his butt in her hands. His fingers never stopped working her.

"I want so badly to make you mine," he said through gritted teeth.

Something hot and wild exploded inside her just then, not allowing either of them to go slowly. He wanted to make her his woman, but she *needed* him to do it. She fisted her hands in his hair, holding him captive while she deepened the kiss. Other men had kissed her, but this was the first time she ever experienced a kiss with her entire body. This was the first time a man had ever made her feel as if she were his entire world.

His thick erection pulsed against her thigh and the need to have it inside her, a part of her, consumed her heart and soul. "You're so thick and hard. I want you, Darius," she told him, the words coming from a secret place within her. The most honest part of herself, a part she couldn't deny, though she knew she should. "I do. Make love to me."

"I—" A hint of reason swept into Darius's consciousness. He couldn't make love to this woman. To do so and then to destroy her would be more vile than anything he'd ever done in the past.

She ran the tip of her tongue over his neck, up his chin, and placed little nips along the column of his jaw. "I want to do this with you every night. Just…" Kiss. "Like…" Nibble. "This."

Every night. The one thing he couldn't give her. He had a duty to fulfill. Touching and tasting this woman was not part of it, much as he wished otherwise. Mired in guilt, he broke all contact, tearing himself away from her and jumping off the bed. He stood, staring down at her, fighting for control. And losing. Her taste was still in his mouth.

Her cheeks were flushed like the barest rose. Moonlight caught the moisture on her lips, making them glisten, beckoning him to sample them once more. Getting near her again was pure folly, he thought with self-disgust. Yet every instinct he possessed screamed that she was his. That she belonged to him and was his sole reason for living. Her conquest—no, her *surrender*—would be his greatest victory.

But even as he entertained the wild thoughts, he denied them.

Javar had fallen to a woman. Many years ago, his former tutor had taken a female dragon as his bride. She had softened Javar, made him lax in his duties. He became less cautious with the mist, no longer so quick to kill. That laxness had most likely earned him death. Or worse. Even now Javar might be imprisoned somewhere, being tortured for his knowledge and authority over the mist.

Darius could not allow the same for himself. Softening would mean the destruction of Atlantis.

Irritation raged through him—for what he couldn't have, for what he shouldn't want. How could the merest touch of Grace's lips and body reduce him to a fire-lizard focused solely on sensation? And how did just being with her let him glimpse everything missing from his life? Warmth. Love. An escape from the darkness.

Allowing himself to know the sweet joy of being in her arms, in her body, could destroy everything he'd striven so adamantly to build. She was life and light, and he was death and shadows. Joining their bodies would be more folly than simply allowing her to live with knowledge of the mist.

"We must stop," he said, the words ripped from him. He summoned all of his strength, all of his resolve.

"No. No stopping." She sat up slowly, a frown marring her features. Her eyes were still heavy-lidded from sleep, still relaxed from the peace spell, and she blinked. "I want you to make love to me. I *need* you to make love to me. I'm close. So close to climax."

"Cover yourself," he said, the words even harsher than before. If she didn't, he might beg her to strip completely.

The front of her shirt gaped open, revealing those perfect curves. When she didn't rush to obey, he leaned down and gripped her shirt, careful not to brush her skin. He was pushed past his endurance already, and one more touch… Whether his will was weakened because of his distance with Atlantis or because of Grace herself, he didn't know. Sweat ran down his brow as he tied the ripped hem together, partially covering her breasts, yet leaving a tempting amount of cleavage.

"What are you doing?" she asked, staring down at his hands, seeing the same image he saw. His darkness against her paleness. His strength against her femininity.

He pulled away, not responding.

Grace blinked. Shook her head. Heady passion still held her in its wondrous fog. She ached. God, she ached. At first she'd told herself Darius was nothing more than another figment of her imagination, but she'd known the truth. She knew it now. He was real, and he was here.

He promised he'd come after her and he had.

A shiver raked her spine. How she'd ever convinced herself those few hours with him in Atlantis had been nothing more than her water-deprived imagination, she didn't know. And it didn't matter now. It didn't matter why he'd come. All that mattered was that he *was* here and he wanted her, too.

Grace's gaze traveled the length of Darius's body. He wore the same black leather pants as before. Instead of being shirtless, however, he wore a black T-shirt that showcased every muscle, every ridge of sinew.

As she watched him, the peaceful lassitude woven so delightfully into her blood began to fade. The corners of her lips turned down as a lone beam of moonlight struck Darius's face, making the golden-brown of his eyes gleam. She paused. Golden? Before, in Atlantis, his eyes had been blue. Ice-blue and as cold as the color implied. Now they were a warm, golden-brown and hinted at untold pleasure, but also an inner pain so staggering she was amazed he hadn't buckled under the burden of it.

His features tightened, and his eyes lightened. Lightened until that cold, crystalline gaze was back in place. How odd, she thought, shaking her head.

"There is much we need to discuss, Grace," he said. The rough edge of his voice sliced through her musings. "When you finish covering yourself, we will begin."

Here she was, offering herself to him despite everything, yet he didn't want any part of her. The rejection hurt deeply.

She must have hesitated too long, because he added, "Do it. Now." His jaw clenched.

Unease dripped past every other emotion working through her, withering her relaxation a bit more. This was the man who had threatened to hurt her. This was the man who had chased her and locked her away. This was not the man who'd held her tenderly, who'd kissed her so passionately.

"Darius?" she said with a wisp of uncertainty.

"Use the sheet," he said.

"Darius," she repeated, ignoring his dictate.

He flicked his gaze to the ceiling, as if praying for divine intervention. "Yes, Grace?"

"What's going on?" It was a silly question, yet she could think of nothing else to say.

"I told you I would come for you, and so I have."

She swallowed. "Why?"

Before she had time to blink, he unsheathed a small blade from the waist of his pants and held the razor-sharp tip at her neck. The contact was light, not enough to draw blood, but enough to sting all the same. She gasped and whimpered, the sounds blending and echoing off the walls.

Darius arched a brow. "We are going to have a chat, you and I."

"You didn't travel all this way to talk," she said. And he hadn't traveled here to make love to her, either. What exactly did he want from her?

"For now conversation is all I require of you." His blade stayed suspended in the air for another fraction of a second before he slid it back into its sheath. "Do not forget how dangerous I am."

Yes, he was dangerous. And if now was for conversation, what was later for?

Fighting a cold sweat and a timorous shake, Grace scrambled up. Her sheet and comforter whisked to the floor in a tangle at her feet. Darius remained in place, as if he feared nothing she could do. Determined, she reached into the backpack on her nightstand, knocking down the empty wineglass in her haste.

She withdrew her Mace and without any hesitation, sprayed him in the eyes. While his roar reverberated in her ears, she bolted out the bedroom door.

CHAPTER ELEVEN

EVERYTHING HAPPENED within seconds.

One moment she was racing through her living room, the next Darius tackled her from behind. He slammed into her, propelling her facedown. They landed on top of her couch, and the impact squeezed every molecule of oxygen from her lungs. As she struggled to breathe, he flipped her over and locked her wrists above her head. Still a favorite position of his, obviously. She didn't have time to panic.

"My soul belongs to you, and yours belongs to me," he chanted, his voice strange, hypnotic. His gaze clashed with hers, ice-blue calculation with turquoise uncertainty. The rims of his eyes were red and swollen, but as she watched, all hint of the toxic spray vanished.

"What are you doing?" she gasped, growing increasingly light-headed.

"Bound we shall be," he continued, "from this moon to another, then set free."

Her blood whirled inside her veins as a strange, dark and oddly compelling essence invaded her. Dark, so dark. Scattered thoughts flashed through her, motionless images in black-and-white—images of a child's terror, hurt, and search for a love never found. Images of desolation and an ultimate withdrawal from emotion.

The child was Darius.

She was poised on the periphery of a vision, gazing down at a bloody massacre. Men, women and children were lying motionless in pools of their own blood. The boy—Darius—knelt over one of the children. A little girl. Long black hair formed an inky river around her face and shoulders, blending with the blood dripping from her neck. She wore a sapphire-colored dress that was bunched around her waist. Her eyes were closed, but there was a promise of beauty in every line of her softly rounded features.

Gently Darius fitted the hem of the dress around her ankles, covering her exposed flesh. He remained kneeling and gazed up to the crystal dome. He slammed a fist into the dirt and howled, the sound more animal than human, more tortured than any child should ever have to endure.

Grace wanted to sob. She found herself reaching out, hoping to wrap the boy in her arms. But even as she moved, she was whisked back to reality. Darius still hovered above her.

"What did you do to me?" she cried.

He didn't answer right away. His eyes were closed, as if he were lost in a vision of his own. When he finally opened his eyelids, he said, "I have bound us together." He looked smug. "For one day, you must remain in my presence. There will be no more escaping."

"That isn't possible."

"Isn't it? Can you not speak my language? Did I not travel here—Gracie Lacie?" he added softly.

She gasped. "How do you know that name?"

"Your father called you that."

"Yes, but how do you know?"

"I saw inside your mind," he said simply. He pushed to his feet, and she scooted backward to the edge of the couch. "Go to your room and dress," he said. "Wear something that covers you from neck to toe. We have much to discuss and not a lot of time."

"I'm not moving."

His gaze slitted. "Then I will change you myself."

With that threat ringing in her ears, Grace jumped up and scurried around him. When she reached her bedroom, she quickly shut and locked the door, then raced to the nearest window. She unlatched the fastener, raised the glass and attempted to throw one leg over.

An invisible wall stopped any movement outside.

Nearly screeching with frustration, she kicked and pounded at the wall but couldn't break past it. Finally, panting, she gave up. How dare Darius do this! she seethed. What had he said? A binding spell. How dare he cast a binding spell, locking her within his grasp.

A hard knock sounded at her door. "You have five minutes to dress, and then I am coming in."

He'd do it, too, she thought. Even if he had to kick in the door. Even if he had to take the apartment building apart brick by brick. With a humorless chuckle, she leaned against the ledge and rested her head on the wooden frame.

How had such a lost little boy grown into such an uncompromising man?

She didn't want to believe those flashes of his life were real, but he'd known her father's nickname for her. And she hadn't shared that information with anyone. Darius's childhood, those things she'd seen, had happened. She didn't like knowing he'd once had a family. She didn't like knowing about the pain he had endured at their deaths. Knowing made her long to comfort him, to protect him. To stay with him.

"I don't want to change while you're inside my house," she called. "I don't trust you."

"That matters not. You will do as I have commanded."

Or he'd do it for her, she mentally finished. Grace dragged her feet to her dresser and tore off her ripped tank. She quickly jerked on her largest, plainest turtleneck sweater and a pair of plain gray sweatpants. He didn't want to see her skin, and she didn't want to show it to him. Glowering, she donned socks and tennis shoes—better to kick him with.

When she was completely dressed, she paused. *What do I do now?* She would go out there, Grace decided, and she would be civilized. She would answer his questions honestly. Afterward, he would leave her, just as he'd found her. The boy he'd been would allow nothing less. She hoped. He'd certainly had the opportunity to hurt her: while she slept, while they kissed. A shiver of remembrance trickled through her, and she scowled. How could she *still* desire him?

Gathering her scattered wits, she unlocked the door and pulled it open. Darius towered a few feet away, his shoulder propped on the opposite wall. His expression was as cold and merciless as ever; his eyes could have been chipped from an Alaskan glacier.

"Much better," he said, eyeing her clothing.

"Let's go into the living room," she said. She didn't want a bed anywhere near them. Without waiting for his reply, she swept around him. She settled on the recliner—so he couldn't sit next to her—and said the first thing that popped into her mind. "Are you going to eat me?"

"What?" he half growled, half gasped. He settled onto the couch, as far away from her as possible.

Was he just as leery of her as she was of him? The thought shouldn't have bothered her, but it did. She had done nothing, by word or deed, to earn his dislike.

"Your friends," she said. "They're cannibals and wanted to eat me." She shuddered at the memory.

His lips curled in what could either have been amusement or fury. "They will never do so. That I can promise you." He schooled his features until they were as blank as a brand-new chalkboard. "Where is the medallion, Grace?"

Uh-oh. Confession time. "I, uh, lost it."

"What?" he roared, jolting to his feet.

"I lost it?" she offered more as a question than a statement.

He sank back into his seat and rubbed a hand down his face. "Explain."

"While I was inside the mist the second time, it ripped from my neck." She shrugged. "I tried to get it back, but failed."

His gaze pierced her with its intensity. "If you are saying this in an attempt to keep the medallion for yourself, I will—"

"Search my home if you want," she interjected defensively.

He massaged his temple with two fingers and continued to stare over at her. Then he nodded as though he'd just come to a monumental decision. "We are going to take a small trip, Grace."

"I don't think so."

"We're going to the cave. We will not stay long."

Heat drained from her face and hands, leaving her cold and pale. Did he hope to send her back into Atlantis? To lock her up? To either kill/torture/molest her—okay, the last one appealed to her in a way it shouldn't have—in his own surroundings?

"Do not think to protest," he said, as if reading her thoughts. "I must go, therefore you must go. We are bound together."

"Atlantis is—"

"Not where I'm taking you. I wish only to visit the cave."

She relaxed, soothed by the ring of truth in his tone. Another trip to Brazil might actually be beneficial, she realized, remembering the postcard Alex had sent her. She could take his picture with her, something she hadn't had last time, and walk through town, asking people if they had seen him. Because maybe, just maybe, whatever lead he'd found, whatever he'd done in Florida had directed him back to Brazil. God knows that's where the portal resided and that portal was what Alex was looking for.

"If I go with you," she said, purposely omitting her change of desires, "will you help me find my brother?"

"You do not know where he is?"

"No. And I've looked. His coworkers haven't seen him. He hasn't been home. He hasn't even called our mother, and he usually does. Someone sent me an e-mail supposedly from him, but I know it wasn't because I found a postcard Alex had written telling me he was in trouble. This entire situation is a mess! The only people who know I'm looking for him are his coworkers, but they're looking for him, too, so I don't know why they'd want to stop me. I just want my brother safe."

A flash of guilt stole through Darius's eyes. "I cannot stay here long, but you have my word of honor that while I am here, I will help you find him."

"Thank you," she told him softly. Why the guilt, though?

He stood and held out his hand, palm up.

"We're leaving *now*?"

"Now."

"But I need to call the airline. I need to—"

"You need only take my hand."

Blinking up at him in confusion, she swallowed, then forced herself to stand. "Give me just…" She rushed to her storage closet. "One…" She withdrew a photo album. "Second." She peeled Alex's picture from the slot, folded it and shoved it into her pocket. She raced back to Darius and, with a half smile, placed her hand in his. "I'm ready."

"Close your eyes." The deep baritone of his voice was hypnotic.

"Why?"

"Just do what I say."

"First tell me why."

He frowned. "What I'm about to do can be jolting."

"There. That wasn't so bad, was it?" She closed her eyelids, total darkness encompassing her. A full minute ticked by and nothing happened. What was going on? "Can I look now?"

"Not yet." His voice was strained, and his hand clenched around hers. "I do not have full use of my powers, so the trip is taking longer than usual."

Trip? And why didn't he have full use of his powers?

"You may look now," he said a moment later.

His dilemma forgotten, she fluttered open her eyelids and gasped. Bleak, rocky walls surrounded her. Water dripped in a constant procession, the sound ghostly. A thick, smoky mist billowed around them, cold and dreary, dusting everything it touched with chill. She was suddenly grateful for her sweatpants.

The only light came from Darius. Even through his shirt, his tattoos glowed bright enough to light a football stadium.

"How did you do that?" she asked, awed. "How did you bring us here so quickly, without walking a single step?"

"I am a child of the gods," he said, as if that explained everything. "Do not move from that spot."

Since that suited her desires perfectly, she nodded. She wasn't going near the mist.

His eyes scanning, searching, he stalked around the cavern, his muscles rippling beneath his clothes with every movement. She easily recalled how all that strength and sinew felt beneath her fingertips. Her mouth watered, and she shifted from one foot to the other. No matter what this man did, he oozed danger and excitement; it seeped from his every pore. He was far too menacing, far too unpredictable, and far too powerful. He'd promised to help her while he was with her, and she believed he would.

If anyone could find Alex, it was this man.

He tried to lift a large branch out of his way, but his hands ghosted through it. As she watched, her eyes widened. She turned toward the wall and ran her own hand over the jagged surface. Shockingly her fingers disappeared inside the rock. "We're ghosts," she croaked out, spinning to face Darius.

"Only while we are here," he assured her.

Knowing she was not a permanent phantom eased her worry, and she relaxed. She was used to new experiences. Most times she went out of her way to have them. But with Darius, things just sort of happened—weird things she could not possibly prepare for. He was excitement personified.

"Are you looking for the medallion?" she asked when he continued his search.

A long silence fell between them. Obviously he didn't want to answer.

"Well?" she persisted.

"I *must* find it."

What was it about that chain? Even she had fought to possess it, had felt its strange, unquestionable draw. "You want it, Alex wanted it and someone once tried to steal it from him. Other than unlocking your bedroom door, what makes that thing so valuable?"

"Dragon medallions are handcrafted by Hephaestus, the blacksmith of the gods, and each one holds a special power for its owner, like time travel or invisibility. What's more, it unlocks doors to *every* room in every dragon palace—as you saw for yourself," he added dryly.

"If I'd known it offered special powers, I might have held on to it more tightly," she said. Time travel. How cool was that? "My favorite novels are time travels, and I've always thought it would be cool to visit the Middle Ages."

"If you had known of the medallion's powers, you would *not* have lived long enough to travel through time."

Well, that certainly put things in perspective, didn't it? "I guess that means I shouldn't ask what yours can do."

"No, you should not. You and other surface dwellers should not even know the medallions exist."

She sighed. "Alex found an ancient text, the *Book of Ra-Dracus*. That's how he knew about them. That's how he knew about the portal into Atlantis."

Darius's chin whipped up and he faced her; his eyes narrowed. "I have never heard of this book. What else did it say?"

"He didn't mention much, but did say the book told of ways to defeat the creatures inside. Alex gave no mention of specifics, though. I'm sorry."

"I must see that book." *I must destroy it,* echoed unsaid.

"Shortly after he found it," she said, lifting her arms in a helpless gesture, "someone stole it from him."

Darius rubbed his neck as he knelt before a muddy mound. "Atlanteans are dangerous beings, stronger than your people and far more deadly. Why those on the surface continually try to invade our land is beyond me. Those who do always die. Every time."

"I didn't," she reminded him softly.

His head snapped in her direction for a second time. Silence. Then, "No," he finally said, "you didn't." He continued to stare at her, and she shifted uncomfortably. His attention wavered between her mouth and her curves. If his eyes became any more heated, her clothing would be incinerated, panties and all. "Where did your brother find the book?"

"Greece. The temple of Erinys," she said, snapping her fingers as the name popped into place.

"Erinys, the punisher of the unfaithful." His brow furrowed. "A minor goddess. I do not understand why she or her followers would possess such a book, a book that tells of ways to defeat us."

"Maybe she wanted to punish those in Atlantis," Grace offered.

His nostrils flared. "We are not, nor have we ever been, unfaithful to anyone."

O-kay. Sore topic. And one she wouldn't bring up again. "I'm sure you weren't, big guy," she said, hoping to placate him.

"We do not attempt to conquer the surface. We serve our gods faithfully. We do nothing to earn ourselves punishment."

"Well, now, that's not exactly true." Even though she'd just promised herself she wouldn't bring this up again, she found herself saying, "You obviously did *something*. Your entire city was cast into the sea."

"We existed. That is why we were hidden in the sea. The way I understand it is we were never meant to be created, yet Zeus cut off his father's—" he paused "—manhood, causing Cronus's blood to splatter upon the earth. He meant to create man, but we were the first to form. Though he was—is—our brother, Zeus feared what we could do, so he banished us from the land he viewed as his playground. We were not unfaithful."

"You were created by the blood of a god?" she asked, beyond curious about him.

"No," he answered. "My parents conceived me through the more traditional manner. My ancestors were the ones created by a god's blood." His lips pressed together firmly, stubbornly, and she knew he'd say no more on the subject.

His parents were dead, she remembered from her vision, and she ached for him. Ached because he'd been the one to find them. Ached because they'd been murdered in ways so cruel she cringed from the thoughts. She knew how devastating losing a loved one was. He'd lost everyone close to him in one fatal swoop.

"Your brother," Darius said, effectively changing the subject. "You said he's been missing for several weeks."

The mention of Alex served as a cold reminder of why she was here. "He hasn't been home, hasn't called, and that isn't like him."

"And there were men chasing him through the jungle, trying to obtain the medallion from him?"

"There could have been, yes. The theft attempt I mentioned was from before."

"Perhaps you should tell me everything that happened before and after you escaped me."

She told him what she knew, leaving out no detail.

"These men," he said, "the Argonauts who found you in the jungle. Would they harm your brother if they knew of the medallion?"

"I would hope not, but…"

Darius pursed his lips as he wondered just how many were involved in this tangled web of mystery—which was becoming more complicated every time Grace opened her mouth. "I wish to find and speak with them." He pushed to his feet. "The medallion is not here," he growled. "I have searched every inch of the cave."

"I didn't lie to you," she assured him. "I lost it in the mist."

He jerked a hand through his hair. Once again he was left unsure whether to believe Grace. Her motives seemed pure, the protection of her brother; yet her claim of losing the medallion seemed too convenient.

As he stood there, warring within himself, his heated tattoos illuminated a dark object, glinting in the corner of his eye. He'd seen the object during his search, but had ignored it. Now he bent down and studied it. Grace's weapon, he realized. The same sort of weapon the human guards carried at Javar's palace. He must have tossed it through the mist.

"Why did you carry this?" he asked her. His fingers drifted through the metal.

"The gun?" She closed the distance between them and knelt beside him. Her heady essence wrapped around him.

"A gun," he echoed. "Why did you carry this?" he asked again.

"To protect myself. I bought it from a peddler in Manaus."

"What does it do?" His voice was solemn, deep. "As I recall, you tried to wound me with it, but nothing happened."

"The cylinder wasn't loaded. If the cylinder *had* been loaded, bullets would have shot out when I pulled the trigger and slammed into you, causing injury. Maybe even death."

Intrigued, he eyed the gun with new expectations. A complicated piece of weaponry, to be sure. The coil, the thin shaft. "I would like to see this in action."

"I just bet you would," she muttered.

He flicked her a glance. "If I make it so that you can hold this weapon, will you show me how to work it?"

"I don't have any bullets," she said.

"Get some."

"Where? We're not exactly in the bustling heart of a city, with eager merchants hawking their wares."

"Later, then. When we return to your home. You can obtain these bullets and show me how this weapon works."

"All right," she said. Though Grace wasn't sure she wanted him to handle a loaded gun. Nor was she sure she wanted to take him to a gun range. "But how are we going to get it home? We can't even pick it up."

He turned back to the gun, letting his hands hover over the top, and closed his eyes. One minute melted into another. Lines of strain bracketed his mouth, and his bronze skin paled. Grace didn't utter a sound, didn't move. She didn't know what he was doing, but she was loath to interrupt.

Finally, he let out a breath and opened his eyes. He scooped his hand under the gun and lifted. Instead of sinking past an immaterial palm, the gun remained cradled.

"How did you do that?" Awe laced her voice. She took the weapon and tucked it in the drawstring waist of her sweats.

He ignored her question. "Come," he said, stalking to the entrance. "I wish to find these Argonauts."

"They have guns of their own," she warned him. "I saw them."

The dire warning didn't cause him a moment's concern, though his gaze gleamed with a tiny flicker of pleasure that she sought to offer it. "They will not even know we are here. We are like ghosts, remember?"

They were forced to crawl on their hands and knees until they reached the cave's entrance. Grace loved the way her knees glided through every rock and twig, but wondered why Darius didn't do his instant transfer thingy. They reached the end, and she eased to her feet. The heat and humidity of the Amazon threatened to roast her, and she was no longer so thankful for her sweats. Familiar scents drifted to her nostrils: dewy foliage, orchids, and recent rain.

"How does one protect oneself from a gun?" Darius asked, ushering her beyond a flourishing green bush.

"Kevlar vests. That's what the police use, anyway."

His expression turned pensive. "I would like some of these vests."

"Maybe we can order you some on the Internet. I'll do a search—"

Her body tingled in strange rippling waves, and she gasped. A piece of fruit had sailed through her and smashed into a tree. Laughter drifted to her ears, not human, but amused all the same. Two more missiles sailed through her as Darius whipped around. He launched himself at her, tossing her to the ground. His weight crushed her.

"How have you been spotted, woman?" he demanded.

"Those damn monkeys!" She glared up at him, blaming him for her trials, slowly becoming aware of the perfect fit of their bodies and the warm, seductive scent of him. "You said no one would know we were here."

"Monkeys are responsible?" His lips compressed, and if she weren't mistaken, amusement twinkled in his golden eyes. She paused. Golden again? The only time they'd been golden like this was right after he kissed her. What made them change? "Animals can see what the human eye cannot," he said.

"Are you laughing at me?"

"Perhaps."

"What I want to know is why he didn't throw anything at you."

"My guess is that he knew I would have him for my next meal if he did so."

She liked this side of Darius, playful and teasing. Grace smiled.

His gaze veered to her lips, and heat suddenly seared his eyes. All traces of merriment fled from his expression. Her own smile faded. Memories of the last time he'd lain on top of her licked through her mind. And just like that, she wanted him again.

The knowledge angered her. How could she desire this man?

She must have moved, must have arched her hips, because Darius hissed a torrent of air between his teeth. His muscles were tense, and he was leaning toward her. Closer, closer still.

In one swift motion, he jerked to his feet.

"Up," he commanded, his tone inexorable. "You're wasting time."

Wasting time? Wasting time! Her? Irritated, Grace stood and anchored her hands on her hips. "It's going to be nothing but good times with you. I can tell."

Darius led her around for the next hour. The heat obviously agreed with him. While he looked as refreshed and vibrant as if he'd just stepped from a yoga class, dirt glued itself to her clothes and body. Even her hair was weighted down and wilted. She was a ghost. Wasn't she supposed to stay clean and untouched by the elements?

"I hate this place," she muttered. Already she was tired and thirsty. And cranky. "I need a coconut smoothie."

The man responsible for her distress finally halted. "There are no Argonauts here."

No shit, Sherlock. Yes, definitely cranky. "I'm telling you, they *were* here."

"I believe you," he assured her, as if that had never been in question. "Their footprints are everywhere." He scanned the trees. "Do you know the names of the men who helped you?"

"Yes. Jason and Mitch. And Patrick," she added.

"I need their surnames, too."

"Sorry." She shook her head. "They didn't offer, and at the time I didn't care to ask."

Darius fought a wave of disappointment. He'd hoped to find the men, question them and finally gain at least some of the answers he sought. The sooner he finished this, the sooner he could reclaim Javar's palace—and the sooner his life returned to normal. No more chaos. No more unquenchable desires.

No more Grace.

His lips lifted in a scowl. She was quickly propelling him to the brink of madness. The way she moved, sultry, swaying. The way she spoke, challenging, lilting. The way she watched him with hunger in her eyes—hunger she couldn't quite hide.

She didn't want to want him, but want him she did. Very much.

And he wanted her right back—alarmingly so.

After he'd uttered the binding spell, he'd seen inside her mind and knew she ran from her own desires. Knew her brother, Alex, did the same. They'd watched their father slowly deteriorate, then quickly die. Grace had loved her father for the kind, gentle man he'd been, but watching him fade had been so painful she'd retreated to fantasy, imagining herself anywhere but home. Imagining herself in all kinds of exhilarating situations. A crime fighter of unequalled strength. A lady pirate who sailed the high seas. A siren who lured men to her bed and pleasured them into unconsciousness. The last intrigued him most.

She craved excitement and passion and all the things she'd created in her dreams, but so far life had offered her none of those things. Nothing managed to live up to her expectations. She'd known one disappointing adventure after another…until she stumbled through the mist. Then she'd finally found the exhilaration she had always craved.

How could he consider ending her life, when she was only just now beginning to experience her dreams? The question plagued him because he knew the answer; he simply could not accept it. Though he might want her to live, he would fulfill his oath.

Darius sighed. He was wasting time here, time that he didn't have to spare. His powers were already weakening. He wasn't sure how much longer he had before he weakened completely.

"Let us journey back to your home," he told Grace. He didn't wait for her response, he simply wrapped his fingers around her wrist.

"Wait. I want to head into town and ask around about Alex," she said. "That's why I brought his pic—" Before she could finish her sentence, he pictured her home and those very walls materialized around them.

CHAPTER TWELVE

THE NEW YORK MORNING announced its presence by shooting rays of sunlight through Grace's living room windows. Cars honked outside; the people above her stomped across their apartment, shaking her ceiling.

"You have got to stop popping me in and out of places. I'm this close—" she told Darius, pinching her thumb and finger together "—to having a heart attack. And besides that, I wasn't ready to leave," she snapped. "I wanted you to take me into town so I could show Alex's picture around and ask if anyone had seen him."

"I did not deem it necessary," he said, releasing her. His face was pale and those lines of tension were back.

He did not deem it necessary, she silently mimicked. What about what *she* deemed necessary? Scowling, she padded to the kitchen, placed her gun inside a drawer and poured herself a tall glass of ice water. She drained every drop. Only after she'd consumed three more glasses did she offer Darius a drink.

"Have you anything other than water? Something with flavor?"

"I could make lemonade." Not that he deserved it.

"That will suffice."

She withdrew several lemons from the refrigerator, beat them against the counter to release the most juice, then sliced a hole in the top of each. She squeezed the tangy liquid into a glass and added sugar substitute—she did *not* keep real sugar anywhere near her—and water. She slid the drink across the counter.

Having watched her mix the contents with a leery eye, he lifted the glass and sipped tentatively. She knew the exact moment the sweet-and-sour flavors blended into his taste buds, knew the exact moment he wanted to howl with pleasure. His strong fingers gripped the cup, curling around the glass with surprising gentleness; his eyelids grew heavy, causing his inky lashes to dip over the sensuous planes of his cheekbones.

As he swallowed, his throat moved. A wicked shiver dripped along her spine, and she had the sudden urge to lick him there. *I'm turned on by a man's trachea. How pathetic am I?*

"Surely that is ambrosia," he said. Thankfully his color had returned. He reluctantly set his empty glass on the countertop.

"I don't mind making more if you're—"

"I would like more," he rushed out.

If he reacted like this to lemonade, how would he

react to chocolate? Spontaneous orgasm? Maybe she had a Hershey bar hidden somewhere…

He consumed two more glasses of lemonade in quick succession. He requested a third, but she'd run out of lemons. His disappointment was palpable, but he shrugged it off.

Watching her with heated eyes, he licked the last drop from the cup rim. "You asked me earlier what power my medallion possessed. I will show you now," he said. "First I will need your brother's surname."

"Carlyle. Like mine."

He arched a brow. "Is that common here? To share names?"

"Yes. You didn't share the same name as your family members?"

"No. Why should we have? We are each individuals and our names are our own."

"How do you show your family relationship, then?"

"House affiliation. My family was House of Py." Darius removed his medallion, and as he held it in his open palm, it glowed a brighter, eerier red. "Show me Alex Carlyle," he said to the dragon heads.

Four beams of crimson sprayed from both sets of eyes. They formed a circle in the air, and the beams grew wider by the second. Grace watched with fascination as the air began to crystallize.

"What's happening?" she whispered.

Alex's image appeared in the center of the circle, and all questions were forgotten. Her jaw dropped open in shock. Dirt, sweat and bruises covered her brother from head to toe, and as she took in his appearance, her blood ran cold. He was pallid, his skin so pale she could see the faint tracings of his veins. He wore only a pair of ripped, stained jeans. His eyes were closed, and he huddled on a muddy floor. Tremors raked him. From cold? From fever? Or fear? The room was sparsely furnished with a small bed and a chipped wooden nightstand.

With one hand she covered her mouth and with the other she reached out, hoping to smooth his brow, hoping to reassure him that she was here. Just like in the cave, her fingers drifted through like a mirage. Feeling helpless, she dropped her hands to her sides. "Alex," she said shakily. "Where are you?"

"He cannot hear you," Darius said.

"Alex," she said again, determined to gain his attention in any way necessary. How long since he'd last eaten? What had put those bruises on his skin? What had made him so pale? She bit back a deep moan of distress.

"Do you recognize this place?" Darius asked.

"No." Lips trembling, gaze never straying, she shook her head. "Do you?"

"No," he sighed.

"It's a motel room, I think. Find him," she beseeched, watching in horror as her brother rolled to his side, revealing two bloody puncture wounds on his neck. Vampire? From Atlantis? Had he made it inside? "You said you would."

"I only wish it were that easy, Grace."

At last she switched her attention, flashing Darius an accusing glare. "You found me."

"We were connected through the spell of understanding. I simply followed my own magic. I have had no contact with your brother, nor does anything bind me to him."

Alex's image began to waver just as a woman approached him. She was the most beautiful woman Grace had ever seen. Where Alex was long and lean, the woman was small and delicate with flowing silvery-blond hair. Pixie features, porcelain skin. She crouched beside him and gently shook his shoulders.

"Who is that?" Grace demanded sharply.

Darius narrowed his focus. "That is Teira," he said, an undercurrent of incredulity in his tone. "Javar's wife."

"I don't care whose wife she is, as long as she leaves my brother alone. Is she cruel? Will she hurt him? What's she doing to him?"

Just as quickly as it appeared, the image faded completely.

"Bring them back," Grace commanded.

"The medallion shows me a vision for only a small period of time, and never the same person more than once."

No. *No!* She controlled the urge to stomp her foot, to whimper. To cry. "Take me to Alex."

"I wish that I could, but I do not know the surface."

"You said you found me because we're con-

nected. I can give you one of Alex's belongings. Or
a photograph of him." Nearing a point of desperation, she jerked out the photo of Alex from her pocket
and wrapped Darius's fingers around the folded
edges. "You can connect with this and find him."

"That is not how my powers work, Grace." There
was no emotion to him now. He'd reverted to his indifferent, unperturbed self, the part of him she so
longed to shatter. Blue eyes hard and cold, he set the
photo aside.

A single tear slowly ran down her cheek. "You
have to help me." Gripping the fabric of his shirt, she
said, "He's sick. I don't know how long he's gone
without food or water. I don't know what that woman
planned to do to him."

"Teira will not hurt him. She is ever gentle and
caring."

"He needs *me*."

"I have given you my word that I will help you
find him while I am here. Do not doubt me."

"I don't doubt that you'll help me, Darius," she
said brokenly. Hollowly. She stared up at him with
watery eyes. "I just wonder if we'll get to him in
time."

At that moment, Darius knew she meant Atlantis
no harm. Knew she only wanted her brother safe and
whole. Her emotions were too raw. Real. He hated
himself for it because he could not let that change his
purpose. He might loathe the man he'd become, the
man he willingly was—a killer and a user—but that
changed nothing.

When Grace learned that he was helping her only to destroy Alex, as well as Grace herself…

Tensing, he forced his mind on the matter at hand. Why was Teira with a human? Where were they being held? Their cell was a surface dwelling, yet Alex had been bitten by a vampire—a fact Darius wouldn't tell Grace.

The female dragon's presence added a new complication. Was she prisoner or captor? A loving woman who possessed a sweet nature and giving heart, she would not make a good captor. Yet Javar would never allow his wife to be taken. Unless he were dead.

That Darius once again found himself back to that line of thought unsettled him. He had, perhaps, another day here before he must return, yet he was no closer to answers than he had been when he first arrived. Instead the mystery had sprouted new, twisted limbs.

"The key is the medallion," he said. "I must figure out which human has the most to gain by possessing it."

"Not necessarily a human." With a shuddering sigh, Grace sank onto a stool. "Any of the creatures in Atlantis could use it to sneak inside your home and steal your valuables. For God's sake, you own jewels of every kind and size."

That's exactly what those humans had been doing inside Javar's palace, stealing, using the gods' tools to pry out the jewels. "Atlanteans must only ask and we share. There is no reason to steal."

"There is, too, a reason. Pure greediness. And I know for a fact that the emotion is inherent to all races, gods and humans alike. All of our myths and legends expound upon such things."

Now *he* sighed. "Humans are responsible *this time*." He thought back to the messenger's words and the gun the boy had drawn. "Humans are even now inside my friend's home, wielding guns and the gods only know what other weapons."

"Could the humans be working with this friend?"

"Never." He would not consider the possibility. "Javar loathes humans as I do. He would never aid one."

She averted her gaze from him, shielding her expression. Several seconds ticked until she said, "Do you loathe *all* humans?" A trace of hurt leaked into her voice.

"Not all," he admitted reluctantly. He liked one tiny female more than was wise. A female with silky red curls and softly rounded curves. With lush breasts and high-tipped nipples.

A female he craved in his bed more with every moment that passed.

"Well, then," she said, straightening her back, pretending she had not a care. "We'll concentrate on humans. I'm willing to bet the same humans who are inside that palace are the ones Alex wrote about. The ones who tried to steal his medallion. The ones who *did* steal his book."

"Wrote?" he lashed out, concentrating on that one word. He could not allow any written record of his home. He already had the *Book of Ra-Dracus* to contend with. "You said he *told* you."

"He did. In his journal. He kept a log of his search for the mist. Would you like to read it?"

"Where is it?" he asked sharply.

"I'll show you." She walked from the kitchen, and Darius followed close on her heels. She led him down a small, narrow hallway laden with the calming scent of chamomile. They entered her bedchamber and it took only one glance at the bed for his stomach to tighten. She stopped at the desk and held up a can for his view. "This looks like an ordinary hairspray can, right?"

"Of course," he said, though he had no idea what hairspray was.

"Well, it's not." With quick, precise motions, she untwisted the end and out popped a key. Her lush, pink lips lifted in a half smile, revealing the hint of straight white teeth.

His stomach didn't tighten this time, but reached up and devoured his throat.

How could one woman possess so much beauty?

With a graceful flick of her fingers, she hooked tendrils of hair behind her ears. She bent down and inserted the key underneath the desk. "My father was too sick to hold a job—that's why we moved from South Carolina to New York, so he could be close to Sloan-Kettering. Anyway, to pass the time and make money in the process, he carved and sold furniture. He built this for me a long time ago."

"I am sorry for your loss."

"Thank you," she said softly. "My dad built one for Alex, too, though his secret compartments are different. I think. We used to get into each other's stuff, which made both of us furious. Alex would read my diary, and I would steal pictures of his friends. So my dad made us each a desk where we could successfully hide our treasures."

The melancholy in her voice remained long after her words faded away. Darius very nearly dropped to his knees and vowed never to hurt her or her brother if only she would smile again. He stayed the impulse, knowing such a promise was impossible to keep.

Inside the secret drawer lay a thin, plain book bound by black leather. As Grace traced her fingertips over the surface, she caught her bottom lip with her teeth, slowly releasing it. She handed the book to him, retaining contact until the last possible second.

He flipped through the pages, frowning at the unfamiliar script. While his spell of understanding gave him complete comprehension of Grace's spoken language, it did not provide him with an understanding of the written. He'd never been concerned with others' opinions of him, but he did not want Grace to perceive any weakness in him. He wanted her to see him as strong and capable, all that a woman could desire.

He handed the journal back to her, saying, "Read it to me. Please."

Thankfully she made no comment, merely

accepted the book and stood. "Let's get comfortable in the living room."

Once there, Grace situated herself on the scarlet couch, and he eased beside her. Perhaps he should have chosen another chair, but he craved physical contact with her and saw no reason to deny himself. Not while he hungered for her scent in his nostrils. Hungered for her touch. Even this, as little as it was.

His thigh brushed hers, and she sucked in a breath and tried to scoot away. Did she think to deny him this minor connection? After everything she'd already allowed? Only hours before, the woman had kissed him as if she couldn't live without the taste of him in her mouth. She had let him suck on her nipples, had let him bury two fingers deep inside of her.

He spread his knees, straightened the wide width of his shoulders, both actions consuming all of her space.

"Do you have to sit so close?" she asked on a ragged breath.

"Yes," was his only reply.

"Want to tell me why?"

"No."

"I don't like it," she insisted, scooting from him for the second time.

He moved closer. "Want to tell me why?" he parroted.

"No," she parroted right back, her expression stubborn.

"Then you may begin reading."

She examined her cuticles and yawned prettily. Only the needy gleam in her eyes gave her away.

"What are you doing?" he asked. "I do not have time to waste. Begin."

"I'm waiting."

He arched his brows. "For?"

"For you to move."

Scowling, Darius stayed where he was for a long while. This was a minor battle of wills, yet he did not want to lose. Did he have any other choice, though? Teeth grinding together, he inched slightly away from her. As he moved, the sweet scent of her lessened and the heat she emanated faded. He wanted to howl.

"That's better." She settled into the cushions and opened the book. Her fingers smoothed over the first page, and a look of sadness filled her expression. She began reading, despair reflected in her tone, as well.

He leaned his head back, locked his hands under his neck and closed his eyes. Her melodious voice floated over him, as gentle as a caress. There was something so peaceful about listening to her, as if her voice, despite its melancholy, was a reflection of joy, laughter and love. As if all three were his for the taking, if only he would reach out and grasp them. But he knew they would never be his. Warriors like him were destined to roam life alone. It was the only way to preserve his sanity.

A cold-blooded killer needed absolute withdrawal.

Much too quickly, Grace closed the journal with

a gentle flip of her wrist and glanced over at him. He worried two fingers over his jaw. "Tell me again where your brother stole the medallion."

"At a charity gala hosted by Argonauts."

Again Argonauts, Darius thought, his determination to speak with them increasing. Alex had stolen it, had almost had it stolen from him, and had been followed.

He frowned as a thought occurred to him. "If you knew someone wanted the necklace," he said to Grace, his voice growing harsher with each word, "why did you even go to Brazil?"

"Did you not hear the last passage? Alex found the hint of danger exciting. And so—" she jutted out her chin in defiance "—did I."

He was furious as he leaned toward her, putting them nose to nose. Their breath mingled, swirling together and becoming a single essence. Exactly what he wanted for their bodies. That quickly he lost his fury in a haze of lust. His dragon's blood roared to life, clamoring for her. Aching for her. Frenzied for her.

"That would-be thief could have found him, could even be the one holding him. Tell me, do you still crave excitement?" he asked softly, menacingly. "Do not think to deny it because I know you do," he added when she opened her mouth to protest. "I sense the need inside you. I sense it pulsing through your veins even now. Such a thing is dangerous for you, but…"

Her throat constricted, and she gulped.

Dismay whirled in the turquoise cauldron of her

eyes, but he also saw hunger, a tempest of desire. She would never be happy with an ordinary life. She needed adventure, needed her deepest fantasies realized, and though it was irrational, he wanted to be the one to give her those things.

His gaze swept to her lips. He found himself closing the rest of the distance, a heartbeat away from possessing her mouth with his own. She jack-knifed to her feet, turning her back toward him, granting him a tantalizing view of her cascading curls.

A lovely view to be sure, but not the one he craved.

"I'm sorry." Grace fingered her lips. Darius hadn't kissed her, had only come within a whisper of her, but still her lips throbbed for him. Of all the things he'd done to her, of all the things he'd made her feel, she feared this the most…this seemingly unquench-able desire she had for him. This need for him, and only him. This consuming ache for his touch that made her forget the only thing she should care about. Her brother.

But…

The more time she spent in Darius's presence, the more she saw past his cold, callous mask and into the heart of a vulnerable man. And that made her want him all the more. That *scared* her all the more. Such intense longing bordered on obsession. No man should have that much power over her. No man should be able to wrap sultry coils around her and consume her every thought.

Most women dreamt of having such a strong, sensual man at their fingertips. A week ago, she would have been in their ranks, thinking there was nothing more a woman could want than a man who looked at her with undeniable hunger, as if there were no other woman who could make him feel that way. Right now, Grace felt too exposed, too vulnerable.

"I'm not ready for this," she said. "Not ready for you. Last night, and even in Atlantis, everything seemed surreal. This…doesn't. This is real and in-your-face and can never be undone. I'm just not ready," she said again. "More than that, the timing is horrible. My first concern has to be my brother's welfare. Not my own…desires."

While she rattled off her list of reasons she shouldn't bed him, Darius's mind formed a list of all the reasons she should. And only one of them mattered. *She's mine,* he thought. His instincts had tried to warn him, had actually screamed it was so when he last kissed her. This undeniable tug had been between them since the beginning, and it wasn't going away. He admitted as much now. He wouldn't forget his oath, but he *would* have this woman. Where she was concerned, he could fight his needs no longer.

He would be doing himself a favor, he rationalized, if he took her and rid himself of this growing curiosity to know what being with her would be like.

He wanted to rise and reach out to clasp her by the

waist. He forced himself to remain in place, hands at his sides. He would take her, yes. But he would take her when it was *she* who was desperate for their loving. Not him. Beads of sweat popped onto his brow and dripped from his temples. He fisted his hands in the soft couch cushions.

Needing a distraction, Darius stood and liberated the journal from between her fingers. She gasped at the sudden loss and spun to glare at him. As she watched, he tossed the little book into a bowl and ignited a fire—with his mouth. He was surprised when the fire quickly dwindled to nothing, and he frowned. The fire should have lasted much longer. His powers must be weaker than he'd realized.

"Fire flew out of your mouth." Grace gaped. "Fire really and truly flew out of your mouth."

"Yes."

"But fire flew out of your mouth."

"I did tell you I was a dragon."

"I just didn't expect fire to fly out of your freaking mouth." Grace struggled to form a proper response. Darius really was a dragon. The concept was laughable—or should have been. All of it should have been laughable. Atlantis, misty portals, the gods. Yet she'd skipped right along, accepting every fantastical experience tossed her way.

But this… She expected her brain to shout *it's too much. I can't accept another implausible happening.* Surprisingly enough, her mind didn't shout. Her mind welcomed.

She toyed with the ends of her hair and expelled

a breath. When she was a little girl, her father had read her a book every night. His favorite had been the story of a long ago prince who rescued a princess from a fierce dragon. Grace had never liked that story. She'd always wanted the dragon to defeat the puny prince so the princess could sail through the clouds on his back. Now a real, live dragon sat in her living room.

"What else can you do?" she asked, her voice raspy.

He merely lifted a brow, a wouldn't-you-like-to-know glint in his eyes.

"Well?" she demanded.

"When you are prepared for the answer, perhaps I'll tell you. Until then…" He shrugged.

"Fine," she huffed. "If you won't tell me about your abilities, at least tell me why you destroyed my brother's journal. I wanted to give it back to him."

"There can be no record of Atlantis." As he spoke, the blue of his eyes swirled and churned with a life of its own, like the very mist he guarded. "I decided to either destroy the book or destroy you. Perhaps I made the wrong choice."

She preferred the other Darius, the honey-eyed Darius. The man who made her blood sing and her deepest fantasies cry for him. The man who twisted her into knots.

"You will obtain the vests now," he told her, crossing his arms over his chest.

Her nose crinkled. "What vests?"

"The ones you promised to buy for me in the cave. The ones that protect against guns."

That's right. She *had* promised him. With a sigh, Grace loped down the hall and into her room. After she booted up the computer—with Darius standing over her the entire time, his hands on either side of her armrests, his chest pressing into her back—she found a site that specialized in guns and other equipment.

"I like this thing," he said. "This computer."

With him so near, she had trouble concentrating. "The vests are two-hundred-and-fifty dollars each," she said, squirming in her seat. Maybe she should turn on the air conditioner. Her skin suddenly felt too tight for her body. "Do you still want to buy one?"

"One? No. I wish to purchase twenty. For now."

"Twenty! Where will you get the money? I doubt you brought any with you."

"I will allow you to pay for them."

Of course he would. "You want extra large, I take it?" Doing this was probably going to place her on the FBI's most-watched list. But Darius wanted the vests, and what Darius wanted, she would acquire for him. They were helping each other, after all.

She placed the order and had to use both of her credit cards. She also requested overnight shipping for double the mailing expense. "They'll arrive in the morning."

"I want to visit the Argonauts," Darius said. "Afterward, we will purchase bullets and you will show me how to use them."

Such a dictator, she thought, and wondered, foolishly, if he'd be that demanding in bed. She stole a glance at the hard angles of his profile. Oh, yes. He'd be demanding and the knowledge made her shiver. With a gulp, she flipped off her computer and swiveled in her chair, dislodging his hands. "Do you think they know more than they told me?"

"Perhaps. Perhaps not."

Which told her nothing. But she had her suspicions. They were not as innocent as they appeared. They couldn't be, and she hated herself for not realizing it sooner. Worry had clouded her mind, she supposed, but that didn't make it easier to take. "If we leave now, we can be there within the hour."

"Not quite yet." He leaned down, replacing his palms on the arms of her chair. Her knees bumped his thighs as his gaze traveled all over her. Burning her. Devouring her in a way that should have been illegal. He saw past her clothes, she suspected breathlessly, and saw the hard pebbles of her nipples. "First," he said, "you will bathe. Quickly," he added.

Blazing red heat stained her cheeks. "Are you saying I—" her mortification was so great she almost couldn't finish her sentence "—stink?"

"You have dirt smudges here." He ran his fingertip over the side of her mouth. "And here." That finger moved to her chin, and his nostrils flared. "While you are beautiful to me as you are, I thought you might wish to wash."

He thought she was beautiful? As she was? Grace nearly melted into her seat. Most men found her a little too plump, a little too red and freckly.

She struggled to form defenses against him, and

reminded herself that she wasn't ready to handle such a dangerous man. "I won't take long." Her legs trembling, she pushed up and raced to the bathroom. She slammed the door shut.

Just in case he entertained any notion of slipping inside, of stripping out of his clothes and getting into the tub with her, of letting the warm, wet water deluge their intertwined, naked bodies, she twisted the lock. She pressed her back against the cool wood, her breathing shallow.

Damn if she didn't pray Darius would burn the lock away.

CHAPTER THIRTEEN

ALEX CARLYLE was hot and cold at the same time.

A single guard shoved him inside his newest prison. A single fucking guard because he was too weak to be any real threat. The drugs his captors were pumping through his system were hell on his body. They kept him compliant, groggy and dependent. Kept him uninterested in escape.

Kept him stupid.

Or maybe his weakness stemmed from low blood supply. Vampires were allowed to suck from his neck anytime they wanted, as long as they didn't kill him. He almost wished they'd finish the job.

For months he'd done nothing but breathe and live Atlantis. He had finally acquired the proof he'd wanted of its existence, but he no longer gave a damn.

He shivered. The room was cold. So cold frost formed every time he breathed. Why, then, did his skin burn? He sank to the hard floor. Another tremor scratched down his spine like long, sharp fingernails.

A woman was shoved into the cell. The only exit slid shut behind her.

Alex closed his eyes, too tired to care. Within moments, small, delicate hands grasped his shoulders
and gently shook him. His eyelids flickered open,
and he found himself staring up into Teira's beautiful, ethereal face.

"You need me?" she said.

He'd lost his glasses, but he didn't need them to
see that her pale brown eyes were alight with
concern. She had the longest lashes he'd ever seen,
as light as her waist-length hair. She claimed she was
a prisoner, just like he was. The two of them had
been "escorted" so many places he didn't know
where he was anymore.

This newest cell was stripped bare, as if someone
had recently scraped everything off the walls. "I'm
fine," he lied. "Where are we this time?"

"My home."

Her home. He inwardly sighed. Somewhere in
Atlantis, then. *If* she was telling the truth. He didn't
know yet if he could believe a word out of the
woman's gorgeous mouth.

He didn't know whom he could trust anymore.

Lately he'd been swindled and double-crossed
by everyone he encountered. Every member of his
team had betrayed him, willingly giving away his
location and his purpose for a few hundred dollars.
The guide he'd hired to see him safely through the
Amazon had been a paid mercenary. Now he had to
contend with Teira.

She was beautiful, exquisitely and guilelessly so,
but beauty often hid a mountain of lies. And she was

too concerned for him, too eager to learn about him. Perhaps she'd been sent to seduce the location of the medallion from him, he thought irritably. Why else lock her in a cell with him? He laughed humorlessly. Why else but to fuck the answer out of him.

Well, the joke was on her. Teira wasn't his type. He preferred women who wore too much makeup, and tight clothes over their even tighter, surgically enhanced bodies. He preferred women who screwed hard and left the same night without a qualm—if they didn't speak to him in the meantime, even better.

Women who looked like Teira terrified him. Instead of makeup and tight clothes, they wore an air of innocence, a marry-me-and-give-me-babies kind of wholesomeness that unnerved him.

He'd spent too many years caring for his sick father, too afraid to leave the house in case he was needed. He stayed as far away from wholesome women as he could. Just the thought of being permanently grounded made him nauseous. His captors should have locked him up with a slutty-looking brunette. *Then* he might have talked.

His jaw clenched. He never should have acquired that damn medallion.

What had Grace done with it? And why the hell had he sent it to her? He hadn't meant to involve her; he simply hadn't realized the extent of the danger until it was too late. He didn't know what he'd do if she were hurt. There were only three people he gave a shit about, and Grace was at the top of the list. His mom and Aunt Sophie claimed a close second and third.

Teira gave him another gentle shake. Her fingers were like ice, and he noticed her teeth were chattering.

"What do you want?" he barked.

She flinched but didn't back away. "You need me?" she asked again. Her soft voice floated over him, as lilting as a spring breeze. Her English wasn't very good, but she'd managed to learn the basics— and quite quickly, too. How convenient.

"I'm fine," he repeated.

"I help warm you."

"I don't need your goddamn help. Go to your side of the cell and leave me alone."

Her innocent features dimmed as she scooted away.

He fought a wave of disappointment. He would never tell her, would never admit it aloud, but he liked her nearness. Dirt might streak the smoothness of her skin, but she still smelled as exotic as a summer storm. The scent comforted him—but scared him, too. She was not his type, but he often found himself gazing at her, yearning to hold her, to touch her.

As if she sensed his inner longings, she moved back to him and smoothed her trembling fingertips over his forehead, down his nose and along his jaw, her touch light. "Why will you not let me help?" she asked.

He sighed, savoring her caress even while he knew he should make her stop. Cameras were probably hidden everywhere, and he didn't want anyone to think he'd finally caved where this woman was concerned.

"Do you have a syringe? Do you have whatever the hell they're giving me?"

"No."

"Then you can't help me."

She began tracing strange symbols over his cheek. An intense concentration settled over her features.

His tremors gradually slowed, and his coldness receded. His muscles relaxed.

"Feel better?" she asked, a trace of weakness to the words.

He managed to give her an indifferent frown and lift his shoulders in a shrug. What symbols had she drawn and what did they mean? And how in God's name had they helped him? He was too stubborn to ask.

"Why you not like me?" she whispered, biting her lower lip.

"I like you just fine." He wouldn't admit that he would have died without her. His captors, the same men who had chased him through the jungle, then plucked him from one location to the other, had been brutal. He'd been beaten, drugged and nearly drained, and shuddered with each memory. Always Teira was there, waiting for him, comforting him. Holding him with her quiet strength and dignity.

"Why do they have you locked in here?" he asked her, wishing immediately that he could snatch the words back. He didn't want to watch her features cloud with deceit as she spun a web of lies. He knew why she was here. Didn't he?

Softly, gently, she lay beside him and wrapped one arm around his waist. The woman craved bodily contact like no one else he'd ever met, as if she'd been denied it most of her life. And he'd be lying if he said her little body didn't feel good curled up next to him.

"They kill my man and all of his army. I try to… what is the word?" Her brow scrunched as she searched her mind.

He gazed deeply into her eyes. They were as devoid of duplicity as always. "Defeat them?"

"Yes," she said. "Defeat them. I try and defeat them."

Whether he believed her story or not, he didn't like the thought of her being tied to another man. And he liked even less that he cared. "I didn't know you were married."

She looked away from him, past him, over his shoulder. Sorrow and grief radiated from her, and when she next spoke, her pain was like a living thing. "The union end too quickly."

He found himself reaching out to her for the first time. He wrapped his fingers around her palm and gave a light squeeze. "Why did they kill him?"

"To control the mist he guarded and steal his wealth. Even here, in this cell, they removed the jewels from the walls. I miss him," she added softly.

To control the mist he guarded… Alex had known she was from Atlantis, though he had failed to realize she was the wife of a Guardian. Or rather, *former* wife. God, he felt stupid. Of course she would be kept alive. She would know things about the mist that no one else knew.

He studied Teira's face with fresh eyes, taking in the elegant slope of her nose and the perfect curve of her pale brows. "How long has your—" Alex couldn't bring himself to say *husband* "—has he been gone?"

"Weeks now. So many weeks." Reaching up, Teira traced the seam of his lips. "You help me escape?"

Escape. How wonderful the word sounded. How terrifying. He'd lost track of time and didn't even know how long he'd been imprisoned. A day? A year? At first, he'd tried numerous times to flee, but he'd always been unsuccessful.

He rolled onto his back, and the action made his bones ache. He groaned. Teira wasted no time tucking her head into the hollow of his neck and placing her leg over his.

"You are lonely like me," she said. "I know you are."

She fit perfectly against him. Too perfectly. As if she'd been made specifically to match his body curve for curve. And he *was* lonely. He stared up at the flat ceiling. What was he going to do with this woman? Was she a heartless bitch who only wanted the medallion and was willing to sell her body to get it? Or was she as innocent as she appeared?

"Tell me about you."

She'd made the same request a thousand times before. It wouldn't hurt to give her *some* information about himself, he decided. Nothing important, just a tidbit or two. He wouldn't mention Grace, of course. He didn't dare. His love for his sister could be used against him, and that he wouldn't allow.

"I'm twenty-nine years old," he told Teira. He placed his hands on her head and sifted his fingers through her hair. Not only did the strands look like pearly moonlight, they felt like it, too. "I've always had a passion for fast cars." And even faster women, but he didn't disclose that part. "I've never been married, and I don't have children. I live in an apartment on the Upper East Side of Manhattan."

"Man-hat-tan," she said, testing the word on her tongue. "Tell me more."

He didn't mention the crime or the pollution but gave her the details he knew she craved. "No matter what time of day or night, crowds of people wander the streets as far as the eye can see. Buildings stretch up to the sky. Shops and bakeries never close. It's a place where every desire can be indulged."

"My people rarely stray to the surface, but your Man-hat-tan sounds like a place we would enjoy."

"Tell me about your home."

Dreamy remembrance clouded her eyes, making the gold darken to chocolate. She snuggled deeper into his side. "We are inside a dragon palace, though you cannot tell by this cell. Outside, the sea flows all around. Flowers of every color bloom. There are many temples of worship," she said, slipping into her native tongue, "but most of us have forgotten them because we ourselves have been forgotten."

"I'm sorry." While he was coming to understand

some of her language, he wasn't close to fluent. "I only understood a little of what you said."

"I say I wish I could show you."

No, she'd said more than that, but he let it go. How wonderful it would be to trek through Atlantis. If he met the inhabitants, studied the homes, wandered the streets and inundated himself with the culture, he could write a book about his experiences. He could—Alex shuddered when he realized he was diving back into his old pattern of thought.

"I wish I had the power to help you understand my language," Teira said. "But my powers are not strong enough to cast such a spell." She paused, traced her fingertips over his jaw. "Who is Grace?"

Horrified, he leapt up and away from her as if she were the devil's handmaiden come to claim him. He swayed as a wave of dizziness hit him, wincing as a sharp pain lanced through his temples. He stumbled to the pitcher of water in the corner and sipped. When he felt more steadied, he glared over at Teira. "Where did you hear that name?"

She was trembling as she sat up and pulled her knees to her chest. "You said while you sleep."

"Don't ever say her name again. Not ever. Understand?"

"I am sorry. I never mean to upset you. I simply—"

The door opened.

Dirt flung in every direction as three men stalked inside. One carried a small table, one a chair and the third a platter of food. Soon a fourth man joined them, cradling a semiautomatic in his hands. He pointed the gun at Alex and grinned, daring him to move. Their arrival meant he'd have his drugs, so he was incapable of fear.

Teira's trembling increased. Every day these same men brought him food, a simple meal of bread, cheese and water. Every day they escorted Teira from the room, leaving him to eat alone. And every day she fought them, scratching and screaming. Alex had always assumed her resistance was an act, that they were taking her away to find out what she'd learned from him that day, but as he looked at her, really looked at her this time, he saw the signs of true terror. Her already pale skin became pallid, revealing the faint trace of veins beneath. Her eyes became impossibly round, and she pressed her lips together—to keep from whimpering?

The table was placed in front of Alex. Hands now free, the guard who'd been holding it strode to Teira and clasped her firmly by the forearm. She didn't protest as he wrenched her to her feet. She merely gazed over at Alex, silently pleading with him to help her.

"Time for you to be by yourself for a while, sweetheart," the man told her.

Whether she worked for or against these people, Alex realized her fear was real. "Leave her alone," he said. He latched on to her other arm, making her the rope in a vicious tug of war.

One of the guards scowled and stalked to him. Something was slammed into Alex's temple. His vision blurred. His knees buckled, and he went down. Hard. Teira cried out, tried to reach him, and Alex watched in growing horror as she was slapped across the face. Her head whipped to the side, and he caught the sight of blood on her lip.

Fury consumed him. Hot, blinding fury, giving him strength where he should have had none. With a roar, he sprang up and tackled Teira's tormentor. All three men flew at him, and he found himself subdued and pinned, helpless once again.

"Alex," Teira cried.

Get up, his mind screamed. *Help her.* As he pushed to his feet, someone grabbed his arm. He experienced a sharp sting as a needle was shoved into his vein. Familiar warmth invaded him, calming, relaxing. The ache in his bones faded. His dry mouth flooded with moisture. When he was released, he sank to the ground, the will to fight completely deserting him.

Teira was dragged away.

He closed his eyes and let his mind float away to nothingness. Footsteps echoed in his ears, tapering to quiet as the rest of the men vacated the room. A new set of footsteps suddenly sounded, these coming closer and closer to him.

"Enjoying the woman, are you?" a man asked, his voice familiar.

Alex fought past the fog webbing his brain and blinked up. Hazel eyes peered down at him, the same hazel eyes that belonged to his boss, Jason Graves. Jason wore an aura of self-importance that was almost palpable. He also wore a dragon medallion around his neck.

Alex's eyes narrowed. He'd never considered the man a friend, but he'd been a dependable employer for the four years he'd worked for him. Betrayal washed over Alex, bitter and biting, as he realized just what this meant.

He'd suspected this, but having actual evidence still managed to shock him. *I never should have stolen the medallion,* he thought again.

"I'm nothing if not hospitable," Jason said. His eyes gleamed bright with smug superiority.

Shards of his fury renewed, sparking past the complacency of the drugs. If only his body had the strength to act. "What are you doing to Teira?" He shuddered at the answer that leapt into his mind, certain now that she wasn't working with anyone, but was merely trying to survive. Just as he was.

"Nothing she doesn't enjoy, I assure you."

If he had a weapon, Alex would have committed murder just then. "Bring her back," he growled. "Now."

"First, you and I are going to have a tête-à-tête."

The extent of his helplessness shone as brightly as a neon sign. He closed his eyes. "What is it exactly that you want from me, Jason?"

"Call me Master," his boss said. "Everyone here does." He claimed the chair that had been set in front of the table and removed the lid from the platter of food.

The scent of spicy meat and fresh fruits wafted in the air, making Alex's mouth water. This wasn't the bread and cheese he'd expected. But then, the meal wasn't for him. How long since he'd last eaten anything that smelled so divine? he wondered. Then he laughed. What did he care? "How about I call you Bastard instead?" he said.

"Do it and I will have you strangled with your own intestines," Jason said easily, almost happily. "Afterward, I'll have the same done to Teira."

"Master it is, then." *Bastard.* Wincing, he pulled himself to a sitting position and crossed his arms over his chest.

Jason swirled his fork in what looked to be pasta and said, "You have been stubborn, Alex, holding out on us."

A prickle of unease worked through him, and he fought to remain expressionless. "What do you mean?"

"Your sister, Grace." Casually Jason bit into his food. He closed his eyes and chewed slowly, savoring the taste. "The picture you have of her on your desk is of a ten-year-old girl."

Alex's unease quickly mutated into terror, and the cold air seeped all the way into his marrow. "So what," he said, striving for nonchalance.

"A voluptuous, very mature Grace was found looking for you in the jungle. She's pretty, your sister." Jason licked creamy white sauce from the fork.

Alex tried to spring up, tried to wrap his hands around Jason's neck. His body refused to cooperate, however, and in midair, he simply collapsed back into a heap on the floor. "Where is she?" he panted. "Did you hurt her? Did you do anything to her?"

"Of course not." Jason's tone actually held an element of affront. "What kind of man do you think I am?"

"You really don't want me to answer that, do you?" He scrubbed a hand down his face. "Where is she?"

"Don't worry. We let her fly back to New York. She's safe—for the moment. We left her an e-mail from you, saying you were okay, and for her sake, I hope she's content with that."

His jaw clenched. "Leave her the hell alone."

"That depends on you, doesn't it?" Jason placed his elbows on the table and leaned toward him. "Where's my medallion, Alex?" he asked, his voice growing harder, harsher.

"I told your men, I lost it. I don't know where it is."

"I think that's a lie," Jason said smoothly. He held a pineapple slice between his fingers and sunk his teeth into it, causing the juices to run down his chin. He dabbed at the wetness with his napkin, mimicking a proper Southern gentleman—the kind of man he'd often teased Alex of being.

"What do you want it for, anyway? You already have a new one."

"I want them all."

"Why? They aren't crafted from gold or silver. They're crafted from metal filigree. They're a worthless decoration, nothing more."

They both knew he lied.

Jason shrugged. "They offer the wearer power beyond comprehension, though we haven't yet learned how to harness that power. In time," he said with confidence. "In time. They also open every door in this palace, offering a banquet of riches. You could have been a part of this... I would have asked for your help eventually, but you chose to work against me."

"You think you can just blithely steal from these people and walk away unscathed?" He snorted. "They are children of the gods. I, at least, meant only to study them."

"No, you meant to expose them. Did you think that would have done them any good? Did you think the entire world could resist coming here and stealing the overabundance of treasures?" Now Jason was the one to snort. "To answer your question, no, I didn't *think* I could blithely steal from them. I knew I could. Quite easily, too."

Alex shook his head at such blatant arrogance. "I suppose you're going to tell me just how you did it. We can have ourselves a Bad Guy Confession Time."

A hard glint entered Jason's eyes, but his need to brag far surpassed his anger. "Before entering the portal in Florida, I tossed in enough fentanyl gas to put a legion of men to sleep. Then I sent in my troops. Most were killed, but casualties of war are expected. The Guardian of the Mist might have been strong, but he couldn't survive multiple rounds of firepower and he quickly bled out."

"What about his men? The *Book of Ra-Dracus* speaks of each Guardian possessing an army of dragons inside his palace."

"Ah, the *Book of Ra-Dracus*." All arrogance, Jason lifted a jeweled goblet and sipped the contents. "Have I thanked you yet for the book's acquisition? It changed my life."

"You stole it from me," he accused, his eyes narrowed.

"Of course. Just like you stole from me. The irony is beautiful, isn't it?" Smiling smugly, Jason added, "You made the mistake of typing your notes into your computer. I keep tabs on all of my employees."

"You hack into their personal lives, you mean."

Jason shrugged. "When I realized exactly what you possessed, I knew I had to have it. So I paid someone to 'acquire' it for me."

"I stole the medallion from you, yes, but I always intended to give it back. I didn't think you even knew what it was."

"Oh, I knew." A soft rumble of laughter escaped. "I'm slowly emptying this palace of every jewel, every piece of gold, every fine fabric and selling them on the surface. How else do you think I afforded those new buildings? My designer clothes?" He paused, tilted his chin. "And I'll do the same to the other dragon palace. But we digress. How did we kill the dragon army? The same way we found them. *Ra-Dracus*. We learned they are weakened by cold and bullets. Quick. Simple."

"You're a monster," Alex whispered, horrified by what Jason had done—and all he would do.

"A monster? Hardly. Those that dwell in Atlantis are the monsters. In fact, let me tell you a little about Teira, the sweet Teira you so wish to protect. She's a dragon. A changeling." He studied Alex's waning color and nodded with satisfaction. "I see you know what I am talking about."

"I read *Ra-Dracus* in its entirety."

"Then you know what happens when you infuriate a dragon? It transforms into a beast. A killer."

"If Teira is a dragon, why hasn't she changed? Why hasn't she freed herself?" He paused. "Why hasn't she killed *you?*"

"She has seen what our guns did to her people, and she fears us. Fear will keep the fiercest of creatures submissive."

"Or maybe that's why you keep it so cold in here. To keep her weak because *you* are afraid of her."

Eyes narrowed, Jason said, "Dragons can go days, weeks without food. Then, suddenly, an intense craving comes over them. Do you know what they eat when this craving comes upon them, Alex?"

He swallowed. He didn't know, but he could guess.

"They eat whatever is in sight," Jason answered, leaning back in his chair. "And do you know what Teira will crave when the hunger hits her? You, Alex. You. She won't have to change to dragon form. She'll just start biting."

A wave of dizziness hit him as he shook his head in denial. "She wouldn't hurt me." He didn't know when he'd started to think of Teira as his ally. He didn't know when he'd lost his animosity toward her. He only knew that hers was the only kindness he'd known these last weeks.

"You sound so confident. So stupid." Jason laughed. "I know the nature of the beast, and I know beyond a doubt that when the time comes, she will feast on your body because you will be the only food in sight. She may not want to, she may hate herself for it, but she will do it."

"Why are you doing this? Why go to all this trouble? Kill me already and get it over with."

"Tell me where the medallion is, and I'll let you go. We'll forget this ever happened."

Liar, he almost shouted. Unless Jason meant to let him go with his head detached from his body.

Lethargy began to weave through the dizziness, and he closed his eyes. "I don't know where it is," he said. His voice sounded far away, lost.

"Need I remind you that I'm not above using your mother? Your aunt? Your sister? Patrick, one of the men who found Grace, would like nothing more than to spread her legs before he kills her."

Alex couldn't manage to open his lids; they were simply too heavy. He said weakly, "If anyone touches a single member of my family, I will—"

"You will what?" Jason said mockingly.

He didn't respond. There was no threat great enough…and there was nothing he could actually do. Not here, not now, and not while the drugs crawled through his system. Not while his body suffered from blood loss. Sleep, he just wanted to sleep.

"We've searched your home, Grace's home and even your mother's home. No one's been hurt yet. That can all change in an instant, Alex. I'm running out of patience." Jason pushed to his feet and walked around the table. He knelt in front of Alex. He gripped his hair and forced his head back, forced him to stare up into his eyes. "Do you understand?"

"Yes," he whispered hoarsely.

"You're pathetic."

His hair was released, but he didn't have the neck strength to keep his head from slamming into the ground. He rolled onto his side and knew nothing more.

How long passed before the sweet fragrance of seawater invaded his senses, he couldn't fathom a guess. But when he opened his eyes, Teira was curled beside him, sleeping peacefully. Instinctively he jerked away as Jason's words flitted through his mind. *She won't need to change into dragon form, she'll just start biting.*

Teira's pale lashes fluttered open, and the corners of her lips gifted him with a sleepy smile—a smile that did odd things to his stomach.

She studied his expression, and her smile slowly faded. "What wrong?"

As he studied her in return, he lost his trepidation. A bruise marred her cheek, barely visible under the dirt covering her. "Nothing's wrong," he said, his throat scratchy. Still a bit groggy, he reached out and gently caressed the discoloration.

"You look in pain," she said.

"How long did I sleep?" he asked.

She shrugged.

His fingers moved from her cheek and cupped her jaw. "What did they do to you?"

"They not hurt me," she assured him. "I think they fear I hurt them."

He chuckled, a low rumble that reverberated in his chest. She looked so delicate, it was hard to imagine her as a fearsome dragon.

"How you feel?" Concern glinted in her golden eyes. She placed her hand over his heartbeat.

"Better." Much better now that she was here. But the shakes would come again, he knew, and so would the need. "Teira." He sighed. "I'm sorry for how I've treated you." Born to a staunchly Southern father, he was ashamed of his behavior toward her. He might live in New York, but like every gentleman, he still opened car doors, still paid for meals and still called women when he said he would. Not that the ones he dated expected it. "I thought you worked for them, but that's no excuse."

Her gaze skittered shyly away from him. "I like being with you."

Her confession pleased him, warmed him as surely as a winter coat. She wasn't his type, but he was attracted to her all the same. A powerful attraction he couldn't hide anymore. Didn't *want* to hide anymore. "I like being with you, too," he admitted. He liked her more than he should.

Leaning up, hesitant, she placed a soft kiss on his lips. He knew she meant it as a chaste peck, a swift kiss of solace, but he pried her lips open with his own and swept his tongue deep. At first, she stiffened. But when she relaxed, she went wild in his arms. She came alive, plunging her tongue into his mouth, moaning her demands, fisting her hands in his hair and fueling his own response.

The air around them sizzled and that sizzle simmered in his blood. Her body pressed to his, her lithe curves a perfect fit. He'd gladly sprint to his death if only to die with her taste in his mouth. He reveled in her flavor, sweet and guileless, like the purest ocean, and unlike any female he'd ever tasted.

With a groan, he gripped her by the waist, clenching the fabric of her sheer gown in his hands. He settled her on top of him. He didn't care if cameras watched them. He didn't care that she was wrong for him. His need for her was too great. He deepened the kiss, exploring more of her mouth, running his tongue over her teeth. He allowed his fingers to trace a path down her spine, allowed them to cup her bottom and anchor her snugly against his growing erection.

She gasped his name, and the moment she did, she seemed to snap out of her haste. She tore her face from him. Their gazes locked, all hot and needy; their ragged exhalations blended. He fought the urge to tug her back down.

"Alex?" she said on a fragile catch of breath.

His hands shook as he smoothed pale strands of hair out of her face. "Yes, Teira." God, yes. His voice sounded slow and slurred, yet it had nothing to do with drugs and everything to do with the woman in his arms. His need for her surpassed any he'd ever known.

She caught her bottom lip between her teeth, and he watched as its plumpness tugged free. His shaft jerked in response. Then she leaned down, placing her lips next to his ear. "I can take us to freedom."

He paused, absorbing her words. "How?" he whispered fiercely, his arms tightening around her.

The corners of her lips turned up in a wry grin. "I stole a medallion."

Alex's smile matched hers. He laughed. They just might be able to escape. Which meant he could feed this woman real food—then spend the next few days with her in bed.

CHAPTER FOURTEEN

DARIUS GAZED at the sights around him.

Buildings towered as far as the eye could see, stretching toward the skyline—a skyline that was wide and open, cloudy, not filled with crystal and water. Colors, so many colors. They glowed from signs; they blurred together as masses of people strode past him. Even the sun shone brightly of yellow, orange and gold. What struck him most of all, however, was the multitude of scents that intermingled and cloyed the air.

The overload to his senses was strangely welcoming.

This place did not offer the lush, green foliage of his home, yet New York was beguiling and lovely in its own right. A place that called out to the beast within him—just as Grace did.

When this was over, he would— No, he could not think that way. He could not allow himself to envision Grace in his future. He must finish this.

Some of his men were surrounding Javar's palace, preventing the humans from spreading their violence further. Still…his fists clenched. The fact that they lived offended him.

And he did not like to be offended.

Beside him, Grace skirted around a table over-flowing with photos. "We'll be there soon," she said, glancing up at him. "Are you okay? You look pale."

She had changed into new clothing after her bath. *She* looked edible. Pale blue pants clung to her legs and a sea-green shirt molded itself to her breasts. She was like an ocean wave, utterly captivating, magical. He could have drowned in her and died happy. "Do not concern yourself with me."

"You could whisk us to Argonauts and save us the walk," she said. "I'm anxious to question them again."

Darius, too, was anxious to question them, but he couldn't whisk about in this city. To do so, he had to visualize his target. He knew nothing of this area, he thought, letting his gaze scan. A trickle of sweat dripped into his eyes, and he wiped it away.

The sun continued to beat down upon him, grow-ing hotter with every step he took. Usually his body embraced heat. Now he fought a deepening lassitude. He stumbled when his foot caught on a rock. One corner of his lips lifted in a scowl as he steadied himself. He despised frailty of any kind, especially his own.

"You're not okay," Grace said, her concern more concentrated. She clasped his arm and tried to pull him aside.

He shook off her hold and kept walking in the direc-tion she'd given him earlier. A woman's concern was not something he knew how to deal with. *This woman's concern was something he couldn't deal with.*

I'm going to bed and kill you before I leave, he almost shouted. *Don't waste what's left of your life caring for me.*

Scowl solidifying, he stepped out onto the street. He wanted his peaceful, emotionless existence back. No more of this I-want-her I-can't-hurt-her nonsense.

No more!

Pain suddenly flashed through his head. A pain more intense than anything he'd ever experienced. He doubled over with it, cursing the gods all the while.

"Darius!" Grace shouted, grabbing him by the arm and jerking him toward her. "Look out."

A honk sounded. A whiz. Cars swerved out of the way.

Fear halted Grace's heartbeat as a taxi nearly clipped Darius's side. The organ kicked back into gear only when she had ushered him to the safety of the sidewalk. Along the way, she accidentally bumped into a young woman headed in the opposite direction. "I'm sorry," she said, jumping out of the way to avoid the coffee spilling from the girl's cup.

"Watch where you're going," the girl fumed, never actually slowing.

"Darius, talk to me. Tell me what's wrong." Too afraid to release him, she clenched his hand and faced him. "We're not moving from this spot until you do."

"My time here is running out," he said.

She studied him. His sculpted features were taut, his lips tight, and the fine lines around his eyes strained. "You've said that before. What happens if you stay too long?"

He shrugged. One minute ticked into another, but he didn't move. Didn't speak. Didn't acknowledge her again in any other way. He simply watched as men, women and children continued to skip past them, some talking and laughing. Some arguing.

Maybe he thought she would use the knowledge against him. She didn't know, but was determined to help him. "Look at me, Darius. Please look at me."

His gaze descended gradually, falling from the building tops, to the neon signs, and finally to her. When their gazes connected, her jaw dropped slightly. As she looked at him, she saw many things. Heart wrenching things. She saw pain in his eyes, as well as traces of guilt and sadness. And, beneath it all, was the slightest glimmer of…hopelessness?

"When we returned from the cave," she said, "you were weak and pale, but after you drank the lemonade you felt better. If you'll wait here, I'll buy you something to eat."

The guilt in his eyes increased, and she wondered at its origin. But he nodded slowly, and her concern for him overrode everything else. "I will wait," he said.

She raced inside the bakery. Fresh ground coffee beans, with a hint of vanilla, and a mouthwatering array of muffins fragranced the air. She claimed a place in line. When her turn arrived, she ordered a bottled water and raisin granola bar for herself. For Darius, she ordered a sinfully rich chocolate éclair and espresso.

With sack and beverages in hand, she rejoined Darius. He hadn't moved from the spot where she'd left him, and he was still too pale.

"Here," she said, handing him the éclair and coffee. Her gaze lingered lovingly on the chocolate. How long since she'd had such a treat? Too long. She and Alex used to spend their allowance on box after box of éclairs. They'd eat as many as their stomachs could hold, and sometimes more.

She blinked away the memory, her determination to find him growing.

"Come on," she said to Darius. "We'll walk and eat at the same time."

As they trudged into motion, Darius sipped at his drink. Some of his color returned, and his steps became more fluid. Men gave them a wide berth, and women gave them, or rather *Darius,* a second—and sometimes third—glance. Grace knew those women were wondering if he looked this savage simply strolling down the street, how savage would he be making love? In his tight black shirt and tight black pants, the man reeked of sexual pleasure.

Darius pinched the éclair between his fingers, studying the sumptuous pastry from every angle. She watched him while she chewed her tasteless granola bar. "Just eat it," she said.

"It looks like creamy mud."

"If that's your attitude, you deserve to eat my granola." Mouth watering, she slapped the bar in his hand and confiscated the éclair.

"Give that back," he said.

"Over my dead body."

"I am hungry."

"Well, so am I."

She was just about to place the chocolate reverently on her tongue, was just about to let the Bavarian cream slide right into her mouth, when Darius ripped the dessert from her hands.

"That is mine," he said and handed her back her granola bar.

Ready to pounce on him, she growled low in her throat.

His lips twitched. "Why did you not buy yourself one of these if you want it so badly?"

"Because— Just because!" Grace chugged down her water, letting the coldness of the liquid bring her back to her senses. *I'm a rational being,* she reminded herself, *and I don't need the extra fat grams. Besides, what does one dessert matter in light of all that has happened lately?*

"Do all the women on the surface refuse to buy themselves the food they want to eat?" Darius asked.

She recapped the lid on the water bottle. "I'm not talking to you right now. You've tackled me to the ground, you bound me to your side, and…and you cast some sort of magic lust spell on me." Once she said the words, Grace blinked in astonishment. Of course! A magic lust spell explained her seemingly unquenchable desire for him, as well as the fact that she often found herself thinking of him when she should be thinking of ways to find her brother.

Slowly his lips inched into a true smile of amusement. The first he'd given her. There was a hint of possessiveness in that smile, too. His eyes darkened to gold. "You lust for me?"

"No, I do not," she ground out, her cheeks scalding hot. "I suspect you're capable of such a despicable deed, that's all."

His nostrils flared in a way that proclaimed he knew, *knew,* exactly how she felt about him—and knew the lust was entirely her own. "If we did not have so much to do this day, I would take you back to your home, sweet Grace, and explore this magic lust spell. Very, very thoroughly."

While she floundered for some type of rejoinder, he at last bit into his food. He stilled. Utterly and completely stilled. Chewed slowly. Closed his eyes. Opened his eyes, revealing a joy tantamount to orgasm. Chewed some more. Swallowed. "This is— this is—"

"I know," she grumbled. She finished off her granola. "It's not mud."

The taste was amazing, Darius thought, and helped restore more of his vigor. What had Grace called this culinary treasure? An ay-klare. The delectable morsel wasn't quite as flavorful as Grace herself, but close. Were he to slather her body with it and lick away every trace, he might find release before he actually entered her.

For so long he'd tasted nothing, and now he tasted everything. He knew Grace was responsible, that she was the catalyst. He just didn't know how. Or why. And he was no closer to the answer than he had been before. But he didn't care. He reveled in these new experiences. When she was dead—was gone, he corrected, not liking her name associated with death—he wondered if he would ever taste again. Or if he'd want to. Without Grace...

He took another bite of the ay-klare and noticed Grace eyeing his mouth with longing in her turquoise gaze. His stomach tightened. Did she crave *him?* Or the food he ate? Most likely the food, he mused, and he bit back a self-deprecating chuckle. She'd very nearly bitten off his hand when he'd snatched the dessert from her, reminding him of a female dragon who'd gone far too long without food.

He waved the remaining piece under her nose, and her eyelids became heavy and sultry. "Would you like to share this with me?" he asked.

She moaned as if he'd just offered to make her dreams come true. Dreams that were forbidden, coveted. Dreams she couldn't acknowledge but craved with every ounce of her being.

"No," she said, that single word sounding raw, like it had been ripped from her throat.

She obviously wished to partake, and quite desperately, so why did she think to deny herself? No matter, he thought in the next instant. Before she could pull away, he placed the food at her lips. "Open," he commanded.

Automatically she obeyed. Then she gasped. Bit. Savored. As she chewed, she made noises of pleasure. Breathy noises he'd only heard from women in his bed. His blood heated, rushing from his head and into his shaft. Gods, he wanted this woman. His responses to her were coming more quickly now. A bit more intently, too. Where she was concerned, he was all beast. Primitive and un-apologetically barbaric. One moment he wanted her slow and easy, tender. The next he wanted her rough, hard. Now.

He needed to sate himself on her. Soon.

Her fingers curled around his hand, holding the ay-klare in place. "Oh, my God," she said, eyes closed. "That is so good."

At the first touch of her fingers, white-hot heat speared him. He jerked away from her, then found himself reaching out again, reaching to take her by the base of her neck and yank her to him. Reaching out to kiss her, hard and deep and wet. He dropped his hands at his sides. Teeth grinding together, he in-creased his speed.

He had to remain focused where this woman was concerned. The time for making her desire him would come after he'd learned all that he could from her and the other humans. Damn this!

"Slow down," she huffed after a few minutes.

He tossed her a glance over his shoulder and noticed a dark smudge marring the edge of her lip. Before he could stop himself, he extended his arm and swiped the smudge away with his fingertip. He

kept the contact light, quick. If he lingered, if he pro-
longed the contact, he would strip her. Penetrate her.
He was near his breaking point already.

He turned his face from her so she wouldn't see
him lick the morsel he'd swiped from her off his
finger.

"Slow down," she said again. As she dictated direc-
tions, she had to pump her arms and jog to keep up
with him. "Will you slow down already? I've had
enough exercise these last few days to last me a
lifetime."

"You may rest when we have completed our
mission."

"I'm not one of your men. And just so you know,
the outcome of this is just as important to me as it is
to you—if not more so—but I'll be no good to
anyone if I collapse."

He slowed.

"Thank you," she said. "I didn't even move that
quickly when I thought I was being followed yesterday."

Darius ground to a halt, causing the couple behind
him to slam into his back. He remained in place,
absorbing the impact without moving an inch. With
muttered curses, the glaring pair scurried around
him.

"You were followed?" Darius demanded, glaring.
"By whom? Man or woman? Were you hurt?"

When Grace realized he was no longer beside her,
that she'd actually passed him, she had to stop and
backtrack, hopping over a piece of chewed gum,

then scurrying around a vender selling pirated DVDs until she reached his side. "I'm not sure," she said. "A man, I think, though I never saw him. And no, he didn't hurt me."

"Then he might be allowed to live another day."

Oh, my, Grace thought, breathless again for a reason that had nothing to do with exercise. Sunlight couched Darius's features, giving his cheekbones and nose a harsh sort of radiance. When he turned on the intensity like this, going all commando, her belly did strange things. Her *mind* did strange things. Like try to convince her to throw herself in his arms, sweep her tongue into his mouth, and rub herself against him, all over him, and forget about the rest of the world.

"I will hold sentry at your side," he said, his gaze already scanning the area, searching. "If this man comes near you today, I will eliminate him. Worry not."

She nodded, fighting an involuntary shiver. Despite everything, or maybe because of it, she knew Darius would keep her safe. As they jolted back into motion, he continually watched the world around him, taking in every detail and missing nothing. Like the guard he'd promised to be, he remained on alert.

If they were being followed, he would know—and she pitied whoever it was.

CHAPTER FIFTEEN

ONLY TWO MINUTES passed before Darius dragged her into a nearby souvenir shop, shoving people aside in his haste to enter.

"I'm so sorry, ma'am," Grace said. "You, too, sir." To Darius, she demanded quietly, "What are you doing?"

The fierce gleam in his ice-blue eyes made her swallow a lump of apprehension. "You were right," he said. "You were being followed." He glanced over his shoulder. "You still are."

"What!" she gasped, just as he pinned her against a rack of T-shirts. She'd felt no menacing presence today, felt no watchful eyes on her back.

"I would have noticed sooner," he said wryly, keeping his gaze trained on the store window, "but my mind was not where it should have been."

"What should we do? Who is it?"

"A human male. Short. He's wearing some type of coat, yet the day is warm."

Grace tried to peek over Darius's shoulder, but it proved too broad and too high. "Can he see us?"

"No, but he's waiting outside this shop."

"Let's go out the back. He'll never know, and we can—"

"No." Darius skimmed his hands inside his pockets, gave a flick of his wrists, and plucked out two daggers. The thickness of his hands and forearms kept the blades concealed from the public, but *she* knew they were there. He gripped each jeweled weapon tightly. "I wish to have a…conversation with the man."

Stunned, horrified, she only managed a choked gasp in response.

Good Lord. There might be a bloodbath this day.

"You can't kill anyone," she whispered fiercely. Her gaze darted around wildly. Tourists were staring at them like they were the morning's entertainment. "Please," she added more quietly, "put the knives away before someone notices them."

"The knives stay," he said, his voice cold, unfeeling.

"You don't understand. This—"

"No, Grace." He pinned her with a glare. "*You* don't understand. Purchase something from this store. Anything. Now."

Too nervous to care what she bought, Grace shakily lifted a plastic replica of the Empire State Building. After she paid for it, she gripped the bag and walked with Darius to the door. Her stomach had yet to settle.

"Good choice," he said, motioning to the small building. "Use the tip as a weapon if you must. Jab his eyes."

Jab his eyes? Grace gulped. *I should have bought a snow globe.* She didn't mind using Mace; that was a spray, for God's sake. But using a model of the Empire State Building, the centerpiece of Manhattan, to blind a human being…

I'm just a flight attendant on extended leave, she thought dazedly. *I do not jab people.*

Darius must have sensed her unease because he stopped just before they stepped outside. Facing her, he said, "I would leave you here if I could, but the binding spell does not permit it."

"Having a *conversation* with this person really isn't necessary." Even to her own ears, she sounded timid, and she winced. She just didn't want Darius injured or in trouble with the law. "I've seen enough movies and read enough books to know that sometimes the safest course of action is to retreat."

"And sometimes the safest course of action is the wrong one."

"When I asked you to help me find Alex, I never meant to place you in danger."

His features softened at her admission, but that flash of guilt was back. "This man might have information about your brother. He could be the one who tried to take the medallion, the one who locked him away. Do you really want to let him go?"

"No," she said quietly. Then more firmly, "No."

"I will be safe. And so will you."

"Let's use violence as a last resort, though. Okay?"

A long, protracted silence enveloped them. "As you

wish," he said reluctantly. "In return for that concession, I want you to stay behind me. And do not speak again until I give you permission. You will distract me otherwise."

Resisting the urge to link her fingers through his, she followed him into the sunlight. A warm breeze greeted them as they began stalking forward. At first she thought Darius meant to lead their tail to a private alley, but her warrior didn't even try to pretend ignorance. He approached the man clad in a brown trench coat who was standing in front of a store window pretending to look inside. At maternity dresses? Puhlease.

Watching their reflections, the man realized Darius meant to grab him. He stiffened, gasped and jolted into motion, running from them as fast as his booted feet could carry him.

"Run, Grace," Darius called over his shoulder, as he, too, started running.

An invisible force wrenched her behind Darius, forcing her body into action. Her feet barely touched the ground as she flew, literally flew, after him. Damn this binding spell!

Darius followed the man through traffic lights and around cars, past people and over commerce tables. Irritated grunts and surprised screams echoed in her ears, blending with the sound of her own panting. Was that a police siren? Air burned her lungs. She clutched the plastic Empire State Building as they ran on and on.

If this kept up, she just might be a luscious size six by the end of the month.

When Darius finally came within arm's reach, he grabbed his target by the neck, quickly cutting off any screams of protest. Using only one hand, he lifted the man up and carried him into a nearby alley. There, he dropped him, watching the flailing man fall onto his butt and scramble to the wall. Darius crossed his arms over his chest, daring him to make a move.

Behind them, Grace huffed and puffed to a standstill, then hunched over, gasping for breath. If she survived the day, she was going to treat herself and Alex to a triple dip hot fudge sundae. Or perhaps a banana split. Or maybe fresh doughnuts dripping with chocolate glaze. Maybe all three. She straightened and saw several men huddled against the brownstone wall. Their clothes were threadbare, and their faces dirty and scared. Did they think they would have to face Darius next?

Forcing a smile, Grace handed one of the men her Empire State Building—she was *not* jabbing anyone today—and reached into her wallet. She withdrew several bills. At the sight of cash, the alley men lost all interest in Darius.

"For you," she said, paying them to go away and keep this "their little secret." *I'm aiding and abetting a criminal,* she thought, an unexpected wave of excitement crashing inside her.

Excitement? No, surely not. Skiing in Aspen hadn't excited her. Paragliding in Mexico hadn't excited her. Most likely what she felt so intently was fear. Any second she expected the police to show up and haul her and Darius away.

"I'll scream."

The threat came as the man pushed to his feet.

Both of Darius's brows winged up. A sheen of sweat glistened on his neck and face, but his expression did not portray a hint of weakness. "Are you a woman, then?" he said. "First you hide in the shadows, and when you are caught, you scream?"

"You lay a single hand on me, the cops will be all over you."

Darius grabbed him by the shoulders, angling his wrists in a crisscross and pressing his knives subtly into the man's carotid artery. Not enough to break the skin, but enough to sting.

That's when Grace received her first good look at the man. Shock held her frozen for a long while. "Patrick?" she said when she finally found her voice. This man worked with her brother; he'd even escorted her to the boat, and had engaged her in several conversations about her family afterward. "What's going on? Why were you following me?"

Silence.

"Answer her questions," Darius demanded. When Patrick still refused to speak, Darius increased the pressure of the blades, making small pricks and drawing blood.

"You won't kill me," he said smugly.

"You're right. I won't kill you. Not with blades, at least." Darius dropped his weapons and wrapped his hands around the man's neck. "You would die too quickly."

"I—I wasn't following her. I swear," Patrick sputtered, his face slowly fading from pink, to white, to blue. He kicked and clawed, losing his smugness with his need for air.

Eyes wide, she glanced from Darius to Patrick, from Patrick to Darius. Intimidation was a good tactic for getting what they wanted, but she knew Darius wasn't trying to intimidate. He really would kill Patrick without a single qualm.

"You are lying, and I do not like liars," Darius said, his voice so bored he could have been commenting on the mating habits of flies. But then his eyes slitted and his voice deepened, no longer dripping with boredom, but with rage. "I recognize you. You are the one who touched Grace while she was sleeping."

Patrick's eyes nearly bugged out of his head. "No, no," he gasped, struggling to loosen Darius's grip. "I didn't."

"I watched you do it," he said, his teeth bared.

Were those fangs? She shivered as she stared at the long, sharp incisors. Then their words sank into her brain. "He touched me?" she gasped, hands anchoring on her hips. To Patrick, she ground out, "Which part of me?"

"Your cheek," Darius told her. "But he wanted to do more. Would have, if his friend hadn't stopped him."

Her jaw gnashed in fury.

"You couldn't have watched me," Patrick said to Darius. "You weren't on the boat."

No, he hadn't been on the boat, but then, Darius hadn't needed to be. He'd used his medallion on her like he'd done to Alex, she realized, not liking that he'd seen her and she hadn't known.

Patrick made a gargled sound, and his battle for freedom intensified. His legs flailed, and his hands slashed.

"Were we in my home," Darius said, "I would have your hands removed for such an offense."

"I didn't hurt her," Patrick squeaked. "You know I didn't hurt her."

"Wrong again," Darius said. A flash of green scales pulsed over his skin. "You touched my woman. Mine. For that alone I want to kill you."

Grace's heart stopped. Literally stopped, suspended in her chest. Which should she react to first? The scales or the "she is my woman" statement? Neither, she decided. Only Alex mattered right now. Not her shock at the fact that there were actually dragon scales under Darius's skin, and certainly not her unwanted joy at his words.

Tamping down her emotions, she forced her attention to Patrick. His lips were moving, but no sound emerged. "I think he's trying to say something, Darius," she said.

Several seconds passed before Darius loosened his hold. "Have you something to say?"

"I—" Patrick sucked in a deep breath. "Just need—" deep breath "—a moment."

"You're supposed to be looking for my brother," Grace told him. "Why aren't you in Brazil?"

"Alex might already be dead. We found evidence to suggest it right after you left. I'm sorry."

Had Darius not shown Grace proof that Alex lived, she would have sunk to her knees and sobbed. Of all the things to say, of all the things to feign remorse about, that was the cruelest. She didn't ask what evidence; she didn't even ask why no one had given her such news before now. She didn't want to hear more upsetting lies.

Her eyes narrowed. "You may kill him, Darius."

Darius flicked her a startled glance, staring at her lips as if he couldn't quite believe what they'd proclaimed. He grinned slowly, then turned that grin to Patrick.

"What the woman wants," he said, "I give her."

Both of Patrick's palms pushed at Darius's chest, but the action had no effect. "I can't tell you anything. I'll lose everything, damn it. Everything!"

"So you would rather lose your life?"

Darius increased the pressure. Patrick gurgled, his mouth opening and closing as he tried to suck in air. Grace snapped out of her murderous inclinations. Thinking about a death and actually witnessing it were two totally different things.

Not knowing what else to do, she laid her hand on Darius's arm. "Perhaps I spoke too hastily," she said. "Let's give him one more chance."

Darius glanced at her hand, then brought his gaze to her face, never releasing Patrick. The blue in Darius's eyes had faded substantially, making them appear almost completely white.

"Let him go. Please." Her hand inched upward, and she stroked her fingers over his cheek. "For me."

She didn't know why she'd added those last words and didn't expect them to work. Yet color began to return to Darius's eyes, not ice-blue but gorgeous golden-brown. The color she was coming to love.

"Please," she said again.

He released Patrick in the next instant. The gasping man collapsed on the dirty concrete, wheezing as he tried to fill his lungs. Red handprints encircled his neck, changing to a blue-black as she watched. She and Darius waited side by side, silent, as Patrick breathed life back into his body.

"Why were you following Grace?" Darius demanded. "I will not give you another chance to answer, so consider your words carefully."

Patrick closed his eyes and leaned his shoulders into the wall. His fingers massaged at his throat. "The medallion," he said, his voice hoarse, broken. "I followed her for the medallion."

"Why?" Every muscle Darius possessed stiffened. "What did you hope to do with it?"

"My boss...he wants your jewels," Patrick choked out. "That's all."

Darius stiffened. "How do you know what I am?"

"You're like the others. The ones we..." His words trailed off. "I was only to keep track of Grace's whereabouts, to record where she went and who she talked to. I wasn't to harm her in any way. I swear."

"Give us a name," she said sharply, though she had already guessed the answer.

His shoulders slumped, and he laughed, a humorless, I-can't-believe-this-is-happening rasp. "I'll tell you, but you know what? You'd better be prepared to wade nose-deep in shit because that's what he's going to throw at you. He's the greediest son of a bitch I've ever met, and he'll do anything, *anything* to get what he wants."

"His name," she insisted.

"Jason Graves." He paused, adding gruffly, "Alex's boss. The owner of Argonauts."

A cold shiver of dread attacked Grace. Argonauts. Jason. Bits of information began to piece together in her mind. Trembling inside, Grace bent down until she and Patrick were eye-to-eye. She cupped his chin with shaky hands and forced him to face her, to stare her directly in the eyes. "Is Jason Graves holding Alex captive?"

Patrick nodded reluctantly.

"Where?" The word lashed from her. "Here in the States? Brazil?"

"Different places. Never the same place for long."

"Was he in Brazil while I was there? Is that why you guys were so eager to send me home?" Why hadn't they hurt her? Why hadn't they threatened Alex with her life? There had to be a reason.

"We didn't want you involved or stumbling on company business. You were to go home and sing our praises for doing all we could to find your brother. Other than that, I'm as clueless as you as to where he is," he added. "I'm told on a need to know basis, and I don't need to know that."

"How long has he been a prisoner?"

"A few weeks." Patrick wheezed, then coughed.

"You were supposed to find the e-mail we sent you and stop searching. Why the hell didn't you stop searching?"

His question was rhetorical, so she didn't bother with a response. The postcard she'd gotten from Alex had been sent a week ago. He must have escaped, sent it, then was recaptured. Her poor brother! "What does Jason plan to do with him? Kill him? Release him later?"

"Who knows?" he said, but the truth was there in his eyes. Alex would never be released. Not alive. "Last I heard, he was fine."

Shoving to her feet, Grace looked up at Darius. "We have to go to the police," she said. "We have to tell them what's going on."

"What are police?"

When she explained, he said sharply, "No." He shook his head, causing black locks of hair to brush his temples. "We will involve no one else."

"They'll help us. They'll—"

"They will only hinder our search. I would be unable to use my...special skills. I will find your brother on my own."

He was asking her to trust him absolutely, to place her brother's life in his hands. Could she? Dare she? Her gaze fell to the ground.

"What will you do with these police of yours?" Darius demanded. "Will you tell them the myth of Atlantis is true and your brother hoped to prove it? Will you tell them you have traveled there? Will you bring more of your people and heartache to my land?"

Her eyes closed for a brief moment. She mentally sighed. Did she dare trust him? she asked herself again. Yes. She dared. No man was more competent. And no other man possessed the magical gifts that Darius did. He could do things the law couldn't; he could take her places the law couldn't. "I trust you," she said. "I won't go to them."

He nodded as if her answer had meant little to him, but she saw the flood of relief in his eyes. He whipped his attention to Patrick, but said to Grace, "Step beyond the building. Don't ask why, don't hesitate, just do it, please."

Shaking, Grace did as he'd commanded. When she turned the corner, she heard a whoosh, a grunt, a thud. She gasped, but didn't look. Necessary, she told herself. Darius's actions were necessary.

Eyes glowing ice-blue, Darius joined her. He wavered suddenly, but righted himself. Grace gripped his arm to help steady him. His skin was pale again as he secured his weapons inside his pockets. He wound his arm around her waist and curled his fingers possessively on her rib cage.

"I kept my word to you," was his only explanation. "Let us pay this Jason Graves a visit."

CHAPTER SIXTEEN

ARGONAUTS WAS HOUSED in a towering building of glass and chrome, and as Grace rode the elevator up to the forty-third floor, she brooded, thinking the company should have been housed in a hut of shame and greed.

Did Jason Graves actually think he could lock her brother away and go unpunished? Her hands fisted at her sides. Underneath her anger, however, were tendrils of fear that refused to leave. She remembered how cold and sick Alex had looked.

"I'm scared, Darius," she whispered.

He remained curiously silent. Solemn, actually.

Grace turned toward him and blinked. Though some color had returned to his cheeks, the lines around his lips were taut, and there was a new hollowness to his cheeks. She didn't like to see this hard, strong, extraordinarily capable man weakened in any way. Not because it made him less able to help her, but because she cared about him. Darius. About all the things that made up who he was. Seeing him distressed was worse than experiencing it herself.

The realization rocked her because it meant…

Oh, God. She didn't just care about him. She loved him. Grace groaned, and Darius cast her a sharp glance. She offered him a forced half smile. Of all the silly things to do. To fall in love with this mighty warrior like a jumper from a plane. No parachute. No landing mat. Just…splat.

When she'd told Darius she wasn't ready for him, she'd meant it. He was too intense. Too stubborn. Too much everything. So how could this have happened?

Don't worry about that right now. Just feed him. Get his strength up. Her hands shook as she dug in her purse and pulled out a tin of mints. Keeping her focus away from his face—she did *not* want him to know what she was thinking—she reached down and grasped his hand. His palm was warm and dry, thick and rough.

He jerked away from her touch.

Before she had time to react, he was reaching out and stiffly relinking their fingers. "Don't do me any favors," she snapped and tried to tug her hand away. She'd just realized she loved him, and he didn't want her to touch him. "Just so you know, I didn't want to hold your hand. I wanted to give you a mint."

"Be still," he said, at last deigning to speak with her.

"Let go of—"

"Close your mouth, or I will close it for you. With my own."

Eyes narrowed, she lifted her free hand and stuffed several mints in his mouth, effectively shutting him up. Close her mouth, would he? His nose wrinkled as he chewed, but his grip on her hand strengthened.

Someone behind them chuckled, reminding her that two men carting briefcases and files were in the elevator, as well. She darted a gaze to them and gave each one a quick, forced smile.

Not about to heed Darius's warning, she whispered to him, "When we get there, let me do the talking. I don't want anyone to know that we know what's going on."

He frowned. "I will allow you to do the talking, since these are your people," he said loudly, uncaring about their audience. "If they do not answer to my satisfaction, however, I will be forced to act."

"You can't threaten everyone who refuses to answer your questions," she told him, still maintaining her sense of quiet. "Or you'll end up in jail—or a dungeon—or whatever you call it."

"Sometimes, sweet Grace, your innocence amuses me. As if *I* could be held in a prison." His frown deepened. "Will this contraption go no faster? We have wasted enough time already." With his free hand, he jabbed his finger into the wall of buttons.

The elevator stopped on the next floor. As well as the next…and the next.

"The stairs would have been faster," one of the businessmen muttered, his voice laced with irritation.

Grace flashed him another smile, this one apologetic.

The man glared at her, as if it were all her fault.

As if she could control a six foot five hulk of a warrior who— Oh, my God! Darius was displaying his fangs again, this time at the poor, innocent businessmen. When the elevator stopped yet again, the two scurried out with fearful gasps—but at least they were alive.

"Did you see that?" one of them said. "He had saber-teeth."

When the doors closed, leaving her and Darius alone, silence gripped them in a tight fist. Over and over the elevator halted. When someone tried to enter, Darius gave them the same scowl he'd given the businessmen and every one of them retreated and waved them on before the doors closed.

After the eighth jostling stop, Grace's stomach threatened to rebel, and she tugged Darius from the elevator and onto the floor. Twenty-nine, she realized with dread.

"Excuse me," she said to the first person she saw, an older woman who carried a tray of vanilla scented cappuccinos. "Where are the stairs?"

"Down the hall. Last door on your right."

"Thank you." Only when they were inside the empty stairwell did Grace speak again. "Perhaps now is a good time to tell me about your dragon peculiarities," she said, chewing her lip nervously. Her voice echoed from the drab walls. "I need to be prepared...just in case."

As they climbed, she retained a firm hold on his hand. He didn't ask her to release him, and she allowed herself to think it was because he needed the contact as much as she did, that they were connected in some intangible way and the physical contact strengthened that bond.

"Dragons can fly," he said on a sigh.

"With wings?"

"Is there any other way?"

"There's no reason to be snide. There's no bulge in the back of your shirt to indicate the presence of wings or any other type of…" She searched her mind for the right words, ending with, "Flying apparatus."

"They are hidden in long slits of skin. When the wings emerge, the skin is retracted. Perhaps I will show you. Later. When we are alone."

There was a promise of something in his voice, something hot and wild and erotically wicked, and she pictured him without his shirt, pictured her fingertips tracing down the muscles and ridges of his back. She shivered. His scent chose that moment to surround, envelop, and submerge her, awakening her to a deeper level of need.

She had to change the subject before she did something foolish, like ignore the outside world and her responsibilities and drag him home. "Are there humans in Atlantis?" she asked.

"Some. The gods used to punish humans by sending them to our land. Not long after their appearance, the vampires ate most of them."

"Gross." She spied a peek at him through the shield of her lashes, then quickly refocused on the stairs before she tripped. "Have you, well, have you ever dated a human woman before? Not that you're dating one now," she rushed on. "I just meant—" She compressed her lips together.

He jumped right to the heart of the matter. "By dated do you mean bedded?"

"If the question doesn't offend you, then yes."

"Are you sure you wish to hear the answer?"

Yes. No. She sighed. She *really* wanted to know. "Yes."

"There's only one human I would willingly bed, Grace, and I have plans to do so." One of his fingers heatedly caressed her palm.

Oh. Ribbons of pleasure wound around her, and her lips lifted in a soft smile she couldn't stop.

By the time they topped the forty-third floor, Grace's thigh muscles burned with fatigue. She'd always dreamt of being a perfect size six, but the torture required for such a task was getting to be too much. Exercise…how she was coming to loathe the word. It was a thing more foul than low-fat ranch dressing.

Darius held open the door, and she swept past him, finally releasing his hand. She stepped inside Argonauts, the carpet beneath her feet a plush burgundy wool. Her gaze scanned the offices. On the wall hung Picasso, Monet and Renoir. Guards manned several corners, and security cameras roamed in every direction. A small rocky waterfall filled the center of the waiting area, and an expensive, exotic perfume floated on the air, drifting like clouds over the sun on a perfect spring day. Both were peaceful, and both mocked her.

That bastard! There was no doubt in her mind how Jason Graves afforded these things. A surge of rage boiled deep inside her. When Alex had first begun working for Argonauts, he'd barely made enough money to pay the rent on a little efficiency in Brooklyn. The past few months he'd brought home substantially more and had moved to his decadent new apartment in the Upper East Side.

Argonauts, too, had moved from their small offices in Brooklyn to here.

Yesterday, or even an hour ago, she had thought this success was because of recent mythological discoveries. Now she knew the truth. Jason Graves afforded these luxuries through the rape of Atlantis.

She stalked to the reception desk. Three women manned phones and computers. The first, the one Grace approached, had short black hair and heavily but perfectly made up features. She wasn't pretty in the traditional sense, but attractive all the same. She frowned with impatience at Grace, then dropped her jaw in awe when she saw Darius. That damn sex appeal of his!

"One moment please," the woman said into her mouthpiece, speaking to a caller. To Darius, she said, "May I help you?" Her voice was cultured, ritzy.

Grace fisted her hands to keep from unleashing her claws.

"We will see Jason Graves now," he said.

So much for doing all the talking, she thought with a mental sigh.

"What's your name, sir?"

"Darius en Kragin."

The woman's fingers flew over her keyboard, her long, oval nails tapping away. Without glancing up, she asked, "Which company are you with?"

"I come on my own behalf."

She finished her typing, read over the computer screen, then leveled him with a stare. "Mr. Graves isn't in today. He's out on business."

Grace rubbed a hand down her face. She was tired of delays and was completely out of patience. "When do you expect him back?" she asked more sharply than she'd intended.

"End of the week. Possibly beginning of next. If you'll leave your name and number, I'll make sure he receives the information when he returns."

Unwilling to wait that long, Grace said, "What about his assistant? Is he in?"

"That would be Mitch Pierce," the woman said. She propped her elbows on the desk, linked her delicate, tapered fingers, and perched her chin in the cradle her hands provided. "And yes, he is."

Mitch…another Argonaut who had *helped* her in the jungle. She contained a scowl. "We'd like to see him. Today."

Arched brows and a superior smile met her words. "Do you have an appointment?"

Grace opened her mouth to say no, but stopped herself. Admitting she didn't have an appointment was the fastest way to get shown to the door. However, she'd be caught in a lie if she said yes. "I'm

Grace Carlyle and if he discovers you let me walk out of here, you'll be looking for a new job."

The receptionist ran her tongue over her teeth. "I'll see if he can fit you in."

One hand rapped at her computer while the other punched a series of numbers in the telephone pad. After requesting Mr. Pierce's schedule, she hung up and glanced at Grace. "He'll see you within the hour. You may wait through the double doors on your left."

"Thank you," Grace said. Trying unsuccessfully to suppress her triumph, she ushered Darius into the waiting room. They were alone in the room. A round, glass table occupied the center and was piled high with books and magazines; along the farthest wall sat a couch and several chairs. All elegant, and all expensive.

During their wait they endured several peek-in visits from security guards. She flipped through a few magazines. (According to the current *Cosmo* love quiz, she and Darius were *not* compatible.) In one of the magazines, there was a feature article about Jason Graves, his recent discoveries, and his recent accumulation of wealth. The article told how he had purchased an apartment building on the Upper East Side and allowed all of his employees to stay there—which was where Alex lived. That she'd known. Jason himself stayed in the penthouse. That she hadn't.

Darius spent the short time splayed out in his seat, his hands locked behind his neck. He kept his eyes closed. She suspected he was gathering his strength and mentally preparing himself for the coming confrontation, which had to be the reason he didn't barge through the offices, demanding to be seen *now*. Or maybe his spirit was ghosting through the building, watching, listening, ensuring their safety.

Finally a woman, slightly older and less hostile than the receptionist, entered and said, "Mr. Pierce will see you now. If you'll follow me…"

Grace jumped to her feet, Darius right beside her. They shared a glance before exiting. Side by side, they strode down a hall and around a corner. The woman stopped and swept her hand out in front of her. "Last door on the right," she said.

Gliding past her, Grace eyed every door she encountered. She didn't see Alex's name. Where was his office? "I'm so ready to nail the Argonauts to the wall," she muttered to Darius.

A genuine smile played at the corner of his lips. "I had not realized before what a bloodthirsty wench you are. Try to contain your bloodlust long enough that we might question this Mitch."

"Bloodlust?" she gasped, then realized he thought she literally meant to nail Mitch to the wall. "I meant—oh, never mind." Whether she meant it or not, the idea had merit. "I'll try to contain myself."

At the end of the hallway loomed a single door. The nameplate in the center announced Mitch's name in bold, black letters. "That's the one," Grace said, smoothing her shirt and jeans. She didn't know what she'd say or do when she saw him.

Darius didn't bother knocking. He simply shoved open the door and strolled inside.

She followed right on his heels. Mitch sat at a large mahogany desk. There was no clutter, no papers scattered around him. He was as average looking as Grace recalled, with broad shoulders and lean limbs, pleasantly attractive with slightly gray hair that gave him a distinguished air. Only one thing about his appearance captured her interest. Sweat beaded atop his brow.

He was nervous.

Very interesting. Her gaze cataloged the office, taking in the sea of wealth and indulgence. Art, vases, glass and wood figurines. Carpet so light her feet felt as if they were traipsing on clouds.

With a visibly forced air of nonchalance, Mitch folded his hands together—hands that were shaking slightly—and propped his elbows on the desk surface. There was something about his eyes, something she hadn't noticed before…they were beady and shallow. Greedy. He offered them a pleasant, if false, smile. "It's nice to see you again, Grace," he said. "You look well after your trials in the rain forest."

"Thank you." Bastard. She didn't offer him the same compliment.

"Please, have a seat." He coughed and flicked a nervous glance to Darius. "Did you really feel it was necessary to bring a bodyguard?"

"He's a friend," she said. "He's staying with me for a while."

"I see. Well, again, please have a seat."

Darius crossed his arms over his massive chest, stretching the material of his black shirt taut over his muscles, silently communicating his refusal. Only a fool would underestimate his capabilities.

Mitch used a plain white handkerchief to wipe at his brow. Obviously he was no fool.

Grace remained beside Darius. She only prayed his dragon fangs were retracted. Watching Mitch pee his pants was not how she wanted to begin this meeting. The only time she might, *might*, be glad to see those fangs was in bed. While he was naked. Looking down at her. Moving into her.

For God's sake, concentrate.

"Very well, then," Mitch said. "How may I help you?"

"Darius," she said, knowing the big guy intimidated him, "feel free to begin."

"Where is your leader, Jason Graves?" Darius demanded.

"Out of town. Still in Brazil, I'm afraid. I'm more than willing to help you with anything you might need." Mitch laughed nervously.

"I want to know why you had a man following Grace." He stressed the word *had*, making it clear Patrick would be following them no more.

With an audible gulp, Mitch leaned back in his seat. Too lost in his apprehension, he didn't try to deny it. "I suppose you cornered the man. May I ask what he told you?"

"He would tell us nothing," Darius lied. "Only that you had sent him."

Mitch's shoulders relaxed. "We *did* send someone to follow Grace, but we did that for her own protection. We feared something had happened to Alex, and we didn't want the same fate to befall Grace."

"You say 'feared,' as in past tense," Grace pointed out. "Do you now know that nothing *has* happened to him, then?"

"No, no. That's not what I meant." The smile he gave her was weak. "As I told you, we've still got men looking for him, both in Brazil and here. I came back because someone has to oversee the company. Don't you worry, though. We'll find him and bring him home safely."

"I'm sure you will." She gripped the edge of her jeans tightly and twisted, wishing it was Mitch's neck instead.

"Is that why you're here?" he asked. "To inquire about our progress with Alex? You should have called me. I could have saved you a trip."

"I'm here because I'd like to search his office, if I may."

"Oh, uh, I'm afraid that's impossible," he said, his smile slipping. "Only Argonauts' employees are allowed in the offices. Client confidentiality, and all that." He laughed shakily. "Are you looking for employment, Grace?"

Her brows raised. "Are you offering me a job, Mitch?"

He paused. "We're always in need of good employees."

Probably because you kill them all, she thought

snidely. She heard Darius suck in a breath and wondered belatedly if she'd actually said the words aloud.

"On your way out," Mitch added, his demeanor unchanging, which meant he hadn't heard her comment, "ask the receptionist for an application. If you're anything like Alex, you'll make a fine addition to our staff."

"I'll be sure to do that." Regarding him sharply, she tilted her chin to the side. "I'm curious. If you suspect something bad has happened to Alex, why haven't you called the police?"

"We don't want to involve the U.S. authorities until we have more concrete information."

Like a body? she mused. "What *have* you done to locate him?"

"Jason can give you more details about this when he returns. Perhaps you should contact the police on your own."

Her eyes widened as a thought occurred to her. Mitch wanted her to go to the authorities. Why? What possible good could that do him? Unless…could they be planning to make her look like a fool, an overly concerned sister? Or worse, guilty of a crime? Blame the sister. Of course. That would be the reason they'd let her leave Brazil, the reason they kept her alive and didn't wave her in front of Alex as an incentive to talk.

The realization rocked her. She owed Darius. Bigtime. He'd saved her from making a huge mistake, from playing right into Jason's hands.

"I haven't yet, no," she told Mitch. "Perhaps I will."

"That might be wise," he said, for the first time offering her a genuine smile. "There's only so much we can do." He paused for a breath. "Would either of you care for a drink?"

How casually he reverted to pleasantries. Suddenly Grace wanted to stomp her foot, to shriek and rail that she knew they had her brother hidden and locked away. She wanted to leap across the desk, magically will on a pair of brass knuckles, and smack Mitch right in his beady eyes. Too, she wanted to find the medallion and offer it on a silver platter. Just return my brother, she inwardly screamed.

It depressed her that she could do none of those things. If they suspected that she knew the truth, they might kill Alex. If she found and gave them the medallion, they might kill Alex. Destroy the evidence of their misdeeds, so to speak. Either way, he could die.

Never in her life had she felt more helpless.

"No drink," she said, surprised at her calm tone. "I do have some questions for you, though. When was the last time you heard from Alex?" If she kept him talking long enough, perhaps he'd slip and inadvertently disclose crucial information.

"I believe I've already answered this question. A few weeks ago," Mitch said. "He called to let us know he was entering the jungle."

"What is the name of the man your search team found? The one who had last seen Alex? He was gone when I woke up on the boat, so I didn't get a chance to talk to him." And now she knew why.

Mitch gulped. "I, uh, can't recall."

"You can't recall an employee's name?" She gave her jeans another hard twist. "Didn't Argonauts fund Alex's trip? Shouldn't you have records with the names of the men you hire?"

"We didn't fund the trip," he offered quickly. Too quickly. "Perhaps Jason can tell you the man's name when he returns."

"In the jungle, I wanted to stay and look for Alex, but was told he'd already bought a ticket home. Do you know which airline he used?"

He chuckled, the sound strained. "I'll be honest with you, Grace. I'm not sure where he is. I wish I could help you, but..." He shrugged. "He could be anywhere."

At least he didn't try to feed her the "he is dead" line. "So tell me, while you were in the jungle, did you happen to run into any...creatures? Hidden lands?"

"I—I—I don't know what you're talking about."

Liar! She wanted to scream. Grace glanced at Darius. His expression was blanketed, stoic, yet she had the distinct feeling he yearned to stalk across the room and beat Mitch into the carpet. Obviously Mitch received the same impression; he shifted uncomfortably in his chair.

With Mitch's complete attention centered on him, Darius strode casually about the office, lifting vases and figurines as if they were no more important than dust mites. His fingers pinched at them, dismissed them, then replaced them on their perches with complete disregard. Mitch tensed, gulped. However, not a single protest oozed from his mouth.

"I do not like you," Darius told him, weighing a jewel-studded goblet in his palms. He offered the words with a kind of still repose, a natural assurance only the most confident of people possessed. "You remind me of a bloodsucking vampire."

Mitch pulled at his plain blue tie. "There, uh, are no such thing as vampires."

"Nor dragons, I'm sure," Darius answered.

All color drained from the man's face, showcasing the thin hollows of his cheeks. His gaze widened, and he transferred his attention between Darius and the goblet. "That's right," he said brokenly, reaching out instinctively for the artifact.

Darius *tsked* under his tongue. He tossed the cup in the air, caught it, then tossed it again. When he caught it for a second time, he said casually, "Since you are an unbeliever, you'll never have to worry about being eaten alive by a dragon." He arched a brow. "Will you?"

On a strangled gasp, Mitch shoved to his feet, his chair rolling behind him as he anchored his palms on his desk surface. "Set that down before I call security. All I've done is try to help, and this is how you treat me. You may show yourselves out."

"I have seen these objects before," Darius remarked, staying right where he was and giving the goblet a few more tosses.

"In *Archeologist Digest,* I'm sure." Mitch cast a desperate, fleeting glance to Grace.

She struggled not to glare at him.

"Now, please," he added. "I have work to do, and I'm sure you don't want to take up any more of my time."

After replacing the goblet, Darius palmed a vase boasting a colorful array of dragons etched around the edges. "Where did you find this?"

A pause. A cough. "Madrid. I really need to get back to work."

"I would swear on my life it belonged to a friend of mine. Perhaps you have heard of him. His name is—or was—Javar ta 'Arda. He gifted his wife, Teira, with a vase identical to this one on the eve of their mating."

"Perhaps you should put that down." Mitch nervously licked his lips. "I meant it when I said I'd call security. I don't want to, but I will."

Darius returned the vase to its perch, letting it wobble ominously at the edge. "As I was saying a moment ago, I do not like you. But Grace has asked me to use violence as a last resort. Still," he added after a loaded pause, "I can say with certainty that you and I will have a reckoning."

With that, he strode from the office. *That's my man,* Grace thought proudly.

"Have a nice day, Mitch," she said, flicking him one last glance. His features were so pallid he resembled a ghost—or vampire. He was reaching out, racing around his desk in his haste to save the vase from annihilation.

As she chased after Darius, she heard the shatter of porcelain, the howl of a man. Both buoyed her spirits, and she bit back a smile.

LOST IN THE INTENSITY of his thunderous emotions, Darius stared straight ahead as he and Grace strode toward her home. "Do you think Alex is okay?" she asked, her voice so low he had to strain to hear.

"For now. He has something they want. Otherwise, they would have killed him long ago."

That kept her quiet for a long while. "Where do you think he's being kept?"

"Atlantis."

She paused midstep, before jumping back into stride. "But you checked. You said he wasn't there."

"He wasn't. Then. The vision of Alex confirmed that, for he *was* here on the surface. However, after meeting the cowardly Mitch I suspect he has already been moved."

"How do we find out where he's being kept in Atlantis? Interrogate Mitch? Break into Argonauts?"

"No," he answered. "We are more likely to find what we need in Jason Graves's place of residence." But more than that, breaking into Jason's home would supply him with a better understanding of the man he would soon fight.

Oh, yes. Fight Jason he would. His anticipation grew with every second that passed.

"You're right." Grace brightened and curled her lush, rosy mouth with anticipation. Her features were so lovely his chest hurt when he looked at her. "Since he's out of *town*," she sneered the word, "today is the perfect day to let ourselves into his apartment."

"We will go tonight, when the shadows can hide us."

"After that are you," she faltered, "are you going home?"

"I must obtain the vests first."

They neared Grace's door, and she withdrew a key. "I want to go with you when you return."

"No. Absolutely not."

Her eyes narrowed.

"Get inside. Now." He gave her a gentle shove past the entrance. "There is something I must do before I join you." A dark storm churned inside him. He needed some type of release, needed to plan his next move. But more than that, he needed some sort of distance from Grace and his growing feelings for her.

He did not give her time to ask him any more questions. He simply closed the door in her stunned, beautiful face. "I will be right here if you need me," he said through the wood.

Perhaps it was his imagination, or perhaps he was seeing more clearly than ever before, but in his mind's eye he watched her fingertips caress the slat of wood, watched her press her lips together, and her gaze sadden. She didn't know what was happening within him and that worried her. This was not the first time she'd worried for him, and each time it touched him deeply, softened him somehow.

He waited until he heard the lock click in place before he stepped away and began pacing back and forth through the hallway. He would have liked to explore this New York, but the binding spell prevented any great distance between him and Grace. Occasionally humans strode past him and gave him a curious stare, but no one stopped and questioned him.

I want to go with you, Grace had said.

He blanched at the thought of taking her back to his home, even as joy flooded him. How he would have loved to splay Grace upon his bed, her naked body open and eager for him. He craved the reality of that.

The thought of being without her left him cold.

And the acknowledgment of that coldness left him reeling.

Tomorrow he would have to leave. He had moments of utter strength, and moments of utter weakness. No matter what he learned or didn't learn, no matter what he acquired or didn't acquire, he would have to return home in the morning, or he didn't think he'd have the strength to transport himself to the mist. Yet he still had so much to do.

He still had to kill Grace.

Could he, though? Could he harm her?

Darius didn't have to think about it. No. He couldn't.

The answer sliced through him as sharply as a blade. He could not hurt sweet, innocent Grace in any way.

She captivated him on so many different levels.

He was coming to depend on her in a way he'd once considered impossible, craving the emotions she made him feel with the same ferocity he'd once hated them. Without her, he was not fully alive.

He'd watched her stand up to that man, Mitch, and he'd felt pride. She hadn't backed down. She'd questioned him without revealing her hurt, without crumbling under the need to administer justice. She was a woman of strength and honor, a woman of love and trust.

His woman.

Silently his boots pounded into the carpet. He drew in the rich scent of food that seemed to encompass this entire building, this city, and steered his mind on to his own home. Javar and all of the dragons of that unit were dead. Dark sorrow wove through his blood as he at last admitted the truth. He'd known it beyond a doubt the moment he spied the treasures of Javar's home displayed so mockingly inside Argonauts.

His friends were dead, he repeated in his mind. They'd died by guns, most likely. Guns…and vampires. Perhaps the *Book of Ra-Dracus* had even helped. No matter what had happened, no matter what had been done, he would have vengeance.

This was what came of allowing humans to know of Atlantis; *this* was what Javar warned him of.

While Javar had not been an easy man to know, he had been like a father to Darius. They had understood each other. When Teira entered Javar's life, the man had softened and the bond between tutor and student had deepened, even as it widened. What a senseless death. A needless death. He'd lost no one close to him since the murder of his family. And now trickles of pain, both past and present, rose within him like a tide of water, seeping insidiously past his defenses and eroding the very fabric of his detachment. A sharp ache stabbed him, and he gripped his chest.

Deny your tears and keep the hurt inside you, boy. Use it against those who mean us harm. Kill them with it.

Javar had said one variation after another of those words. He wouldn't want Darius to mourn him, but mourn him Darius did. He would not have survived those first years without Javar, without the purpose his tutor had given him.

He should have killed the human man, Mitch, Darius thought dispassionately. He should have killed both human men. Mitch and Patrick. They each had knowledge of the mist, had most likely entered and had played a part in Javar's death. Had he destroyed them, however, he felt certain Grace's brother would have been killed in retaliation. So he'd knocked Patrick out—punishment for what he'd wanted to do to Grace—and walked away from Mitch. What was wrong with him?

He knew the answer. Part of it anyway. He hadn't wanted Grace to view him as a killer. Protector, yes. Lover, most definitely. But ruthless slayer? No longer.

He could only guess at how she would react if she

fully beheld the beast inside him. Tremble with fear and disgust? Run from him as if he were a monster? He didn't want her scared of him; he wanted her pliant. Welcoming. He just wanted her, all of her. Now…and perhaps always.

He'd come so close to losing control with the one called Patrick, and it had required a conscious effort to calm himself. Coming face-to-face with the man who had run his fingertips over Grace's sleeping body had infuriated him. Only he was allowed to touch her. Only he, Darius, was allowed to gaze at her luscious curves and imagine her stripped and open, ready and eager.

She belonged to him.

He wished to give her the world, not take it from her. He wished to fill her days with excitement and her nights with passion. He wished to protect her, honor her and devote himself to her needs. He could not let her go, he realized now. Not ever. He needed her for *she* was his heart. His emotions had never been mild where she was concerned but as unstoppable as a turbulent storm.

I'll never be able to harm her. The admission solidified inside him. His deepest male instincts had known since the beginning. The woman was a part of him, the best part, and hurting her would destroy *him.*

There was a way to have it all, he decided. A way to keep her from harm, a way to keep her for himself and still honor his oath.

He had only to figure out what that was.

CHAPTER SEVENTEEN

WITH THE STOLEN MEDALLION in his pocket, Alex clasped Teira's hand in his, grateful for her warmth, her softness and her strength.

A tremor racked him. Not from the cold or blood loss, but from the forced drug-induced hunger. He craved, oh, how he craved more of that damning substance. His mouth was dry. His head pounded, creating a dull ache he knew would soon become a raging inferno of pain. He needed those damn drugs and was appalled that a part of him wanted to stay here and await another dose.

The other part of him, the saner part, flashed pictures of his sister and his mother through his mind. Next came an image of Teira being dragged away, being hurt in the worst possible ways. This picture lingered, fueling a spark of anger. And that anger overrode the hunger.

He was leaving this place tonight.

Saving Teira was necessary for his peace of mind. He owed her. They were in this together; they had only each other.

"Are you ready?" he asked. They'd waited for the

palace above to quiet, and now silence held them in its grip.

"Ready," she answered.

"I'll keep you safe," he promised her, praying he spoke true.

"And I will keep you safe," she replied, her tone more assured than his own.

How could he ever have doubted her? Alex wondered. He gave her hand a squeeze. "Let's do this."

Together they stepped toward the doors, and the thick ivory barriers slid open smoothly, as if they'd never offered any hindrance. *How simple,* he thought. *Carry a medallion and come and go as you please.* Drawing in a steadying breath, Alex hurried Teira from the cell. He kept his footsteps light, but all the while his heart thudded in his chest.

The deeper he roamed from the cell, the more frigid the air became, chapping his skin. Fog billowed about like a frenzied snowstorm, so thick he could only see what was directly in front of his face. Dry ice, he realized, recalling how Jason had bragged about sending bags of it through the portal. The shards crunched beneath his boots.

He was grateful for the fog. It embraced him in its chilly depths and kept him hidden from view. Using his free hand, he trailed his fingertips over the wall, letting the rough texture be his guide.

Beside him, Teira's body shuddered. He released her hand and wrapped his arm around her slim waist, pulling her into the warmth of his side, rubbing his hand over her ice-cold arm. Her delicate scent wafted to his nose, heating his blood. He wished he could see her face, wished he could see the glistening fog create a halo around her because he knew beyond a doubt that it would be the most erotic sight he'd ever seen.

"I'm here," he soothed.

"The cold…it makes me weak," she said, stumbling.

His own weakness had him stumbling, as well, but he used his weight to hold them both steady. "I'll get you warm," he said. As they trekked deeper through the palace, Alex expected alarms to erupt. He expected men with guns to surround them. Instead, silence.

The wall ended all too quickly, and he was left with only air and fog to guide him. Where did he go from here? The ghostly whiteness was too thick. Protective, yes, but also slowing.

A lone figure suddenly parted the fog and rounded a corner.

Unseen, Alex forced Teira quietly behind him, waiting until the man closed the distance. The hairs on the back of his neck prickled with tension as each new second passed. When the guard stepped close enough, Alex didn't allow himself to think. He simply slammed his fist into the man's exposed trachea, cutting off his air. Gurgling, he went down hard and fast. Alex didn't know if he'd killed him, and he didn't care.

Motions shaky, he removed the man's coat and fastened it around Teira's shoulders. The thick brown material swallowed her slight frame. He looked for a gun, but didn't see one. When he spotted a fallen fire extinguisher, he hefted it up and looped the straps around his shoulders. Not a great weapon, but it would have to do.

"Which way is the portal?" he whispered to Teira.

"You cannot use the portal here. I tried to escape before, when they took me from you. Too many guards. Too many weapons."

He uttered a frustrated sigh and pushed a hand through his hair. He hadn't come this far to be stopped now. "We'll have to take them by surprise." Though how the two of them were going to pull that off, he didn't know.

"There's another way," she said. "A second portal on other side of the island. Darius en Kragin is Guardian there and we will con-convince—is that right word?—him to allow you to pass. He will destroy these men."

A grin of relief lifted the corners of his lips. He placed his face so close to hers their noses touched, and he gazed into her golden eyes. "You lead the way, baby. I'll follow you anywhere."

She returned his grin, though an air of sadness clung to the edges of hers. "I do not want to lose you," she said. "I do not want you to go."

"Then come with me." When she opened her mouth to protest, he interjected, "Don't give me your answer now." He didn't want to lose her, either, he realized, and would actually fight to keep her with him. After clinging to his freedom all these many years, he was finally willing to surrender it in favor of permanency with a woman. *This* woman. "Just think about it, okay. Right now we need to get out of here."

He curled his fingers through hers again, and Teira weakly led him up a winding staircase. The room they entered next was even more frigid, but not as thickly fogged. Alex surveyed these new surroundings. There was no furniture, yet there was more wealth than he'd ever seen. Ebony at his feet, jewels at his side, and crystal above. He halted midstep and could only gape.

This is why Jason desires the mist. Hell, I want it, too.

A sense of greed momentarily choked his throat. There had to be a way to take some of this home. Conceal a few jewels under his shirt. Fill his pockets. He'd be able to keep his family in luxury for the rest of their lives.

The thought of his family drowned him in a desperate need to see them. Jason claimed they were unhurt, but Alex couldn't believe a single word out of that murderer's deceitful mouth.

No one would ever have to know what he'd done, and that was a heady thought indeed. He reached out and traced his fingers over the jeweled wall. As he did so, the exotic scent of jasmine wafted around him, loosening the tightness in his throat and reminding him that he already held a treasure. Teira. He glanced down at her, and she smiled slowly up at him—a smile of trust. His hand fell to his side.

Atlantis had to be kept secret. Men like Jason would continue to plunder, never ceasing their quest for riches, killing men, women and children in the process. *God, how stupid I've been, how caught up in my own need for glory.* He'd endangered his entire family for *this.* For prestige and money. His stomach churned with shame, making him all the more aware of his body's need for drugs.

"Come on," he said. "Let's get out of here."

"Yes."

They maneuvered around corners, stumbled through empty rooms, making Alex feel like he was navigating a maze. Most walls were bare, ripped of all jewels. Several guards were posted throughout, but they never detected Alex and Teira, hidden as they were by fog and shadows.

Two ten-foot panels of glistening dragon-inlaid ivory ended their winding search. The pair of doors opened, welcoming them into the night. Crashing waves created a calming lullaby, and warm air laden with the fragrance of salt and sea cascaded gently. Teira stopped, allowing the warmth to thaw and strengthen her. Color returned to her cheeks, and her back straightened.

She dropped her coat and spread her arms wide.

Alex drank in the mesmerizing beauty of both Teira and Atlantis. There was a dusky glow over the breathtakingly lush green foliage and stunning array of colorful blossoms. Blossoms Teira seemed to be a part of. How did a city under the sea have night and day? There was no sun, no moon. Crystal prisms stretched above to form a dome as far as the eye could see.

Vibrancy and vitality pulsed all around, strengthening him to his very core, making him forget his dry mouth, making him forget his bitter need.

"If we follow the forest path," Teira said, her voice stronger than it had been inside the palace, "we can reach Darius by morning."

"Then let's go."

One of the guards scattered along the bastion noticed them. "Down there," he shouted.

Someone else called, "Stop them!"

Pop. Whiz. Bullets flew, peppering the ground a few feet behind them. Alex increased his speed, sprinting for all he was worth, the fire extinguisher slamming into his back. Later, he would feel the bruises. For now, he felt only the blessed numbness of his adrenaline rush.

Still hand in hand with Teira, he forced her to keep pace beside him. He launched into the safety of the trees before finally slowing. Alex liked to think he was in top physical condition, or had been, thanks to his daily workouts. But right now his breathing was ragged, and his pulse leapt like it was connected to a live wire.

"You need rest," his companion panted. "We are safe here. We can stop—"

"No. No resting. Keep moving."

She claimed the lead, and he forced his suddenly heavy feet to step one in front of the other. Forced his mind on the task at hand and not the drugs he was leaving behind. For a moment, his vision blurred and he swayed. Teira glanced at him over her shoulder, her expression concerned.

"Keep moving," he said again.

When they swerved around a large elm, a giant of a man jumped from the shadows, followed quickly by another. Their features weren't visible in the growing darkness, but Alex felt the anger coiled so tightly in their bodies.

Teira screamed.

Acting instinctively, Alex sprayed the liquid nitrogen, spinning in a circle as he did so. A thick foam of white coated the men, and they growled indistinguishable curses as they wiped at their faces. He tossed the red canister to the ground and jerked Teira through the thick foliage. Then they ran. Ran around trees and bushes, flowers and stones. They waded through two crystalline rivers along the way, and through it all he heard the men racing in pursuit, their footsteps fast, determined.

"Which way?" he called.

"East," she said, panting a little. The white gown she wore swished and swirled around her ankles, and her moonbeam pale hair whipped behind her. "There is…a town…nearby. We can lose ourselves."

Alex veered east, pushing himself past his endurance. The longer he ran, the less he heard of his followers. Either he'd lost them or they'd given up. Or were somehow able to silently follow. He didn't relax his defenses. Only when Teira was safely ensconced inside his apartment would he rest—after he made love to her. Several times.

After what seemed an eternity, they reached the town. One moment they were surrounded by dense forest, and the next by shimmering gold and silver buildings. He slowed when he found himself on a crowded stone road. Throngs of people strolled in every direction. No, not people. Winged men, bull-like animals and horned women. Interspersed throughout were tall, lean humanoid creatures with skin the color of new fallen snow. They glided rather than walked.

Alex felt their dynamically surreal eyes boring into him hungrily, as if they could already taste his every drop of blood. Vampires. He shuddered. They moved with fluid, catlike grace, mere slashes of white skin and flowing, black clothing. The only color they possessed was in their eyes, an inhuman blue that hypnotized and promised every desire sat-isfied.

His shudders intensified, and he reached up and massaged his neck, covering the marks of his last encounter with a vampire. The *Book of Ra-Dracus* told of their insatiable thirst for blood—more so than earth legend proclaimed. He knew that firsthand.

"In here," Teira said. She ushered him inside the nearest building. "We will hide here until we are sure we are safe."

Loud music, more fluid than rock, less structured than classical, boomed in every direction. Voices and laughter blended with the music as people mingled and danced. He and Teira swept through the crowd, trying to remain unnoticed. There, in the back, was an empty table, and they hurriedly claimed it.

He plopped into his seat. The adrenaline rush he'd experienced in the forest had helped mask his need for drugs, but now, as the surge receded, he became increasingly aware of his shaking hands and aching temples.

A woman approached them and clanked two glasses onto their table. Two small brown horns protruded from her forehead. She gave them a brittle smile and said something in the same language Teira sometimes used. He was beginning to catch on to its unusual inflections and pronunciations, so he didn't need an interpreter to know the waitress had said, "Drink up and leave, or tonight will be your last," before she flittered away, suddenly lost in the crowd.

"There are many vampires here," Teira said, gazing around. "More than usual."

A wisp of dark cloth. A shiver of electrifying power. Then someone was there, standing behind Teira, caressing her shoulder. The laughter and music slowly tapered to quiet, and the patrons stared over at them.

"You smell good, little dragon," a vampire male said, his voice hypnotic and dark. Seductive. "I wonder, though, how you will taste."

It took Alex a moment to translate. When he did, he saw red. He didn't care how much stronger the vampires were, he didn't care that he might be inciting a fight, he would not allow threats to Teira's life. "Back off," he said, glaring up at the blood-sucker. "Or it will be *your* blood that is spilled this night."

The vampire snickered.

"I taste like death," Teira finally responded. Her gaze flicked from Alex to the vampire nervously. "Now leave us. We wish only to rest. We will depart soon."

"No, you won't. Not until I've sampled both you *and* your human."

Another vampire joined them, his mouth a blood-red frown. "We are not to harm the human, Aarlock. You know that."

"I will not kill him. The dragon, however…"

Still another vampire approached, crowding their table further. "The human doesn't wear the mark. We can kill them both if we so desire."

All three bloodsuckers glanced at Alex's neck. The one called Aarlock smiled slowly. "No, he doesn't wear the mark of the other humans. He is fair game."

Alex could almost see the knife and fork clanging together in their minds, and he wondered what mark Jason and his minions wore to prevent vampire attacks. *I have to do something,* he thought, vaulting to his feet. Not knowing what more he could do, he drew back his fist. Before he had time to blink, the vampire caught his arm and held him in a bruising grip. Those eerie eyes turned to him, gazing deeply, probing.

A strange lethargy worked its way through him,

as if he'd been shot full of those delicious drugs. Suddenly he wanted only to feel this vampire's fangs sink into his neck, wanted only to give himself to this powerful man.

Dainty, gentle Teira, who loved tender contact, snarled a sound more animal than human, jolted up and bared amazingly sharp claws. She shoved the vampire backward, causing him to stumble as he released Alex.

"Do not touch him," she snarled. "He is mine."

The rest of the vampires gathered around them, some baring their fangs, others hissing. Alex shook himself out of his stupor just as Teira flashed her own set of fangs, hers longer than the vampires. Alex's eyes grew round. He'd known she was a dragon changeling, but he hadn't really expected her body to physically change.

"We must leave," Teira mouthed, once again speaking his language, never taking her attention from the creatures in front of her. "We will need a distraction."

Determination rushing through his veins, his palms sweating, he glanced around, searching for a spear, a torch, something. Anything. When that failed, he looked for a back door—not that they could have used it. The vampires had formed a circle around them, their bodies nearly transparent and vibrating with hungry energy.

His protective instincts sharpened. He'd have to use his own body to divert their attention. He'd never battled a vampire before—obviously—but he'd always welcomed new experiences. "I'll distract them." His muscles tightened, readied. "Run, baby, and don't look back."

She sucked in a breath. "No. No!"

"Do it!"

The front doors burst open, saving her from another reply.

Three of the largest men he'd ever seen tramped inside. An air of menace surrounded them, as dark as their clothing. Their faces were red, their eyes puffy from some sort of toxin. Alex concluded almost instantly that they were the giants from the forest.

The vampires uttered a collective hiss and inched away.

Teira peeked over his shoulder, and when she saw who had entered, she gasped. "Braun, Vorik, Coal!" Smiling with relief, she waved with one hand and laced the other on Alex's shoulder. "They will help us."

The three men flicked them a glance, gave a barely imperceptible nod, then spread out and assumed a menacing come-and-get-me-you-blood-suckers stance.

Alex had yet to fight past his shock. "You know them?"

"They are Darius's men."

"Then why did you scream when they approached us in the forest?"

"I not realize who they were. Come. We go to them."

While he was grateful for the help, Alex was oddly disappointed. He'd wanted to be the one to save Teira. He'd wanted her praise to be all his own. How foolish, since he wouldn't have lived to hear such praise.

As Alex and Teira skidded toward the front door, the vampires and dragons divided the bar, each group taking one side, facing the other. The moment Alex came within striking distance of his rescuers, he was roughly shoved behind them. Teira was gently lifted out of the way.

"What were you doing in the forest, Teira?" one of the warriors asked. He never removed his piercing gaze from the enemy.

"Escaping," she answered.

A hard, dangerous glint consumed his golden eyes. "Escaping? You will tell me more of this later." He motioned toward Alex with his chin. "What of the human?"

Teira cast a glance at Alex. *What of the human?* The question had plagued her over the last weeks. If only he were like the others of his kind, she could have ignored him. If only she hadn't been so completely drawn to him… He was nearly as tall as a dragon warrior, with wide shoulders and a lean, strong body. Short, curly red hair framed a strong, square face. His lips were wide and soft, his jaw angular. But it was his eyes that truly captivated her. They were big and green and filled with so many dreams. Those dreams called to her in so many ways.

"He's my friend," she said to Vorik. "No harm is to befall him."

Having listened to the conversation, Braun whipped around, facing her, radiating fury. "What of Javar?"

She hated to give him the news, here and now, like this, but she would not lie or evade. "He is dead," she said sadly.

"Dead!" all three dragons exclaimed at once.

Remorse flitted over Braun's expression, but he quickly hardened the emotion into determination. "There were other humans at the palace. They carried strange objects that fired some type of disc."

"Those discs stayed inside the dragon bodies, keeping their flesh open and preventing them from healing."

"That alone would not—"

"That alone *would.* The palace has been made into an ice land. When our strength was drained, the humans attacked us with their weapons." She remembered how easily her people had been destroyed. One moment, healthy, happy and whole. The next, gone. Murdered.

Her hands clenched, making the sharpness of her claws bite into her flesh. She barely felt the sting. Why the humans kept her alive and imprisoned, she could only guess. A threat to Alex, perhaps? A bargaining tool? They had kept her weakened by the cold, had tried to keep her hungry, as well, but she'd stolen bits of food here and there. More than anything, however, the humans had kept her frightened. For herself, for Alex.

She would not rest until the intruders were destroyed.

She had loved her husband, had loved the time she spent with him, and even missed him, but he had never filled her with such great longing as Alex did, as if she couldn't breathe without him near. She sighed. What was she going to do with the handsome human? She wanted him to stay here, with her. Wanted him to hold her in his arms every night, and wake to his kisses every morning. If he wouldn't stay, she would lose him. She could not survive on the surface.

The sound of guttural curses sliced at her reverie.

"You are not welcome here, dragons," a vampire snarled.

"We came for the human and the woman," Vorik said calmly. He kept his hands over the hilts of his swords—swords that could pierce a vampire's chest, sending poison through the creature's body and striking a lethal blow. "We mean you no trouble."

"We claimed them first. They belong to us."

"Perhaps you'd like to fight us for them." Coal offered his opponents an anticipatory smile.

"That is an invitation we cannot refuse." The vampire offered his own anticipatory smile.

Dragons were stronger, but vampires were faster. Years ago, the two had warred and the dragons had emerged the victors. But both races had suffered horribly. If they fought now, Teira was not sure a single man would be left standing.

"Let them go," a vampire said to his brethren, surprising her. "These dragons will bow to us soon enough."

"We will never bow to you," Braun spat.

The words, "We shall see," were delivered with supreme confidence. "Yes, we shall see."

Vorik arched a brow. "We shall see *now*."

Without emitting a single sound, the dragons flew at the vampires, teeth bared and gleaming a hungry white, a vision of silent death as they transformed from man to beast. They dropped their swords, relying instead on their natural reflexes. Vampires moved quickly, gliding to the ceiling, then launching themselves at the dragons before gliding upward once again. It was a dangerous dance.

There were snarls and grunts of pain, the sound of ripping cloth. The flash of claws, and the scent of blood and sulfur.

"The stench of dragon can be smelled miles away," one of the vampires snarled, lashing out with his sharp nails as he slipped past.

"Since you can smell me, Aarlock, you might as well feel my flames." Vorik spat red-orange sparks out of his mouth, catching the vampire in the side.

A tormented scream erupted, blending with the sound of sizzling skin. Eyes glowing with hatred, the vampire retaliated, attacking straight on, fangs bared. Before Vorik had time to move, their bodies slammed together and Aarlock sank his teeth in Vorik's neck. Vorik gripped him by the neck, ripped him away, and tossed him to the ground.

"I see you still bite like a girl, Aarlock," he seethed.

"I see you still breathe like a hatchling."

They were on each other again.

"Hand me a dagger," Alex said to Teira over his shoulder. When the fight first began, he'd shoved her behind him. He didn't know if he'd be any help, but he couldn't let these dragon men fight alone. He had to do *something*.

She tried to maneuver around him for what seemed the hundredth time. The woman wanted to guard *him* instead of the other way around. "No," she said. "We must not interfere. We would only distract them."

Alex continued to search for a weapon, catching glimpses of the brawl at the corner of his gaze. Each of the species fought hard and cruel, biting and slashing. The dragons drew blood with teeth, claws and tails, while the vampires relied on speed, moving from one end of the bar to the other to slash and run. Their rusty-brown blood dripped onto the dragons, acting like acid.

In the end, speed and poison blood weren't enough.

The more fire the dragons produced, the stronger they became. Even Teira seemed to soak up the heat like a flower turning to the sun. All color had returned to her cheeks. Alex wiped at the sweat dripping from his face.

When the battle finally ended, burning embers and vampire ashes littered the ground. Braun, Vorik, and Coal were still standing. They were covered in blood and wounds, but by God, they were standing.

One of the dragons, Braun, pushed Alex outside. The others, Teira included, followed. She quickly made the introductions. Alex had never been more aware of his human frailty. The men he knew did not behave like these warriors, ready and eager for bloodshed.

"What do the humans at the palace want, Teira?" Vorik asked.

"The riches. They are taking them back to the surface."

"Damn this," Coal snarled. He threw a withering glance toward Alex.

Alex backed away, palms up. "I'm not with them. I'll help you in any way I can."

"He was a prisoner, like me." Teira met each man's stare. "Are there other warriors with you? Can we retake the palace tonight?"

Braun shook his head. "We cannot act until Darius returns. Our orders are to stay outside of the palace, detaining any who try to enter or leave."

Vorik frowned down at her. "The time for war will come, and then we will act. Until then, we do nothing." His gaze became piercing. "Understand?"

"When will Darius return?" she demanded. "I am eager for vengeance."

Ignoring her question, Coal exchanged a concerned glance with Braun. "As are we. As are we."

JASON GRAVES STUDIED the vampire stronghold with assessing eyes. While this fortress lacked the same magnitude of wealth as the dragon palace, it held enough to capture his attention. Silver walls. Gold inlaid floors. A violet ram's fleece rug.

Perhaps he needed to rethink his alliance with the vampires.

They had supplied the tools necessary to strip the dragon walls of their jewels, as well as the location of coins and other treasures. And in return, Jason was to slaughter the dragons. A good bargain, in his estimation. Or so he'd thought. He was beginning to suspect that the moment the dragons were exterminated, the vampires would feed off of him and his men, the alliance forgotten. He swallowed, allowing the idea of striking first to take root in his mind. That way, he would not only save his own life, but also gain vampire riches. He had heard they knew where to find the greatest treasure of all. The Jewel of Atlantis. A powerful stone, granting the owner unimaginable victories.

Right now, his unlikely allies knew that any human wearing a medallion was to be left alone. Jason had made it clear in the beginning that if one of his men were harmed, just one, he would join forces with the dragons instead.

That threat would no longer work when the dragons were gone.

"You have defeated Javar," Layel, the vampire king, said. He stroked deathly pale fingers over the seam of his red lips and leaned back in his throne. A throne comprised of bones. "It is time for you to defeat Darius, as well."

"We haven't emptied out the first palace yet," Jason hedged. He stood in the center of the room and shifted nervously. He hated coming here and never stayed longer than necessary. Knowing his men waited outside the throne room doors, weapons cocked and ready, did not soothe his unease. Layel could have his neck ripped open before he managed a single scream for help.

"No matter. I want them killed immediately." The king slammed a fist onto his armrest—a femur, Jason thought. "The dragons are cruel, evil murderers. They must die."

"And they will. We just need a little more time. I cannot divide my forces, and I will not leave the first palace until it is completely emptied."

Heavy silence encompassed them.

"You dare tell me no?" Layel said quietly.

"Not no, exactly. I'm merely asking you to have more patience."

Layel slowly ran his tongue over his razor-sharp teeth. "I knew you were greedy, human. I didn't know you were also stupid."

Jason scowled. "You are more than welcome to fight the dragons on your own." He didn't need the vampires anymore—he already possessed the tools. But they both knew Layel *still* needed him. Jason might be intimidated by this creature, but damn if he didn't enjoy what small power he held over him.

Intense fury blazed in Layel's eerie blue eyes. "How much longer?" he ground out.

"A week. Two at most."

"That is too long! The only reason you were able to defeat Javar was because you surprised him. Without that surprise, you will not defeat Darius." In a hiss of rage, Layel hurdled his jeweled goblet at Jason's head.

Jason ducked and the cup sailed past him. Barely.

"He is stronger than his tutor ever was," Layel said.

Jason glared up at him, a heated retort pressed at the gate of his lips. The doors burst open before a single word escaped.

One of his men ran inside. "Alex and the female escaped."

"What!" Jason shouted, spinning.

"Word arrived only seconds ago. They escaped through the forest."

"How?" Scowling, he strode toward his man and met him halfway.

"We aren't sure."

"Damn it! Search the forest. I want him found within the hour and brought back to me."

"Alive?"

"If possible. If not..."

The man hastened to do as he was bid.

Jason stood there, grinding his teeth. A part of him didn't care that Alex had escaped. The bastard would probably be found and killed by any number of vicious creatures. But the other part of Jason, the part that acknowledged wars could be lost by a simple mistake such as this, recognized the damage that could be done. Alex could stumble upon Darius, could warn him.

"Jason," Layel said.

The hairs prickled at the base of his neck, and

without looking, he knew the vampire king was directly behind him. Jason slowly turned, hoping his features remained emotionless. "Yes?"

"Fix this. Fail me and I'll add your bones to my throne."

CHAPTER EIGHTEEN

HOURS TICKED BY as Grace thinned the carpet in her tiny living room, pacing back and forth, from one wall to the other. The hallway had fallen silent half an hour ago. Every time she blinked, she pictured Darius sitting just beyond her front door, his eyes closed, expression pensive, his mind thinking of ways to leave her behind. She scowled. Darius might travel home in the morning, but not without her. Whether he approved or not, she was going.

Pushing out a breath, Grace rubbed her temples. Her shoulders slumped dispiritedly. *What am I going to do?* Beneath her frustration with Darius hovered a constant fear for Alex, and she knew that was the true catalyst to her riotous emotions. Helplessness ate her because she knew there was nothing she could do but wait and pray Darius was right. That Jason Graves would keep Alex alive because her brother had something he wanted.

The medallion.

She laughed humorlessly. It always came back to that. If she'd suspected the true value of that damn chain, she would have held on to it tighter. Where the hell was it?

She needed Darius. She needed him to reassure her. She needed him to wrap his arms around her and reaffirm wrongs would be righted and life would continue with promises of pleasure and happiness.

"Darius," she said in frustration. What was he doing?

The air in front of her thickened and blurred, sparkling with crystallized raindrops. A whisper of heat, a waft of masculine scent, then Darius materialized right before her eyes. His features were taut as his gaze darted left and right. "What is wrong?"

"I need you," she said. "I need you. That's all."

His visage relaxed, fraying his worry but leaving behind lines of tension.

Their gazes locked. She stood frozen, drinking him in. More than strained, he looked…changed. Different somehow. Sexier than ever before. Scorching. Needy. He sensed her growing desire, perhaps, because his nostrils flared and his eyes lit with fire.

Grace's heart flip-flopped in her chest. Darius didn't resemble the man who accosted her in the cave, a sword raised over his head, death in his gaze. Nor did he resemble the man who had nearly choked the life from Patrick. Right now he reminded her of the man who found delight in colors and chocolate, who had tenderly kissed her lips, savoring her every nuance. He had licked her palms and soothed her bruises.

Oh, God, how she wanted *this* man.

But guilt swam through her, locking her in place. How could she want him, *enjoy* him, when Alex was hurt?

"You cannot help your brother right now," Darius said, as if divining her thoughts. His gaze reached across the space between them, caressing her with quiet strength.

"I know," she said softly, yearning for him all the more. She tried to absorb his comfort from a distance, but that wasn't what she needed. Only full-body, skin to skin contact would work.

He stretched out his hand. "Then come here."

Without another word, Grace launched herself into Darius's arms. He caught her with a *humph* and banded his arms around her waist, anchoring his hands on her bottom and backing her into a wall. Instantly he smothered her mouth with a kiss. No, not a kiss. A devouring. He worshipped her taste, and she reveled in his, and as their tongues danced, she became a part of him. He became a part of her. She moaned, and her legs tightened around him.

He pulled away. "I will not stop this time," he said raggedly.

"Good, because I wasn't going to let you."

He trapped her earlobe between his teeth and gently tugged. The time had come; the wait was over.

One hand cupping his neck, the other kneading his back, she fit herself against his erection. The contact sizzled. A tremor moved through her, leaving a desperate arousal in its wake. He reclaimed her lips in total possession, branding her very soul.

She was his woman, and he was her man.

His tongue swept inside her mouth, and her desire raced toward the point of no return. No, that wasn't exactly true. She'd reached the point of no return the first moment she saw him.

She quivered with the force of her need, with the intensity of his heat, and the consuming ache to finally know him. All of him.

"Darius," she whispered.

"Grace," he whispered back.

This is where he belonged, Darius thought savagely, gazing down at Grace. Right here. With this woman. He'd never felt more alive than he did right now, in her arms. She showed him a world he'd never thought to see again, a world of colors and tastes... and emotion. True emotion. And he exalted in it. In *her.*

Slowly, seductively, her fingers crawled up his chest. She smiled a feminine smile. He nearly spilled his seed just then. The deepest, most primitive part of him had recognized her the moment she'd stepped through the mist. She was his mate.

His reason for being.

He would wed her, Darius decided in the next instant.

As he continued to watch her, Grace licked one of her fingers and drew a moist heart around his right nipple. Air hissed between his teeth.

By mating with him, Grace would become a citizen of Atlantis. His oath stipulated only that he kill surface dwellers who passed through the mist. If she were Atlantean...gods, yes. He would make her Atlantean.

The relief, the joy, resonated through him like a torrid rain.

He claimed her mouth with more ferocity, growling his need. She responded by weaving her hands in his hair and slanting her lips over his more fully. She rubbed herself against his erection, gasping, taking, giving. Their clothing only added to the friction. His fingers dug into the soft roundness of her buttocks, quickening her rhythm, and their kiss continued, hard and fast, then slow and tender.

"You are so beautiful," he said brokenly.

"No, I—"

"You are. I burn for you. I flame."

She melted against him. Into him. Her breasts meshed against his chest, her nipples pearled, waiting. Tasting them became as necessary as breathing. In all of his other couplings, Darius had rushed. He'd been savage, giving the woman pleasure, taking pleasure for himself, but offering nothing more. Never more. There would be no rushing now.

He wanted to savor and give.

"I will take care of you," he whispered. "Do you trust me?"

"So much, I ache."

With her legs still wrapped firmly around him, he sank to his knees and laid her tenderly on the carpet. He gently gripped her chin and forced her to meet his gaze. "This will not just be a coupling, sweet Grace. I am giving you me. All of me." He paused and studied her features. "Do you understand?"

Something he couldn't read leapt into her eyes. Uncertainty? Or excitement? She chewed on her bottom lip, then shook her head.

"I want to make you mine for now and always," he explained.

Her brow crinkled. "Do you mean…get married?"

"More than that. Life mates."

"There is a difference?"

"One that cannot be explained. One that must be shown."

"And you want to do this here?" Her eyes widened. "Now?"

He nodded.

Grace gulped. Surely he wasn't serious. He had to be teasing her. But the lines of his face stretched, determined, and an air of vulnerability clung to his shoulders. He refused to relinquish his hold on her gaze.

He meant every word.

And she didn't know how to react.

Grace en Kragin, her mind whispered.

Though she didn't understand what had brought him to this decision, the thought tempted her on every level, and a great need welled inside her. She'd already admitted that she loved him. Why deny her feelings in this? *I want to be his wife.* She did. Now and always, like he'd said.

How wonderful to be the one who snuggled in bed with him each night, the one he pulled tightly to his side, his breath on the back of her neck, his whispers of love in her ears. How wonderful to be the one who gave him children. Her mind easily supplied the image of a plump baby. Their baby. A boy as strong as Darius, or a girl as intense and focused.

"You saw the violence of my past," he said, mistaking her silence. "You know the things I've done and can guess the things I will do. I'm asking you to accept me regardless. If you can do this, I will give you my life, my riches and my vow to always protect you." The last words left his lips with all the desperation inside him. With all the longing. With all the need.

Her expression softened; her lashes dipped to half-mast. "I don't need your riches," she said. "Only you."

At her words, the possessiveness Darius had always felt for Grace raged to the surface. Raw, primal arousal burned inside him, hotter than ever before. Everything inside him cried for her. Not just part of her, but her entire essence.

He joined their hands, palm to palm.

Not pausing for a moment, lest she change her mind, he uttered, "To you I belong. My heart beats only for you." He held her gaze with the strength of his own. "No other will tempt me, from this day and beyond. To you I belong."

As he spoke, the places where his body touched hers warmed, became blistering, and a strange swirling unfurled in the pit of Grace's stomach, sweeping through her from head to toe.

"Say the words back to me," he intoned harshly.

Yes. *Yes.* "To you I belong. My heart beats only for you." As she spoke, he inched his lips closer to hers. "No other will tempt me, from this day and beyond. To you I belong."

The moment the last word left her mouth, he fit his lips directly over hers. She cried out, and he caught the sound. His eyes tightly closed as his entire body clenched and bowed.

A part of her soul ripped out of her body and into his. Instantly the void filled with his essence, sweeping through her like wildfire. The exchange was powerful, wholly erotic. Her stomach heated and tingled, and she lay there, panting. The fine hairs on her body clamored for him.

"What happened?" she asked between breaths.

"Our joining."

No more needed to be said because she understood. They were joined, not physically—not yet— but joined in a way that was even more tangible. Undeniable. She didn't understand the implications or mechanics of it. They were not two separate entities. They were one. She'd needed him before, but now she would die without him. She sensed it, knew it in the deepest part of her being.

"I am nothing without you," he said, echoing her thoughts. "Do you feel how much I hunger for you?"

She did. God, she did. His hunger mingled with her own, purring within her veins.

"You are more important to me than air," he said. "More important than water. You, Grace, are my only necessity."

"I love you," she said, at last giving him the words in her heart. As she spoke, the contentment that had always remained elusively out of reach was suddenly there and hers for the taking. So grasp it she did, holding Darius closer. He encompassed everything missing from her life: danger, excitement, passion.

Fire flashed in his eyes. Reaching back, he peeled his shirt over his head. "I'm going to give you everything you crave, sweet Grace." His lips lifted in a fleeting smile. "Everything."

Anticipation shivered through her. She threaded her palms up the strength of his chest, over his ribs and nipples, over his tattoos. He sucked in a breath. His tattoos were slightly faded, not as red and angry as before, but still there. Still sexy and warm. Her mouth watered for a taste of them, and she rolled him onto his back. Leaning down, she licked a path along the colorful dragon wings, savoring the salty taste. His muscles jumped at the first stroke of her tongue.

He slithered his hand between her legs and played; the fabric of her jeans created a dizzying friction. She moaned, arched her neck, and became lost in the breathtakingly sensual caress. Everything within her sprang to life, even places she hadn't known existed, starved for more of his attentions. She ached to be filled. By Darius. Only Darius.

He claimed he had done horrible things, but deep down she hungered for that fiercest part of him. For the wildness. The danger. She might have tried to deny it upon occasion, but she'd always known the truth. He was her every fantasy; his presence alone offered her more excitement than any challenge or adventure. When she was with him, she felt whole. She felt alive.

She felt vital.

"I want you naked." Darius didn't wait for her response, couldn't. Impatient for her as always, he did exactly what he'd done before. He gripped the neck of her shirt and ripped. Underneath he found lacy green fabric, her sexy belly ring and a light outline of a dragon tattoo.

He traced the edges with his fingertip. "Look," he told her.

Lost in sensation as she was, a moment passed before she obeyed. When she did, she gasped. "What the— I don't understand. I have a tattoo." Shock dripped from her tone, and her stunned gaze went from the tattoo, to him, to the tattoo. "I've never gotten a tattoo in my life."

"You bear my mark," he said, rolling them over once again and easing her down. "I am a part of you forever."

He tore the green material in half, just as he'd done to her shirt. Her breasts were lush and lovely, and the sight of them made him tremble. Tremble like a boy. He palmed one then the other, loving the way her eyes closed and her back arched, a silent entreaty for him to continue. He moved down her body and sucked a nipple into the hotness of his mouth. She gasped his name like a reverent prayer.

He sucked harder.

"Oh, God," she groaned.

Her knees clenched around his waist; her hands gripped his hair. He continued to knead one glorious breast, abrading the pearled nipple between his fingers while he laved and sucked the other. Like raspberries, they were, pink and rosy, sweet and delicate. One of his hands gravitated to her belly, fingering the delicate silver loop.

Losing control of his resolve to go slow, he teased himself between her legs. She moved wantonly against him, then with him. When she was gasping, begging, he jerked at her shoes, then her pants, tugging them down and kicking them from her ankles with his foot. The sight of her, lying under him in only a pair of lacy emerald panties, nearly made his heart stop. Such beauty. *His* beauty.

He drove his fingers past the delicate lace and found the silken heat of her. She was wet and hot. Ready. But he wanted her beyond ready. He wanted her desperate. Using the tip of one finger, he smoothed her moisture over her soft folds, gently grazing the center of her desire.

"Yes," she said, curving into his touch. "Yes. Touch me there."

"You need to be filled, Grace."

"Yes. Please."

He slowly sank one finger inside her, then another. "Are you ready for more?" A bead of sweat trickled down his temple. He bit her neck, making a small sting, then he licked it away as he thrust those fingers in a delicious rhythm.

She cried out and lifted her hips. His shaft strained for her, but he worked another finger inside her. How he loved the feel of her tightness. Her moist heat.

Soft, mewling sounds escaped her lips when he circled his thumb around her clitoris.

"I'm ready," she said. "I promise I'm ready."

With a growl, he latched on to her mouth and drank from her. He didn't deserve her, but the gods had given her to him and he was going to do everything within his power to make her happy. She would never regret giving herself to him.

"I want to kiss you here," he said, again circling his thumb around the very heart of her wetness.

Her eyes closed in surrender. As generous as she was, his Grace wasn't content to take pleasure only for herself; she insisted on returning it. "I...want to kiss...you here," she said, between panting breaths, slipping her own hand between them and cupping the long, thick length of him. "Who gets to go first?"

Those beads of sweat grew into a fine sheen over his entire body. She craved excitement, he thought, and so he would give it to her. "We will both go first."

Her tongue shot out and traced her own lips, taking in the residual taste of himself he'd left behind. "Really? How?"

In a total of two seconds, he removed his pants, then her panties, leaving them both completely naked. He gathered her into his arms and settled on his back, placing her on top. He'd never given a woman a chance to take him in her mouth. Picturing Grace's red curls spilled across his abdomen, over his thighs and cock, picturing her teeth grazing his length and her mouth sucking him deeply, nearly made him come.

"Straddle me," he said, surprised he still possessed a voice. His need pounded through his veins. "Do not face me. Face the other direction."

Her nipples pebbled further, and she gazed down at him with an expression of utter longing. Slowly she did as he instructed. Her back was long and slender and perfectly proportioned. He caressed a fingertip down each vertebra, and tiny bumps of pleasure appeared on her skin.

He clasped her hips, tugged, scooting her closer and closer to his waiting mouth.

"Now lean over," he instructed.

Languidly sensual, she moved her mouth toward his thick erection. Her warm breath fanned his heavy testicles as he lifted his head and licked into her slick heat.

At that first contact, Grace screamed her pleasure. Not an orgasm, but close. So close. Her hands clenched Darius's hips. He continued to lave her, and she inched the thick length of him into her mouth—and almost screamed again. The eroticism of having his shaft nestled in her mouth while Darius tasted her very essence proved earth-shattering.

"This is what I meant when I said I wanted to eat you," he rumbled, the vibrations resonating into her.

His words and actions combined, bringing her swiftly to a torturing climax. Her body jerked and quivered as a thousand lights sparked past her mind. Pleasure, so much pleasure. She tore her lips from him as his name ripped past her throat. "Darius, Darius, Darius." The heat of it branded.

When her climax faded, she should have been sated, completely fulfilled. But she wasn't. She wanted him buried deep inside her, so deep he'd leave his mark on her for days.

Desperate, Darius lifted her and spun her toward him. He tumbled her over and gazed down at her. "Now?" The word emerged hoarse and eager. Frantic. He needed to be inside her.

She spread her legs wide, fitting his hard length where it belonged, almost—but not quite—at the sweet edge of penetration. "I'll always be ready for you."

"You're my woman. Say it."

"I'm yours. Now. Always."

"And I am yours." He slanted his mouth over hers at the same moment he impaled her. He cried out at the joy of it, the heady bliss, his enjoyment so intense his wings burst unbidden from his back, stroking a heated draft over their bodies. Those majestic wings stayed suspended in the air for a breathless moment, two deceptively sheer extensions that at last lowered, surrounding him and Grace in an iridescent cocoon.

Shocked, he stared down at her. Her eyes were closed, and her lips pressed together. Instead of a pained cry, she murmured in surrender.

For Grace, the sharp pain of virginity left as suddenly as it appeared, leaving only the thickness of him. The hardness.

"You are…this is…I am your first lover," he said, when the realization struck him. "Only lover." A possessiveness more potent than orgasm shuddered through her.

"Don't stop," she said. "Mmm. You feel so good."

"Your only mate," he said with awe. He moved slowly at first, but that wasn't enough for her. She gripped his hips, raised her own and ground herself into him. He needed no more encouragement. He clasped her bottom and pumped into her, over and over, again and again.

He rode her hard, unable to slow. His kisses grew fervent, plunging in sync with his powerful thrusts. Exquisite tension held her in its grasp, held tighter, tighter, then suddenly exploded, gifting her with the most shattering gratification she'd ever experienced. She shuddered with it, gasped and screamed with it.

"By the gods, you are sweet," he said through clenched teeth. Anchoring her legs atop his shoulders and sending him deeper inside her, he quickened his strokes further and joined her, chanting her name.

Unexpectedly she climaxed again.

DARIUS CARRIED GRACE to bed and neither of them rose for several hours.

He wanted to spend the rest of his life right here in her arms, her plump backside nestled against him, but knew that wasn't meant to be.

Midnight had settled over the land.

Moonlight crept through the windows, its silvery fingers intertwining with darkness. The city pulsed with life, even at this later hour. Time to leave. Still...

He allowed himself a few more minutes of quiet luxury, of holding Grace in the protective shield of his embrace. Her intoxicating scent surrounded him, and her warmth seeped into his bones. Virgin. She had been virgin. This beautiful, sensuous creature had given him what she'd given no other man.

She was a treasure more rich and satisfying than any other. He would protect her with his life.

"Darius?" she sighed, snuggling closer.

"Hmm?"

"Are we married? I mean, we didn't sign anything or—"

"We are joined. Never think otherwise."

"I'm glad." She eased up on her elbow and offered him a satisfied smile.

"As am I," he said.

"What we did—I don't think there's even a word to describe the bliss."

He nipped the softness of her shoulder with his teeth. "I meant to go slowly, wife, meant to savor you."

Her eyelids fluttered down. "Say it again."

"I meant to go—"

"No. The part where you called me your wife."

His arms tightened around her. "We belong together, wife."

She rolled onto her side and faced him. "Just so you know, I happened to like it the way you gave it to me, *husband*."

His cock should not have stirred for hours— perhaps days—but as he looked at her and basked in her words, need unfurled through him. If they did not get up, he would take her again, and he knew he wouldn't have the strength to leave afterward.

"Get dressed," he said, patting her bottom. "Time for us to visit Jason Graves."

Grace lost her dazed expression. The sensual reprieve ended as real life intruded. She lumbered to her feet and stumbled to her bathroom. Wincing at the soreness of her body, she took a quick shower and slipped on a pair of black pants and a matching black, short-sleeved shirt.

When she glanced up, Darius stood in the bathroom doorway, watching her through intense, golden eyes. Golden eyes! Her pulse fluttered in time with a single thought: *he is my husband!* His pants hung low on his waist, giving him a sexy, rakish air. She found herself taking a step toward him, intent on slipping her fingers beneath the black material and—she stopped that line of thought before it was too late. Before she lost herself in him.

He didn't appear aroused in any way. He looked…pained, like that strange weakness afflicted him again. Proud as he was, he didn't say a word.

"Come with me," she said. She led him into the kitchen. There, she hurriedly fixed him a sandwich, and once he finished eating, he leaned back in his chair. He looked the same. Why hadn't that helped? She frowned and took his hand, meaning to gauge his temperature. But as she held his palm in hers, his color returned. It wasn't food that strengthened him, she realized, but her. Her touch.

"You have to tell me what's going on," she said, holding his gaze and retaining her grip on his hand. "What causes your illness?" When he remained silent, she persisted. "Tell me."

He sighed. "When the gods banished us to Atlantis, they bound us irrevocably to the land. Those that try to leave, die."

Her stomach twisted, and her body went cold. If staying here meant his death, she wanted him gone. "You have to go home. Now." She allowed all of her concern, all of her anguish at the thought of his demise, to seep into her voice.

"I will return in the morning as planned."

"I'll search Jason's home on my own, then fly to Brazil. I can be in Atlantis in two days."

"No. On both counts."

"But—"

"No, Grace."

She had to convince him to leave. But how? She released him and began clearing away the dishes, keeping her back to him. In seconds, he was directly behind her, holding her captive between his arms.

"You are upset," he said.

She paused, saying, "I'm scared for you. I'm scared for Alex. I want this to be over."

An undercurrent of menace suffused his voice when he said, "Soon. Very soon."

CHAPTER NINETEEN

BRIGHT NEON LIGHTS blazed from nearby buildings. Grace sucked in a deep breath as her gaze darted left and right. *I'm a criminal. I'm breaking and entering— or committing a B and E as the arresting officer would say.* She pursed her lips together and fought a shiver. She'd never admit this aloud, but hidden beneath her nervousness surged an intense adrenaline rush.

She and Darius stood outside Jason's swanky apartment building. A slight breeze drifted past, cooling her heated skin. She pressed her back to the brownstone, and cast another glance to her right. Unfortunately Darius couldn't magically teleport them inside. He had to visualize a room first, and he'd never been inside Jason's. She wondered, though, how he planned to get them in undetected.

"What if we set off the alarms?" she asked softly. Did the people strolling the streets suspect the truth? She was wearing all black, after all. Criminal colors.

"We will not," Darius answered confidently.

"Security guards observe screens of every corridor, maybe every room."

"That does not matter. I will cast a spell to guard

us before we set a single foot inside." He leveled her with an intense stare. "Are you ready?"

She gulped, nodded.

"Put your arms around my neck and hold tight."

After only a slight hesitation, Grace intertwined her shaky fingers around his neck, pressing her breasts into the hardness of his chest. Tingles raced through her nipples. "We could get into serious trouble for this," she said. "I don't know why I suggested it."

He grazed her lips with his own. "Because you love your brother."

Ripping fabric drifted to her ears a split second before Darius's shirt fell to the ground. His long, glorious wings unfurled. Her heartbeat galloped as her feet lost their solid anchor on the ground. *Whoosh. Whoosh.* A cool breeze stirred.

"What's happening?" she gasped, but she knew the answer. "Darius, this is—"

"Do not panic," he said, his grip on her tightening. "I have not forgotten how to fly. All you need do is hang on to me."

"I'm not panicked." She laughed. "I'm exhilarated. We're flying on the Darius Express." They moved quickly, smoothly, higher with every second that passed.

He uttered a chuckle of his own and shook his head. "I expected fear from you. Will you ever cease to amaze me, sweet Grace?"

"I hope not." She looked down, loving how the cars and people appeared like small specks, loving the giddiness of hovering in the air.

The moon loomed closer and larger, growing in intensity until she could only gape at its luminance. Darius chanted under his breath, and a strange vibration unfurled from him, a vibration that began as nothing more than a slight tremble, then grew into an intense shaking through the entire apartment building. No one below seemed to notice.

The shaking stopped.

"We are safe now," he said.

She didn't ask how exactly since they had reached Jason's upper balcony. As his wings glided them slowly forward, Darius set her firmly on the ground. The action drew a grunt from him, and she glanced up at his face. His cheekbones stretched taut and lacked any color. He kept his gaze from her as he drew in a shaky breath.

"You're weak again," she said, concerned. "Perhaps you should go home and—"

"I am fine." Irritation—with her or himself?—lashed from his tone.

She gulped, determined to get him out of here as quickly as possible. "Let's hurry, then."

White gauzy drapes billowed around the French double doors. Grace brushed them aside and tried the knob. Locked. "Do you know how to pick these?"

"No need." Darius ushered her aside, positioned himself in front of the doors and spewed rays of fire. The wood around the glass panels quickly charred. The tinkle of glass erupted as the panels fell and hit the ground.

"Thank you." Stepping over the jagged pieces,

Grace waved her hand in front of her nose to whisk away the smoke. Unabashedly she entered Jason Graves's home. "It's so dark," she whispered.

"Your eyes will adjust." He didn't use a breaking-and-entering voice. He used a why-are-you-whisper-ing-you-silly-woman voice.

Even as he spoke, her vision opened and objects became clear. A chaise longue, a glass coffee table. "What about motion sensors and security cameras?" she asked. "Are we one hundred percent protected from those?"

"Yes. The spell disabled them."

Allowing herself to relax, she padded throughout the living room, tracing her fingertips over the paint-ings and jewels—yes, jewels—hanging on the walls. "So much wealth," she said. "And none of it belongs to him. It's like we've stepped through the mist and into Atlantis."

Darius remained at the threshold, his teeth bared in a red-hot snarl as he took in the stolen Atlantean artifacts.

"I know you're a child of the gods," she said, hoping to distract him from his fury, "but you're not technically a god. Where does your magic come from?"

"My father," he said, losing his infuriated edge. He entered, his steps clipped. "He practiced the ancient arts."

The image of his parents' lifeless bodies flashed in her mind again, exactly as she'd seen them in her vision when he'd cast his binding spell. She ached for the little boy he'd been, the child who'd found his family slain. She couldn't imagine the pain he must have suffered—and still suffered.

"I'm sorry for their deaths," she told him, letting her remorse and sorrow seep out with the words. "Your loss of family."

Darius stilled and glanced over at her. "How did you know they were…gone?"

"I saw them. In your mind. When you cast the binding spell."

His shoulders straightened, and surprise flashed through his eyes. "They were my life," he said.

"I know," she said softly, aching for him.

"Perhaps one day I will tell you of them." The offer emerged hesitant, but there all the same.

"I would love that."

He nodded, a little stiff. "Right now, we must search for any information this Jason has about Atlantis and your brother."

"I'll check the library for the *Book of Ra-Dracus.*" She looked around. "I'm willing to bet *he's* the one who stole it from my brother."

"I will search the rest of the home."

With a last, lingering glance, they branched off. The floors were polished mahogany panels, and the decor something out of a medieval home and garden magazine. Upstairs, Grace quickly found the study. Piles of books littered every corner, and some appeared old and well used. She flipped through each one, finding references to dragons and liquid nitrogen, magic spells and vampires, but none were the *Book of Ra-Dracus*. A large walnut desk consumed the center and a world globe made completely of…what was that? Some sort of jewel, perhaps? Purple, like an amethyst, but jagged like crystal. She studied it more closely. In the center, a waterfall churned around a single body of land. Around Atlantis. And a pulsing sapphire.

Though she wanted to study it more closely, she forced herself on the matter at hand. She moved toward the desk and shuffled through the papers on top. Finding nothing of importance, she withdrew a letter opener and, after struggling for several minutes, pried open the drawer locks. Inside the bottom drawer, she discovered photos that shocked and repelled her. She covered her mouth to muffle her horrified gasp. The graphic images depicted dragon and human warriors covered in a white foam, blood flowing from multiple bullet wounds. Some showed Alex and Teira. The two were lying in a jewel-encrusted cell, dirty but alive. Several held grotesque imprints of tall, pale creatures with eerie blue eyes feasting off the dragon bodies. The humans standing off to the side watched, their expressions a mix of fear, disgust, and titillation.

Why take photos of his crimes? As a memento? To prove the existence of Atlantis? Or did he hope to write a book, *How I Like to Kill?* She scowled.

She replayed the vision of her brother that Darius's medallion had supplied. This room wasn't the one Alex first occupied. This was a different room, one she knew resided in Atlantis. Those jeweled walls were very similar to what she'd seen inside Darius's home. When her husband returned to his home, she thought, more determined now than before, she was going with him.

Perhaps Darius sensed her growing disquiet, because the next thing she knew, he stood over her.

"What do you—" He paused, then very slowly, very precisely, reached over her shoulder and slipped the photos from her hands. She tried to pry them from him because she didn't want him to see the travesties done to his friends. He held tightly. "This is Javar and his men. And these are vampires."

Vampires. She shuddered. Having proof of their actual existence settled like lead in her stomach.

"I'm so sorry," she said, turning to face him. His eyes narrowed, but even from those tiny slits she could see their color glowed ice-blue. Fragments of grief radiated from him and into her.

"What else is in there?" He set the photos aside with one fluid motion, a deceptively calm motion.

Allowing him to change the subject, she said, "That's it. Did you find anything?"

"More artifacts from Atlantis." Radiating cold determination, he clasped her hand. "Jason Graves deserves so much more than death. He deserves to suffer."

Another shudder worked through her, because she knew he would do everything in his power to see that Jason got exactly what he deserved.

And she planned to help him.

GRACE WANTED TO BANG her head against the wall.

She and Darius arrived home several hours ago, yet he still remained rigid with tension. He refused to speak. She hated this, hated the remorse radiating from him.

He sat on the couch, his head back, his eyes closed. Not knowing what else to do, she quietly approached. "I want to show you something."

His eyelids reluctantly opened. When he offered no reply and made no move to rise, she added, "Pretty please with a cherry on top."

Not a single word left his lips, but he stood. Grace wrapped her fingers around his and ushered him into the bathroom. She didn't explain her actions; she simply removed his clothing, then her own. He was in need of loving—and she was going to give it to him. All the loving he could stand.

After turning the knobs and allowing the water to heat, she stepped inside the tub and tugged Darius in behind her. Still he remained silent. Hot water cascaded down their naked bodies, and as she stood in front of him, she lathered his chest with soap.

"I've got a joke for you," she said, mentally converting jokes she knew into dragon jokes.

He frowned—his first reaction. It didn't matter that he'd only given her a frown. She'd take anything she could get.

"What did the dragon say when he saw a knight in shining armor?"

His brow wrinkled, and he sighed.

"Oh, no, not another canned meal."

Slowly, so slowly, his lips inched up in a smile.

I did that, she thought with a surge of pride. *I made him smile.* She basked in the warmth of it and all the while his smile continued to grow. So sweet, so endearing, it lit his entire face. His eyes darkened, becoming that golden-brown she loved. He traced his fingertip over her cheekbone.

"Tell me another one," he said.

She nearly sank to her knees in relief at the sound of his rich, husky voice. Grinning happily, she slipped behind him and traced her soapy hands over his back. "It's long," she warned.

"Even better," he said, tugging her in front. He nibbled on her ear, dragging the sensitive lobe through his teeth.

"There was a dragon who had a long-standing obsession with a queen's breasts," she said, growing breathless. "The dragon knew the penalty to touch her would mean death, yet he revealed his secret desire to the king's chief doctor. This man promised he could arrange for the dragon to satisfy his desire, but it would cost him one thousand gold coins." She spread her soapy hands over his nipples, then down his arms. "Though he didn't have the money, the dragon readily agreed to the scheme."

"Grace," Darius moaned, his erection straining against her stomach.

She hid her smile, loving that she had this much power over such a strong man. That she, Grace Carlyle, made him ache with longing. "The next day the physician made a batch of itching powder and poured some into the queen's bra...uh, you might call it a brassiere...while she bathed. After she dressed, she began itching and itching and itching. The physician was summoned to the Royal Chambers, and he informed the king and queen that only a special saliva, if applied for several hours, would cure this type of itch. And only a dragon possessed this special saliva." Out of breath, she paused.

"Continue," Darius said. His arms wound around her so tightly she could barely breathe. His skin blazed hot against hers, hotter than even the steamy water.

"Are you sure?"

"Continue." Taut lines bracketed his mouth.

"Well, the king summoned the dragon. Meanwhile, the physician slipped him the antidote for the itching powder, which the dragon put into his mouth, and for the next few hours, the dragon worked passionately on the queen's breasts.

"Anyway," she said, reaching around him and lathering the muscled mounds of his butt, "the queen's itching was eventually relieved, and the dragon left satisfied and touted as a hero."

"This does not sound like a joke," Darius said.

"I'm getting to the punch line. Hang on. When the physician demanded his payment, the now satisfied dragon refused. He knew that the physician could never report what really happened to the king. So the next day, the physician slipped a massive dose of the same itching powder into the king's loincloth. And the king immediately summoned the dragon."

Darius threw back his head and barked with laughter. The sound boomed raw and new, and she fell deeper in love with him at that moment. She'd never heard anything so precious because she knew how rare such amusement was for him. She hoped he found such joy every day they spent together.

When his laughter subsided, a sensual light glowed in his eyes. His features were so relaxed, so open. "I'm intrigued by this breast feasting," he whispered, rubbing his nose against hers.

"I am, too," she admitted. "I have an itch."

"Allow me to help you." He pressed his lips to hers in a lazy, delicious kiss. His fiery flavor, his heat, his masculinity, still managed to enthrall her. Need and desperation wrapped around every inch of her body, and she threaded her wet hands around his neck.

His palms caressed a slippery path down her spine and stopped at the small indentation at the base. When those scorching fingers dipped lower, cupped and pulled her tightly against him, she sucked in an eager breath. She pressed her lower half into him, cradling his erection. Her nerve endings were alive with the memories of making love, and longed to repeat the experience.

"I'm going to have you again," he said.

"Yes, yes."

"Tell me you want me."

"I do. I want you."

"Tell me you need me."

"So much I'll die without you."

"Tell me you love me."

"I do. I love you."

She was living passion in his arms, Darius thought, and she was all his.

"Kiss me. And don't ever stop kissing me," she said.

He did more than kiss her. He gifted her with sweet nips and erotic licks, then proceeded to suck every drop of water from her body. He invaded her senses until all she could see, all she could feel, all she could taste was him. She shivered when the tip of his tongue swirled along the edge of her ear.

Suddenly he paused. A slow, suspended moment dragged by. "Help me forget the past," he whispered brokenly.

She nuzzled his neck and dipped her hand over his ridged abdomen. When she clasped his thick erection, he hissed in a breath. She didn't hold him long, just long enough to stroke him up and down. Then she released him, granting him one last fleeting, teasing caress before cupping the heavy sac of his testicles.

While her fingers gently tugged, she swirled her tongue around his nipples. They felt like little spikes in her mouth, and she lapped at the masculine taste of him mingled with the water.

"How am I doing so far?"

"I need more time to decide," he said roughly, raggedly. His fingers tangled in her hair, then massaged her neck…her breasts.

The sight of his strong, bronze hands on her soft,

white flesh proved the most erotic thing she'd ever seen. Once more she curled her fingers around his length. He was so hot and big, so hard. Up and down, she tormented him. She wanted so badly to fill his days with happiness, to help him "forget" his pain, as he'd said. No, not forget, but heal. She would do whatever was necessary to give him the peace he craved.

"What's your naughtiest fantasy?" she murmured against his collarbone. She bit down, not hard enough to break the skin, but hard enough to leave her mark. "Perhaps I can make it come true."

"You are my fantasy, Grace." His hands cupped her jaw, and he forced her to look up at him. "Only you."

If she hadn't already loved him, she would have fallen just then. "I have a fantasy," she whispered. She licked the seam of his lips. "Want to hear?"

He trailed his hands down her back, making her shiver, then cupped her bottom and jerked her into him for deeper contact. "Tell me."

"Well, I like to read books about big, strong warriors who love as fiercely as they fight, and I've always wanted one for my very own."

His lips twitched. "Now you have one."

"Oh, yes." The warm water made their skin slick and she rubbed against him, letting the peaks of her nipples abrade his chest, letting the plump head of his penis catch between her legs. "What I fantasize about is my big, strong warrior lifting me up, pressing my back into the shower tile and filling me."

He pressed her back against the cool tile and shoved inside her, deep and hard and scorching. Steam billowed around them, but it was the spicy scent of dragon and soap that filled her nostrils. He felt so good inside her, more exciting than climbing a mountain or bungee jumping from a bridge.

He pumped in and out of her, and she wound her arms around him. His strength beneath her palms filled her with heady power. He bit her neck, making her shiver. He spread her knees wider and pounded harder. She panted his name. Moaned his name. Gasped his name.

"Grace," he growled. "Mine."

And she was. Completely.

DARIUS HELD A SLEEPING Grace in the tight clasp of his arms.

She possessed inner strength, a giving heart and a deep capacity for love. Her smile gleamed brighter than the sun. Her laughter healed him. Actually *healed* him.

As he lay in the stillness of the night, with hazy moonlight enveloping him, he remained weak and sated from their loving. Long forgotten memories finally resurfaced, bits and pieces of his past, pieces he'd thought buried so deeply they'd remain lost forever. He didn't fight them, but closed his eyes, saw his mother laugh down at him, her smile as gentle and beautiful as the pristine waters that surrounded their city. Her golden eyes flashed merrily.

She had caught him with his father's sword,

brandishing the weapon through the air with a dramatic flourish, trying to mimic the warrior strength his father possessed.

"One day," she said in that sweet, lyrical voice of hers, "your strength will far surpass that of your father." She claimed the sword from him and leaned the gleaming silver against the nearest wall. "You will fight beside him and protect each other from harm."

That day never came.

He saw his father, strong and proud and loyal, striding up the cliff that led to their home. He'd just come from a battle with the Formorians, had washed away the blood on his skin, but his clothing still bore traces. When he spied him, his father smiled and opened his arms. Seven-year-old Darius ran to him and threw himself into the waiting embrace.

"I've been gone only three weeks, but look how you've grown," his father said, squeezing him tightly. "Gods, I missed you."

"I missed you, too." He fought back a tear.

His strong, warrior father wiped the moisture from his own eyes. "Come on, son. Let's go greet your mother and sisters."

Together, they walked side by side into the small house. His three sisters danced around a fire, laughing and chanting, their long dark hair bouncing about their shoulders. They each possessed identical features, plump cheeks and such innocence it hurt to gaze at them.

"Darius," they called when they saw him, running

to him first, though they'd seen him only a few hours ago. They shared a special bond with him that he could not explain. It had always been there, and would always remain.

He hugged them close, drawing in the sweetness of their scents. "Father has returned. Give him a proper greeting."

Their faces lit with their grins and they propelled themselves at the warrior.

"My precious hatchlings," he said, laughing through more tears.

Their mother heard their mingled joy and rushed inside the chamber. They spent the rest of the day together, not a single member of the family straying far.

How happy they'd been.

Here, in the present, a lone tear slid from the corner of Darius's eye. He did not wipe it away, but allowed it to trickle down his cheek and onto his ear.

As tuned to him as she was, Grace sensed his torment. She shifted to face him, her features alight with concern. "Darius?" she said softly. "It's okay. Whatever it is, it will be okay."

Another tear came, then another. He couldn't stop them, and wasn't sure he wanted to. "I miss them," he said brokenly. "They were my life."

She understood immediately. "Tell me about them. Tell me the good things."

"My sisters were like sunlight, starlight and moonlight." Their images filled his mind once again, and this time he nearly choked from pain. And yet…the pain was not the fearsome destroyer he had expected, but a reminder that he lived and loved. "Every night they created a small fire and would dance around the flames. They were so proud of their ability and were determined to one day create the biggest fire Atlantis had ever seen."

"They didn't fear being burned?"

"Dragons welcome and thrive in such heat. I wish you could have seen them. They were all that is good and right."

"What were their names?" she asked softly.

"Katha, Kandace and Kallia," he said. With an animalistic growl, he slammed his fist into the side of the mattress. "Why did they have to die? Travelers tortured and killed my sisters as if they were garbage."

Grace wrapped her arms around him and laid her head in the hollow of his neck. There was nothing she could say to ease his anguish, so she held him more tightly.

He rubbed at his stinging eyes. "They did not deserve such a death. They did not deserve what they suffered."

"I know, I know," she cooed.

He buried his face in the hollow of her neck and cried.

At last, Darius mourned.

CHAPTER TWENTY

GRACE RIFFLED THROUGH the box of Kevlar vests she'd picked up downstairs. Darius knelt on the other side and pinched one of the heavy black vests between his fingers. His lips curled with distaste.

She watched him. His eyes shone with vitality, alive with gold, glistening with contentment. They had been like that since last night and hadn't changed. Hadn't even flickered with blue. The fine lines around his eyes and mouth had relaxed, as well, and there was an ease about him that warmed her heart. Oh, he still possessed that dangerous aura. Danger would always be a part of him. But the coldness, the hopelessness, were both gone.

How she loved this man.

"Try one on," she said.

Frowning, he tugged the material over his shoulders. She leaned over and worked the Velcro for him. "It's too tight," he said.

"If a bullet smacks into you, you'll wish it was even tighter."

He snorted. "How can these do any good?"

"Maybe you'll understand better after I show you

how to use a gun." She raced to her kitchen and dug out the gun she'd stuffed into one of the drawers. She doubled-checked to make sure no bullets rested in the cylinder.

"This is a revolver," she explained when she stood behind Darius. Wrapping her arms around him, she placed the cold metal in his hands and curled his fingers in the correct places. "Hold it just like this."

His shaking fingers squeezed.

"Gently," she said, noticing how unsteady he suddenly seemed.

He tossed her a glance over his shoulder. "Who taught you these skills?"

"Alex. He said a woman should know how to protect herself." Fighting a wave of sadness, Grace steadied Darius's wrists by locking her palms underneath them. He might be more relaxed and at ease than ever before, but he battled that damn weakness and she didn't like it. The only time he seemed to recover his full strength was when he was sexually excited.

Grace wet her lips and purposefully meshed her breasts into the hard ridges of his back. "You want to keep your finger on the trigger and pick a target. Any target. Do you have one?"

"Oh, yes." His voice grew stronger and deeper. If she allowed her hands to slide inside his pants, she knew she would find him hard and thick.

"Good," she said. "Aim down the sight on the barrel."

Pause. Then, "What?"

She blew on his neck. "Aim down the sight on the barrel," she repeated.

Another pause. "How can I concentrate when your body is pressed to mine?"

In response, her fingers tickled up his arms. If sexual arousal kept him strong, she'd use everything in her power to arouse him. "Do you want to learn how to shoot or not?" she whispered huskily.

"I do," he ground out.

"Is your target in sight?"

He felt the heat of her, Darius thought, the sizzle of her, throughout his entire body. Yes, he had his target in sight. The couch. Exactly where he wanted her, naked and open.

He flicked a glance to the window. The sun arrived hours ago, vanquishing the binding spell. He should have left for his homeland. He possessed everything he needed from the surface. Atlantis called him, and it was long past time he destroyed her invaders.

But he wasn't ready to say goodbye to Grace.

He couldn't take her with him. She would be safest here, and her safety mattered more to him than anything else.

When this whole mess with the Argonauts ended, he would come back for her. He would whisk this woman, *his* woman, his *wife*—gods, he liked the sound of that—to Atlantis. They were going to stay in bed for days, weeks, perhaps months, and they were going to make love every way possible, then invent some new ways.

"Target in sight," he said.

"Squeeze the trigger," she said.

He easily recalled how she had squeezed him. How her inquisitive fingers had slipped beneath the hem of his shirt and skimmed the taut flesh of his lower abdomen. He ground his teeth together.

"Darius?"

"Hmm?" he bit out.

"Squeeze the trigger." She blew in his ear.

He squeezed. He heard a *click*.

"If the couch were human, and this a loaded gun, a bullet would have shot out and punctured skin, causing grave injury," Grace the temptress said. The woman who had sneaked past his defenses and infiltrated his senses. The woman who had captured his heart. "The lining inside these vests stops bullets and keeps them from entering bodies."

Darius spun, keeping her arms locked around him. The gun fell from his hands. He wrapped his fingers around her wrists and directed her aim lower.

"I have another target in mind," he said. And he kept his "target" busy for the next hour.

SATED AND REDRESSED, Grace tucked her gun in the waist of her jeans, filled her pockets with bullets and helped Darius gather the remaining vests. With that done, they squared off, facing each other. Neither moved.

"It's time to go," he finally said.

"I'm ready," she said with false confidence. She

raised her chin, not removing her gaze from him, but daring him to contradict her.

He regarded her silently for an inexorable moment, his expression blank. "You will remain here, Grace."

She bit back a scowl. She'd known he would do this, but knowing didn't stop the anger, the hurt. "Wrong," she said. "Alex is my brother, and I'll help find him."

"Your safety comes first."

"I'm safest with you." Her eyes narrowed, showing him the first sign of her increasing ire. "Besides, I'm your wife. Where you go, I go."

"I'll return for you and bring back your brother."

She gripped his shirt, tugging him close. "I can help you, and we both know it."

Pain flashed in his eyes, but was quickly overshadowed by determination. "This is the only way. I must lead my dragons into war, and I will not allow my woman near battlegrounds."

"What about the binding spell?" Ha! She watched him with almost smug expectation. "I can't leave your presence."

"The spell broke when the moon disappeared."

Her shoulders dropped. She racked her brain, searching for anything, anything at all, that might change his mind. When the answer arose, she smiled slowly. "Perhaps you're forgetting the Argonauts. That they had me followed."

Arching a brow, he crossed his arms over his chest. "What are you saying?"

"They could have me followed again. They

could try to hurt me this time, instead of simply watching me."

He stroked his jaw as he considered her words. "You are right," he admitted darkly.

She relaxed, thinking she finally convinced him of her point—until he next opened his mouth.

"I will simply lock you inside my palace."

Her earlier scowl broke free, and she poked him in the chest. "I like this macho thing you've got going on. I really do. But I won't stand for it."

Without a word he clasped her wrist with one hand and held the handle of the suitcase with the other. The air around them began to swirl. Bright-colored sparks flickered like dying lightbulbs, then quickly sped past them. The temperature never changed, the wind never kicked up, but suddenly the cave closed around her.

Grace didn't have time to catch her bearings. Never breaking his momentum, Darius pulled her inside the mist. The moment she realized exactly where she was, she threw herself in his arms.

"I've got you," he said.

His voice soothed her racing heartbeat. Only a minute or two passed before Darius unhooked her hands from his neck, gave her a quick kiss and ushered her into another cave.

Not even slightly dizzy, she cataloged her newest surroundings. A man—Brand, she recalled—stood off to the side. He held a sword above his head, and there was a deadly gleam in his eyes as he stared at her. Before she could utter a protest, Grace found herself shoved behind Darius.

"Brand," Darius barked.

At the sound of his voice, Brand's gaze finally flicked away from her. He glanced at Darius and relaxed. He even lowered his sword. "Why does the woman still live?" he demanded.

"Touch her and I will kill you."

"She is from the surface," he spat.

"She is my mate."

"She is—"

"My mate," he said firmly. "Therefore, she is one of us."

A childish part of Grace wanted to stick her tongue out at Brand. She hadn't forgotten that he'd once called her a whore.

Brand considered those words, and his fierce expression softened. He even grinned. "Tell me what you learned."

"Gather the others and meet me in the dining hall. I will tell you when I tell them."

Brand nodded, and with a final glance in her direction, he rushed off.

"I am glad to be home," Darius said. His strength had returned in its entirety the moment he'd stepped through the mist, and now he breathed deeply of its familiar essence. "I need you to demonstrate the gun and vests to my warriors."

She shook her head. "Not unless you're willing to compromise with me."

"I do not compromise." His tone was as stern as his expression. "Come."

She glared at him the entire way to the dining hall.

The dragon warriors were gathered around the table, standing with their arms locked behind their backs and their feet braced apart. When they spotted her, they each glanced to Brand who wore a smug, I-told-you-so frown. The youngest of the group offered her a smile, if you could call baring of teeth a smile. She waved nervously.

"Hi, again," she said.

Darius squeezed her hand. "Do not be scared," he told her, then glanced pointedly at each man present. "They will not muss a single hair on your head."

In the next instant, questions were hurled at Darius. "Why did you take a human for your mate? When? What happened while you were gone? What happened to Javar?"

"Give him a minute," Grace told them.

Darius smiled at her and tenderly kissed her lips.

Madox gasped. "Did you see that?"

"I did. I saw," Grayley said, awed.

"A human female has succeeded where we failed," Renard said. "She made Darius smile."

"I've made him laugh, too," she pronounced.

Darius rolled his eyes. "Show them what we have brought."

Despite his failure to compromise, she did as he asked. His safety, and that of his people, came before her sensibilities. "This is a Kevlar vest," she explained, demonstrating how to maneuver the Velcro fasteners.

"You must remain in human form to wear it," Darius said. "Your wings will be trapped by its wrappings. However, it will protect your chest against the enemies' weapons."

"I have a more important part I'd like to protect," Brittan said with a smile of his own.

A round of laughter followed.

"Now demonstrate the gun," Darius said.

Grace nodded and withdrew the gun from the waist of her pants. "This expels bullets, and those bullets cut through clothing and skin and bone, and sometimes lodge themselves inside the body. You can't see them, but they leave a hole and make the victim bleed. If you want to survive, you must dig them out."

Silence reigned as they considered her words and actions.

Each of the men wanted to view the gun. She once again double-checked to make sure she'd removed the bullets, then passed it around. "They come in many sizes, some much bigger than this, so be prepared."

After everyone viewed the weapon, Darius returned it to her. "Guns such as this were used to destroy Javar and his army."

Some warriors gasped. Some hissed. Some blinked in shock. "So they are dead?" Madox asked sharply.

Darius didn't flinch his gaze. "Yes. Both humans and vampires seized the palace."

Their fury became a palpable force, wrapping around each of them. "Why did you make us wait? Why did you not let us slaughter the vampires days ago," Tagart shouted.

"Had you approached them, you would be dead," he said flatly. "Vampires are already powerful, but aided as they are by the humans…"

Tagart had the grace to nod in acknowledgment.

"An entire dragon army wiped out," the tallest said, shaking his head. "It hardly seems possible."

"We will claim vengeance this day," Darius said. "We will reclaim Atlantis, our home. We go to war!"

Cheers of anticipation erupted.

"Gather what you need," Darius finished when the cheers died down. "We leave within the hour."

"Wait!" Grace called as the warriors shuffled out of the room. They paused and glanced back at her. "There's a man, a human with red hair. He's my brother. Keep him safe."

They looked to Darius. He nodded. "He is to be protected and brought to me."

The men filed out. All except Brand. He approached Darius's side. "The men need you to lead them. I will remain behind and guard the mist."

"Thank you," Darius said, and clapped him on the shoulder. "You are a true friend."

When they were alone, he turned to Grace. "Come," he said, an order he'd obviously become quite fond of.

She didn't protest as he led her to the entrance of his room. "Are you sure you don't want me to guard your back?" she said as he hustled her inside.

His golden eyes darkened. "I do not mind a woman going into battle. I mind *my* woman going into battle."

"Darius—"

"Grace." He closed the distance between them and meshed her lips with his. His tongue swept inside, conquering. She wound her arms around his neck, accepting him fully. Loving him completely. When he pulled away, they were both panting.

"Darius," she whispered again.

His heated gaze met hers. "I love you," he said.

Of all the times to give her those words!

"Tell me what I want to hear," he demanded.

"I love you, too," she sighed. "Here, take my gun."

He already had bullets.

He took it and gave her one final kiss. Without another word, he left her in his room. Alone. The doors slid firmly shut behind him, and Grace looked down at her hands. They were shaking, not from the lust that sluiced through her body; that was always there and would never go away. This time a gut-wrenching fear caused her tremors. Fear for Darius. For her brother.

She had thought about stealing a medallion, but had changed her mind at the last moment. Waiting here would be hard, but she would do it. For Darius. She would pray and she would plan, because one way or another vampires and Argonauts were going down. Hopefully, her men would not be harmed in the process. If they were…God help the citizens of Atlantis. Guns would be the least of their worries.

CHAPTER TWENTY-ONE

DARIUS STOOD in the forest, gazing down at the carnage before him. He'd flown here at lightning speed, only to learn the unit he'd sent to guard Javar's palace had been bested. They were covered in a white film and blood streamed from bullet wounds. Some were alive. Most were dead. His wings retracted and he dropped his vest. His hands curled into fists. Those humans *must* be stopped.

"Find the survivors," he called. Then he and the dragon warriors branched off, searching for the living.

He cursed under his breath as moans of pain filled his ears. How many more would die before this ended? Frowning, he strode over to Vorik, who lay prone and still. He knelt down.

Vorik's eyelids opened slowly and Darius pushed out a breath of relief that his man lived. He withdrew a sharp silver blade from his back scabbard and blew fire on the metal. When it cooled, he dug out the bullets just as Grace had shown him. Vorik grimaced and tried to pull away.

"Tell me of the attack," he said to distract him.

"Their weapons…" Vorik said, calming. "Strange."

Renard approached and crouched beside him just as Vorik fainted. "What happened to them?" He touched the white, dusty coating and jerked his hand away. "What is this cold substance that covers their bodies?"

Darius turned stark eyes in his friend's direction. "I do not know what it is. Don gloves if you must, but do as Grace advised and dig out the bullets."

The carnage reminded him of the day he'd found his family slaughtered, and as he worked, he had to bite back a groan. Had he not shared his pain with Grace, he might have collapsed from the weight of it now. With shaky hands he continued on to body after body. The dragon's recuperative blood helped them heal as soon as the small bullets were removed. If only Javar had known this, how many of his warriors could he have saved?

When he finished, Darius gazed down at his blood-soaked hands. He'd had blood on his hands before, and hadn't reacted. But this affected him. How much more blood would he wear before this day ended? He knew the answer: by the end of the day, blood would flow like a river. He only prayed the blood did not belong to his own forces, but his enemies.

He shoved to his feet, gripping the hilt of his blade. "We must reclaim what belongs to us," he shouted. "Who will fight with me?"

"I will." "Me," rang out. Every warrior standing wanted the chance to avenge the wrongs done.

"May the gods be with us," he said under his

breath. His wings sprang from his back. He swooped up his vest, gripping the black material and smearing it with blood. Using the strength in his legs, he pushed off the ground. The glide of his wings kept him in the air and moving higher, faster. His army followed behind him. He heard the rustle of their wings, felt the intensity of their determination.

Human guards roamed the top of Javar's palace. When they spotted Darius, they shouted, aimed and fired. In the air, he dodged the multiple rounds of bullets and spewed his own fire. His warriors did the same, burning the humans and their weapons. Then, one of his warriors grunted and was suddenly falling from the sky. He didn't see who it was, but continued breathing his fire.

A gong sounded, loud, high-pitched.

The humans atop the ledge didn't live long enough to hear it. Their scorched bodies withered into ash and floated on the breeze. Darius settled his feet on the jagged crystal. His wings retracted, and he quickly drew on his vest and fastened the straps. When his warriors were properly protected, as well, he met each of their stares one by one and waited for nods of readiness.

He withdrew a long, silver blade with one hand, the gun with the other, and approached the dome seam. Sensing his medallion, the two sides silently parted. He gazed down, but could not see anyone inside, surrounded as they were by a thick fog. He heard the shuffle of their panicked footsteps, however, and the murmur of their fear.

He would have preferred *flying* into the unknown, but the vest would not allow it.

He jumped.

His men quickly followed suit.

Down, down he fell. When his feet hit the ground, his entire body reverberated with the impact. He grunted and rolled.

Humans screamed and scrambled out of the way. Their shock delayed their reaction, and Darius used that to his advantage. He jolted to his feet, sword raised and struck his first victim. The human gurgled in pain, clutching his chest, then collapsed.

Behind him, his warriors fought valiantly. Breathing fire. Always breathing fire. He didn't pause, but advanced on his next target. A look of sheer terror contorted the young man's features when he realized Darius was coming for him. The man aimed a long black gun at Darius's chest and fired. One bullet after another slammed into Darius, causing only pinpricks of pain. He laughed. Eyes widening, the man dropped his gun and gripped a thick tube that rose from a red canister on his back. White foam sprayed out and over Darius's skin, so cold his blood hardened with ice crystals. His dark laughter increased.

A Guardian of the Mist welcomed cold. Was strengthened by it. He raised his own gun and fired, aiming for the head. The man's body spasmed, then sank lifeless at his feet.

The alarm grew louder, screeching in his ears and soon blending with the sound of gunshots. He winced at a sharp sting in his thigh, glanced down, and saw trickles of blood where a bullet had pierced. Never slowing, he rocked forward, using the momentum to slay an enemy with his blade.

Having destroyed every human within striking distance, he darted his gaze throughout the room, searching where to fight next. He watched through horror-filled eyes as Madox fell, his body covered in white foam, blood seeping from numerous wounds in his arms and legs. Darius emptied his gun of bullets, all of them slamming into a human many yards away.

He didn't know if his friend lived or died, and his stomach twisted. With a growl of pure rage, he raced forward and spewed a stream of fire, catching the last of the humans and igniting them like a bonfire. They did not dodge it fast enough. Their screams echoed from the walls, and the scent of burning flesh filled his nostrils. He tossed his gun to the ground.

The moans soon quieted and smoldering corpses littered the floor. With the battle over, he counted how many of his men still stood. Only three had fallen. He carried Madox outside and laid him on the ground. The others followed, some limping, some relatively unharmed. Renard rushed to his side and examined Madox, then helped remove the bullets.

"He'll live," Renard announced with relief.

Filled with his own relief, Darius gripped the dagger he held and sank the tip into one of the wounds on his leg. He grimaced. The bullets hurt more coming out than they had going in, but he welcomed the pain.

As he continued to work the knife in his other injuries, he realized he and his warriors reigned victorious. Yet…where was the sense of joy and accomplishment he should have had?

"What do we do next?" Renard asked, sitting down beside him.

"I do not know. Their leader, Jason, was not here," he fumed.

"How do you know?"

"The cowardly bastard is—" Darius did not finish his sentence. Something stirred in his soul, something dark, and he knew Grace was in danger. His blood curdled. He ripped off his medallion and held it in his hands. Because he couldn't call on Grace's image, he said, "Show me Jason Graves."

The twin eyes lit with glowing red beams. Jason's image formed in the middle. He was standing in front of Grace—who was chained to a wall. Vampires surrounded the two, eyeing Grace hungrily. She struggled against the chains. "What have you done with my brother?"

"I recaptured him and that dragon whore of his. And if you don't shut your mouth, I'll kill him while you watch," he said with an evil smile. "Mitch told me how protective Darius is of you. I wonder how much he's willing to give up for you."

"Leave him out of this," she spat, then pressed her lips together. Her face and clothes were dirty and her bottom lip was swollen. Darius's world darkened to one emotion: rage. It was a cold, calculated rage that wanted Jason's blood drenching his hands. They had sneaked into his home and taken her. They would pay.

He forced himself to study the rest of the vision, searching for clues as to where Grace was being held. When he saw Layel, king of vampires, he knew—and his fear for Grace grew in intensity.

The vision faded all too quickly.

He squeezed his fingers over the medallion. "Those who are well enough, come with me. We fly to meet the vampires. *Now.*"

Wings sprouted from his back, ripping away his vest. Every dragon still breathing unfurled his wings, as well. He experienced a moment of pride. These warriors were injured, but they remained faithfully by his side. They would fight—and die if they must.

THE VAMPIRE STRONGHOLD loomed on the horizon.

Black stone gave the large structure a haunted aura, casting shadows in every direction. Even the windows were blackened. No foliage grew here, for no living thing could thrive among the destruction and decay. Drained bodies hung from pikes, acting as a visual warning of the death that waited within, ready to strike.

Grace was inside.

Swallowing back his fear for her, Darius flew to the highest window and motioned for his warriors to do the same. The thin railing provided no ledge to stand upon, so he simply hovered there. A cold sweat covered his skin, and his teeth gnashed together. He was a man who liked to wait and study his enemy before attacking. But he couldn't—wouldn't—wait. Not this time. His warriors watched him, floating on silent wings. He couldn't see through the darkened glass, but could hear voices.

A woman's scream filled his ears. *Grace!*

He immediately gave the signal. Glass shattered as they propelled inside. Vampires hissed and humans aimed their guns. No longer protected by the vests, the dragons were vulnerable—and they knew it.

Darius pushed, shoved and sliced his way toward Grace. Careful not to burn her with his fire.

When she spied him, she struggled fruitlessly against her chains. "Darius," she called, her voice weak, hollow.

Jason Graves stood beside her, his expression one of shock and rage. Seeing Darius, the coward trained his gun on Grace's temple. Darius did not allow himself to look at his wife's face; he would have crumbled, and he had to stay strong. So it was then that he saw the blood oozing down her neck and onto her shirt.

"We both know I'm going to kill you this day," he told Jason, deceptively serene. "Your actions merely dictate whether you die quickly." His gaze narrowed. "Or whether I make you suffer endlessly."

Jason's hand shook as his gaze darted between Darius and the raging battle. Dragons breathed fire, scorching vampires and humans. Howls and shrieks blended together, creating a symphony of death. Sulfur coated the air.

"Kill me," Jason said, desperate, "and you'll never recover the *Book of Ra-Dracus*."

Intent only on saving Grace, Darius stalked toward him. "I care not for the book."

"One step closer, and I'll kill her. Do you hear me?" he screamed. "I'll kill her!"

Darius stilled completely. Yet…intense fury boiled in his blood, hotter and hotter until finally transforming him into his dragon self. He howled at the suddenness of the change, at the way his body elongated and sharpened. Scales armored his skin. His teeth lengthened and thinned, honed to razor-sharp points. His claws unsheathed. He felt the heat of the change and welcomed it.

Jason's eyes grew round, filling with undiluted terror. "Oh, my God," he gasped. He whipped his gun to Darius and squeezed the trigger.

Darius absorbed the impact of each bullet and launched himself at Jason. He twisted in the air, slashing the man's face with his tail. The bastard screamed, collapsed to the ground, blood seeping from the deep gashes, jewels tumbling from his pockets. Darius reached for him again, but gunfire came at him from a different direction. Another bullet pelted his arm, and he spun, spraying fire at this other enemy. Protecting Grace.

Having regained his breath, Jason scrambled up and stuffed the fallen jewels back into his pockets, the battle forgotten in his greed. Darius swung back to him just as Jason glanced up. Their gazes clashed for one startling second, terror against determination, before Darius bit his throat. Unsatisfied with that, Darius lashed him with his tail, clawed with his hands and slammed the man into the wall. A sickening crack followed as Jason's neck snapped, and he collapsed to the ground in a lifeless heap.

Jason's eyes stared transfixed upon a huge blue sapphire, and his fingers gave one last twitch, perhaps reaching for the sparkling diamond that rolled across the floor toward Grace's boot.

It happened too quickly and wasn't nearly enough. Not for the harm Jason had done. But Grace whimpered, and he suddenly didn't care. Vengeance didn't matter. Justice didn't matter. Only his wife mattered.

"Grace," Darius said, Jason already forgotten. His concern overshadowed all else as he rushed to her. His scales receded, revealing smooth skin. His fangs retracted. His wings curled into his back. When he reached his wife, he ripped her bonds from the wall, and she sank into his arms.

"Darius," she murmured. Her eyes were closed, her face pale.

He laid her gently on the floor and crouched beside her. As if sensing his vulnerable state, the vampire king swept before him, his eyes glowing that eerie blue. His sharp, white teeth were bared, ready to strike. The urge to leap up and attack was there, but Darius resisted. He wouldn't risk hurting Grace further.

Layel dove for him. Darius hunched over, protecting Grace with his body. He made no other move toward his opponent. The vampire's teeth sank into his shoulder, but as quickly as Layel attacked, he withdrew.

"Fight, you coward," Layel growled. "We end this here and now."

He glared up at him. "You cannot provoke me. The woman's life is more important, and I will not risk it. Not even to rid our world of your existence."

Blood dripped from Layel's mouth, slashes of red against his pale skin. He looked ready to pounce again, but instead offered, panting, "What are you willing to do for me to save your woman?"

"Call off your bloodsuckers, and I will not burn down your home."

"Burn my home and I will ensure your woman burns with it."

Grace uttered another whimper. Darius smoothed his hand over her brow, whispering soft words in her ear, though he never removed his gaze from Layel. "My warriors will disengage as soon as the woman is safe."

"I like having your warriors here. Easier to kill them." As he watched them, something indistinguishable came over Layel's expression. Something... almost human. He licked the blood from his mouth. "You love her?"

"Of course."

"I loved once," he said as if he couldn't hold back the words.

Darius studied the taut lines of Layel's features. "Then you understand."

The vampire king gave an almost imperceptible nod, then closed his eyes for a long moment, pensive. When he refocused, he said, "To save the woman, I will allow you and your men to leave my castle in peace. But there will not always be a woman to shield you and we will fight again, Darius. That I promise you."

"I welcome the day."

Layel unfurled his cape and turned, but he wasn't about to leave without offering one final blow. "I now possess many dragon medallions. Won't be long before your home is mine," he said, grinning over his shoulder.

Before Darius could reply, smoke erupted around him, and the vampire disappeared. Just like that, the rest of the vampires disappeared, as well, and the dragons were left in midbattle stances. Confused, they swung around, their expressions feral as they hunted for their opponents.

"Search the dungeons," Darius called. He continued to hold and rock and coo at Grace, willing his strength into her body.

Long moments later, Renard dragged a human man by the arm. Teira raced at his side, shouting that he was not to be hurt. Alex, Grace's brother, Darius realized. The human paled when he saw Grace.

"Grace," he shouted and fought to free himself. Renard held tight.

"These two were in the dungeon," Renard said. "This is the man your woman spoke of, is it not?"

"Release him."

The moment Alex gained his freedom, he sprinted to Grace. "What have you done to her," he snarled, trying to rip her from Darius's arms. "Let her go."

"If you do not remove your hand from my wife, I will remove it for you," he snapped. "The woman is my mate. *Mine.* That you are her brother is the only reason you will live. No one touches her but me."

Wisely Alex dropped his hands to his side. He lost his fury and desperation, both replaced by confusion. "Your mate?" He knelt beside them. "Is she…"

"She lives. She is merely weak from blood loss."

"She's pale."

"Give her time," Darius said, gazing down at this woman he loved and caressing a fingertip down her nose.

"I'm awake," she said quietly. "I'm sorry I let them get me. I tried to fight, but…"

Relief shuddered through him, and he couldn't hold back his next words. "I love you, Grace Carlyle."

"That's Grace en Kragin." Her eyelids fluttered open, and she smiled slowly. "And I love you, too."

Darius didn't know where Javar's medallion was, how many medallions Layel had or when the vampire would try and use them. Nor did he know where the *Book of Ra-Dracus* was, but he had Grace, and that's what mattered.

"I was so afraid…"

He cupped her cheeks in his hands. "Hush. All is well. Your brother is here."

To verify this, Alex leaned into her line of vision and grinned. "I'm here, sis. I'm here."

"Oh, thank God." With a grimace, she sat up and wrapped her arms around him, hugging, her grip fragile. "I missed you. God, I was so worried about you."

Darius allowed her a few minutes to reunite with her brother, then reclaimed her in the circle of his arms, exactly where she belonged.

She glanced up at him. "So what do we do from here?"

"I want you to live here with me. We can build a life together and raise our children."

Her eyes filled with tears. "Yes. *Yes.*"

Chuckling, he smoothed back her hair, then kissed her nose, her lips, her chin. "I think your brother will be staying, as well."

"Really?" Grace glanced at her brother curiously.

Alex wagged his brows and motioned to the beautiful blonde. "He means," her brother said, putting his arm around Teira, "that I've found love, too. Grace, I'd like to introduce my future wife, Teira."

She and Grace shared a secret smile, then Grace turned to Darius. "We can't leave my mom and aunt Sophie on the surface without us."

"I'm sure Layel has room for them."

"No!"

He smiled at her, a true, genuine smile. "I was teasing, Grace."

She stilled. Blinked. Darius? Teasing? How… shocking.

"You do find teasing acceptable, do you not, sweet Grace?"

"Of course. I just didn't expect it from you."

A tender light consumed his golden eyes. "You thought I lacked humor?"

"Well, yeah," she admitted. She drew in the masculinity of his scent, closed her eyes and savored. "But I love you anyway. You'll adore having my mom and aunt with us."

His lips twitched. "I'm not sure my men are prepared," he said with an undercurrent of humor. "But for you, anything."

"I love you," she said again. "Have I told you the one about the dragon who couldn't say no?"

* * * * *

You asked for Layel's story…
And now the wait is over.
Return to Atlantis in
Gena Showalter's
THE VAMPIRE'S BRIDE.

Turn the page for your sneak preview!

NIGHT HAD LONG since fallen.

The air was warm, fragrant and fraught with danger. The insects were eerily silent, not a chirp or whistle to be heard. Only the wind seemed impervious to the surrounding menace, swishing leaves and clicking branches together.

Delilah's every survival instinct remained on high alert. No telling where the other creatures were. She'd spied a few here and there as she'd gathered stones and sticks. And then they had disappeared, hiding amongst the shadows. She could have hunted them down, could have challenged them, but she hadn't.

The gods' warning refused to leave her mind. What if she killed one of her own team members? To begin at a disadvantage would be the epitome of foolish. She'd been foolish a little too often lately.

She and Nola had opted to sleep in the trees, making them harder to find, harder to reach. Right now she was stretched atop a thick branch, legs swinging over the side, handmade spear clutched tightly in her palms. Wooden daggers were strapped to her legs, waist and back.

Sharp bark dug into her ribs, helping keep her awake, alert. What were the other creatures doing just then?

What was *Layel* doing?

Layel…beautiful Layel. She'd only interacted with him twice, yet that had been enough to utterly, foolishly fascinate her. He was like no one she had ever encountered. Constantly she found herself wondering what his body looked like underneath his clothes, what his face would look like lost in passion, what he would feel like, pumping and sliding inside her.

He despises you. He is best forgotten.

Forget that his skin was pale and smooth as silk? Forget that his eyes were blue like sapphires and fringed by black lashes that were a striking contrast to his snow-white hair? Forget that he was tall with wide shoulders and radiated a dark sensuality women probably salivated over? Impossible.

What kind of females did he enjoy? What type of females had he allowed into his bed?

Sparks of something…dark flickered in her chest. Jealousy, perhaps. She wanted to deny the emotion, but couldn't. *Mine,* she thought. He might want nothing more to do with her, but no way in Hades would he be allowed to have another woman. Not while they inhabited this island.

What's come over you? Men were no longer something she prized. To her, they were something to destroy, a threat to her loved ones. Since her one and only mating had ended so disastrously, she had not thought to find herself possessive of a male. How many times had she watched her sisters fight over a particular slave? *He's mine,* they would shout. *It's my bed he will warm this night.* A clash of daggers always followed, as well as cut and bleeding warrioresses. How many times had she watched those "prized" men leave when the loving was over? Without a backward glance at the brokenhearted they were leaving behind.

Delilah had thought herself immune. Until now. She'd straddled the vampire's shoulders and he'd looked between her legs with undiluted heat. A shiver followed the thought, drowning her in another wave of that deep and inexorable desire. What would it be like to be bedded by Layel? Would he be gentle, taking her slowly? Or would his passion be as ferocious as his wild, blue eyes promised? Perhaps even a little wicked?

"You're aroused, Amazon. Why?"

Layel's whispered entreaty was so close, so husky, she wasn't sure if she'd imagined it. She stiffened, fingers tight on the spear, as she searched the darkness for him. Only treetops and night birds came into focus. Not even where thin slivers of golden moonlight seeped through the canopy of leaves overhead did she make out the form of a man. Slowly her muscles released their vise-hold on her bones.

Why am I aroused? Because of you, she wished she could tell this fantasy.

"Well?"

She gasped. Too real, too real, too real…

Before she had time to react, however, a hard

hand settled over her mouth while another shoved her to her back. A heavy, muscled weight slammed into her body. She lost her breath, barely managing to remain on the branch.

In seconds, Layel had her stretched out and her legs restrained. Her eyes widened as her spear was torn from her grip and thrown to the ground. A mocking *thump* echoed in her ears. She balled her hand and moved to strike him, but he released her mouth to catch the action. Next he caged her arms between their bodies.

"You will not hurt me," he said.

"I'll do anything I want."

"Try."

One word, but it was so smug she longed to slap and kiss him at the same time. She didn't panic. Yet. Nola was nearby. Probably sneaking up on Layel…now. But no. A moment ticked by, then another.

Nola never arrived.

Delilah's heart began to drum erratically in her chest. Her blood rushed through her veins with dizzying speed, and need quivered in her belly. Here was her fantasy, in the flesh. Hers for the taking.

You are an Amazon. Act like one. Forcing herself into action, she raised her head and sank her teeth into his neck until she tasted the metallic tang of blood. He hissed in her ear, the sound one of pleasure and pain. *You are biting him to escape, yes? So why are you writhing?*

Mmm, so good… Her tongue flicked against his racing pulse.

His hands now free, he fisted her hair and jerked her away. He was panting, anger and arousal bright in his eyes. "Think yourself a vampire, do you? Or are you half vampire? I know your kind consorts with all races and your father could belong to any of them."

She opened her mouth to respond but he shook his head, stopping her. "Scream and you'll regret it."

"As if I would scream," she muttered, offended that he thought so little of her abilities. *You did allow him to sneak up on you.*

Oh, shut up.

He blinked in surprise, as if he'd expected her to scream despite his threat.

Her irritation intensified, and she glared at him. "Did you hurt my sister?"

"She was gone when I reached you. I did not touch her."

"Then I will allow you to live. For now. But very soon I'm going to grow tired of letting you overpower me."

He snorted.

"Be thankful I haven't already killed you."

"Do not fool yourself, Amazon. You would be dead right now had I not stayed my hand."

There was fury in his voice and hate in his expression. Stayed his hand? So he *had* come here to kill her? Bastard! Except, despite everything he had said, despite the genuine loathing directed at her, his legs were between hers and she could feel the length of his shaft hardening, growing, filling.

Just like that, her blood sizzled another degree.

Blistered her veins. *I am callous, and I care for no one but my sisters.* If they were in Atlantis, she might agree to take him as her slave. If only for the month males were allowed inside the Amazon camp. But here on this island, with a dangerous competition in the works, they might very well be enemies.

"Afraid, Delilah?" he asked silkily.

Her name, spoken on those red lips…a hot ache bloomed between her legs, moisture pooling here.

"Of what?" The words emerged breathless, wine-rich.

"Dying. Pain."

"No," she answered honestly. Dying didn't scare her. Pain didn't scare her. But her reaction to this man petrified her. He made her feel vulnerable, as if she couldn't rely on herself. As if she needed him to survive. He'd already overtaken her thoughts.

"You should be very afraid," he said….